Must Love Mistletoe

"Finn . . ." Bailey whispered.

"What?" He pressed a kiss to the rim of her ear.

"Finn?"

He froze. That wasn't her voice calling his name.

It was part of his sixteen-year-old world, though. And his thirty-year-old world, too.

He broke free of Bailey. Then of her spell.

They stared at each other from opposite sides of the hedge, and he wondered how he'd gotten so stupid. Why had he let his mouth get him into trouble again?

At the same moment they turned from each other. The older dark rebel and the wiser golden girl beating hasty retreats from the traitorous, beguiling past.

He could only hope it wasn't like it had been all those years ago . . . already too late.

Christie RIDGWAY

Must Love Mistletoe

AVON BOOKS
An Imprint of HarperCollinsPublishers

This is a work of fiction. Names, characters, places and incidents are products of the author's imagination or are used fictitiously and are not to be construed as real. Any resemblance to actual events, locales, organizations, or persons, living or dead, is entirely coincidental.

AVON BOOKS
An Imprint of HarperCollins*Publishers*
10 East 53rd Street
New York, New York 10022-5299

Copyright © 2006 by Christie Ridgway
Something Sinful copyright © 2006 by Suzanne Enoch; *Angel In a Red Dress* copyright © 1988, 2006 by Judith Ivory, Inc.; *Billionaires Prefer Blondes* copyright © 2006 by Suzanne Enoch; *Must Love Mistletoe* copyright © 2006 by Christie Ridgway
ISBN-13: 978-0-06-114020-4
ISBN-10: 0-06-114020-1
www.avonromance.com

First Avon Books paperback printing: December 2006

Avon Trademark Reg. U.S. Pat. Off. and in Other Countries, Marca Registrada, Hecho en U.S.A.
HarperCollins® is a registered trademark of HarperCollins Publishers Inc.

Printed in the U.S.A.

10 9 8 7 6 5 4 3 2 1

With thanks to the "Mayberry Moms,"
who didn't hesitate to help me out
by scheduling our Christmas happy hour,
uh, "meeting" in Coronado.
Cheers!

December 1
St. Nicholas took pity on a family of penniless girls and tossed bags of gold through their window for dowries. The bags landed in their stockings that had been hung by the fire to dry, initiating the worldwide custom of Santa leaving gifts in stockings or shoes.

Chapter 1

Fingers hovering at the switches by the front door, Bailey Sullivan glanced over her shoulder at the interior of The Perfect Christmas and wondered what would happen if she set Santa's beard on fire.

But the happy, arsonistic notion died a swift death. That wasn't the answer to her problems. Surely the manufacturers of the dozens—hundreds!—of Santas in her family's shop would have treated their respective fabric, resin, wood, or cotton-floss facial hair with flame retardant.

Damn it all.

And anyway, a visit from the Coronado, California, fire department would only make bigger the mess she'd been forced back home to put to rights. With a resigned shrug, she doused the lights and cut off Marilyn mid–"Santa Baby." For the first time in ten hours Bailey's ears experienced a grateful reprieve from holiday assault. Until the rattle of the jingle bells as she exited the front door, that is. But that noise was mercifully brief, and after she locked the door behind her, she closed her eyes and leaned her forehead against the cold plate glass.

One day down, twenty-four to go.

She sucked in a deep breath of night air, cooled and salted by the Pacific Ocean just a block away, and let it clear out the lingering notes of cinnamon-and-clove potpourri that was The Perfect Christmas's signature scent. Customers Internet-ordered the stuff from all over the world, claiming it captured their very best holiday memories.

As far as Bailey was concerned, *captured* was the operative world. From the day she could be trusted to unwrap merchandise to the day she could run the cash register with her eyes closed, she'd been a prisoner in the two-story Victorian that housed the almost sixty-year-old family business. She'd managed to escape for the ten years between eighteen and twenty-eight, but now, just as surely as Hermie's dental skills came in handy, just as inevitable as the foggy night that required Rudolph's very shiny nose, she was once again held hostage.

Until December 25. Then she was outta here and back to Los Angeles and her happy holidays-less life.

Giving an emphatic nod, she almost lost the green-and-white striped hat jammed over her blond hair. With a grimace, she yanked the thing off and stuffed it in the front pocket of her red cotton and fake-fur-trimmed apron. This morning she'd driven straight from her condo in L.A. to the shop and found them hanging on their customary hook in the back office. Along with her customary nametag—her name between two peppermint sticks—that read:

BAILEY
(Yes, like George!)

Just about everyone except the Japanese tourists recognized the identity of the main character of the movie classic *It's a Wonderful Life*. Just about everyone loved the idea that she'd been named after a famous Christmas character.

Just about everyone.

Gee, thanks, Mom.

Which made her think about the next item on her today's to-do list. Heading the eleven blocks to her childhood home and confronting her mother. Bailey rested her head another moment against the cold glass, then straightened. There was nothing to it but to do it. And there was no one else to do it but Bailey.

She turned, pointing herself in the direction of her car that earlier she'd moved to the end of the block beneath one of the streetlights. Her gaze lifted to the holiday decorations suspended from the metal poles along the avenue. When she was a kid, they'd been tired-looking tinseled bells and dusty angels, but in the new millennium they were bright polyester flags depicting holiday icons like nutcrackers and snowmen. Over her silver Passat hung one stamped with a multicolored tree ornament, and beside her car was a little man in a uniform holding a ticket book.

A ticket book?

"No!" she called out, rushing down the walkway and along the sidewalk. She wasn't going to get a citation. She couldn't. Wasn't being back in the shop enough? Wasn't it already unfair that she'd be spending the night in her old twin-sized canopy bed, sleeping with her Nirvana posters instead of on her Posturepedic mattress and with her framed Picasso prints? Her day wasn't supposed to get any worse. "Hey!"

The elderly man didn't look up.

Bailey was going to break his busy little pencil in half. "Listen," she said, in her meanest I-manage-a-hundred-attorney-law-firm voice, the one even the toothiest of shark-lawyers feared, "what do you think you're doing?"

The man looked up. "Eh?" His fingers went to the hearing aid nestled in his right ear. "Bailey? Bailey Sullivan?"

"Mr. Baer?" He used to live down the street from her family home. She supposed he still did. "What are you doing?"

He gestured to the car parked on the other side of hers. The one with "Retired Citizens Service Patrol" emblazoned on its side. It was gleaming white, official enough to have a cherry-red light on top and a sturdy-looking something that might be a cattle prod attached to the front grille. "I'm on the job."

"Oh, well." She tried smiling at him, hoping he'd remember some good deed she'd done for him as a kid. Maybe she'd retrieved his morning newspaper from the bushes once upon a time. "Me too. I put in a *long* day at the shop."

He leaned against the side of her car as a fond smile added new wrinkles to his liver-spotted cheeks.

Inside Bailey hope surged, until she realized he was gazing not at her, but over her shoulder, at the store that was the new albatross around her neck.

"I bought my daughter her first Christmas ornament there," he said. "She bought *her* daughter her first Christmas ornament there."

"Yeah, yeah, yeah," Bailey said. "It's an institution." *Albatross*.

"A landmark," the old man added, then bent his head back over his book of triplicate forms.

She wasn't going to take a ticket. "What are you, uh, writing there, Mr. Baer? Because, you see, I'm in a bit of a hurry. Mom's home alone, probably keeping dinner warm for me, and—"

"Dan's really moved out then?" He stopped writing to squint at her over silver-rimmed bifocals. "Heard he's in one of those ugly condos on the bay side."

"Um, well . . ." Bailey wasn't sure if her mother and stepfather's recent separation was public knowledge, but heck, this was 7.4-square-mile Coronado. Secrets were impossible to keep, plus perhaps she could use the sympathy to wiggle out of whatever the Retired Citizen Patrolman had written on that little form. "They've been living apart since September."

Mr. Baer nodded. "Heard one won't step inside the shop if the other one's there."

"That's true too." Which had resulted in the frantic phone calls she'd been fielding from the part-time assistant manager and the guy who did the books—both old family friends. With her mother and Dan refusing to share the same air space, no one was minding the store. During the season when they made seventy-five percent of their year's profits, this meant the likely end to a Coronado institution. A landmark.

The bankroll that kept her mother, stepfather, and freshman-in-college younger brother living in the style to which they were accustomed.

So she'd been guilted into coming home to save the day.

"I'm leaving on the twenty-fifth, though," she murmured.

"Eh?" Mr. Baer squinted at her again. "What's that?"

"I'm running the store," Bailey explained. "But only until Christmas." By then her mother would have accepted the hard lesson Bailey had taken to heart a decade ago. She even had her own private axiom to cover it, a Christmasy twist on the famous phrase from the Robert Frost poem. "Nothing flocked can stay."

"Eh?"

"My take on 'Nothing gold can stay' and my personal motto, Mr. B." A reminder that trusting in pretty promises and the lasting strength of romantic relationships was about as sensible as believing in Santa and all his itty-bitty elves. That kind of magic didn't exist.

"Now, about that ticket you're working on, you can't mean that . . ."

But of course he meant it for her. He even had a special measuring stick he'd made that proved she was nineteen inches away from the curb, one inch over what Coronado parking regulations allowed. And since she was an admitted perfectionist herself, Bailey took the ticket with as much good grace as she could muster.

Which meant that when he wished her a "Merry Christmas," she managed not to flinch.

After that it was in the car and the short trip to Coronado Island's Walnut Street. The "island," really a peninsula, had once been a wheat farm, a whaling station, and then, in the late 1880s, it had been turned into a tourist destination thanks to the founder of a piano company and his partner, a telephone executive. The superlative Hotel del Coronado had been built first, then more streets, housing tracts, a ferry landing.

To maximize all this prime real estate, the home lots were small, hence the houses were close together. Back in the day, presumably the community planners assumed vacationers wouldn't mind the close quarters. In modern times, the result was that the year-round residents inside the cheek-by-jowl Victorians, Craftsman cottages, and suburban ranches lived in a cozy, nosy community.

Everyone had always known her business, from the day in first grade when Jeremy Barger had kissed her, to the day she'd been caught kissing—

What the heck is that?

As she accelerated around the next corner, she could see a radioactive glow up the next block.

The block of her childhood home. Spooked by the strange light, Bailey braked and peered into the distance. Maybe things had changed recently. One end of Coronado was fenced off as the North Island Naval Air Station. Perhaps the military had moved in on the residential community and built a new runway or something. Up ahead it was just that bright.

With a gentle foot on the accelerator, Bailey moved cautiously forward. At the corner of Walnut and Sixth, she stopped again, dazzled. Lights were everywhere. On mailboxes, flowerpots, bicycles. Across bushes like fishnets, rimming rooflines, marching up tree trunks, running over anything that didn't move. Make that things that moved too. A cat skipped past, wearing a collar studded with red and green Christmas bulbs.

And music. Piped out of windows and doors and from the mouths of plastic carolers, cardboard snowmen, and poster-painted plywood angels. "Hark the Herald" clashed with "Silent Night" clashed with "O Tannenbaum."

"Oh, ton of crud," Bailey cursed. They'd turned her block into Christmas Central. Giant-sized presents were stacked on porches. Overstuffed Santa butts were heading down chimneys. Reindeer pawed at patches of grass.

And there, in the middle of the block, stood her childhood home. The solitary oasis of darkness. She headed for the simple porch light like it was a homing beacon. As she braked her car in the driveway, she glanced over at the neighboring drive, just a tire's width away. A sleek SUV sat at rest, and the dark gleam of it sent another spooky little chill down her spine. It didn't look like the kind of car their eighty-something neighbor Alice Jacobson would drive. And there was a tasteful, lacy edging of icicle lights hanging from her eaves. In the old days, Christmas lights at Mrs. Jacobson's meant only one thing.

Finn was back.

Her driver's door jerked open.

Bailey gasped, her heart jumping, just as it used to when she saw those Christmas lights. When she saw Finn for the first time on his biannual vacation visits.

But of course it wasn't Finn. Thank God. "Mr. Lantz." Recognizing her mother's across-the-street neighbor, she held her hand against her chest to calm her heart. "Good to see you."

So much better than Finn, whom she never expected to see again.

"Bailey-girl, it's good to see you too." He was beaming at her, the lights from the holiday ostentation reflecting off his bald head. "Your mother's thrilled you're coming home. Heck, we're all thrilled."

"Oh. Well. Nice."

He was nodding. "Worried about the store, you know. It's an institution."

The albatross tugged hard on her neck. "A landmark."

"Exactly." He patted her shoulder as she slipped out of the car. "But you'll take care of everything, sharp girl like you."

Surrounded by overdone dazzle, nearly deafened by the dueling carols, Bailey thought longingly of the quiet and order of her anonymous Los Angeles condo building. The housing association there posted rules and regulations that prohibited just such displays as those that were right now smothering her.

It was why she'd chosen the place.

Mr. Lantz didn't seem to notice her disquiet. He beamed at her again. "I know you'll fix things. Save the store, save the season."

Bailey sighed, wondering what he'd think if he knew she hated the holiday. If he knew that from the day she'd left home she'd never once celebrated on December 25—except for the fact that she didn't have to celebrate it at all. What he'd think if he realized that the "sharp girl" assigned to save The Perfect Christmas was in fact a certified, holiday-hating Scrooge.

Bailey speed-rolled her suitcase along the path to her mother's front porch, eager to escape the cacophony of merry tunes tumbling down the narrow street. But with the solid brick steps leading to the front door beneath her feet, she paused.

Just as The Perfect Christmas had been her maternal grandparents' store, this had been her maternal grandparents' house. The most stable thing in her life. The idea gave a little lift to her spirits, and the weight of the albatross eased some too.

Maybe she'd overreacted to the phone calls. Maybe she only needed a face-to-face with her mother to straighten out all their lives. *Mom, here's the deal. Dad left, and now Dan. Get over it, get back in the store, and I'll get on my way.*

It could work.

On the strength of that thought, she pushed open the front door, wearing an almost-smile. "Mom?" she called out. "It's me. I'm here."

Silence was the only reply, but there was the scent of food in the air, and her mother had said she'd be home all evening. Bailey left her suitcase in the entry hall and wandered past the living room in the direction of the kitchen. "Mom?"

A light glowed over the stovetop, but there wasn't a plate on the counter or any dishes in the sink. Ghost fingers feathered over Bailey's skin as she hurried to the staircase. The walls were lined with photos, and she couldn't help but slow to look at them. Baby Bailey with two teeth and a pink-bowed topknot. Her brother, Harry, in footed pajamas. Stiff school photos, group shots of gymnastic teams, Little League, soccer.

Prom photo of Harry and some tall bombshell whose pinkie—and svelte figure—he'd been wrapped around until graduation last June. Then, oh . . .

Prom photo of Bailey and Finn. She tried forcing her gaze away—God, what had she been thinking when she bought that silver dress?—but then it snagged on Finn. Finn, two years older, eons more fascinating than any boy she'd ever known.

She'd chosen silver to match the thick steel hoops he wore in his ears. Of course the color washed out her blond looks, but who wouldn't look washed out compared to Finn, with his bad-boy bleached-on-black hair and his brooding brown eyes? He'd worn motorcycle boots with his dark-as-night tuxedo, and by the time they'd arrived at the dance, he'd already yanked free from his neck the bow tie his grandmother had been so careful to tie for him.

He'd never been careful with anything but Bailey.

It had only made him more dangerous, more imperative to run away from. She'd done it ten years ago.

Move feet, move. She could do it again now.

Forcing him out of her mind, she climbed the last of the steps. "Mom?"

A scuffle down the hall sent her toward Harry's room. In the doorway, she halted, relieved to finally find her quarry sitting on Harry's bed, her back half turned. Surely with a little forthright conversation she could convince her mother to swallow her pride or her heartbreak or whatever was keeping her out of the store. Bailey could jump back in her car and drive away from Christmas and from Coronado. Maybe tonight!

"Mom, I've been calling you."

Tracy Willis swiveled to face her. "Oh, I didn't hear you, honey."

Bailey swallowed. The last time she'd seen her mother had been at Harry's high school graduation. But the older woman looked as if years had passed instead of months. Her face and neck were thin, her blunt-cut hair straggled toward her shoulders. It looked gray instead of its usual blond. She wore a pair of muddy green sweat pants and shearling slippers. A football jersey.

Another unwelcome memory bubbled up from the La Brea tar at the back of Bailey's mind. Her mother, lying in an empty bathtub in Bailey's father's flannel robe, sobbing, unaware that her kindergarten daughter was peering through the cracked door. Her kindergarten daughter who was wondering why her daddy had left and made her mother so miserable. It could have been yesterday, an hour ago, ten minutes before. There'd been a bumpy mosquito bite on Bailey's calf and she'd stood there, silent, scratching it until it bled like red tears into her thin white sock.

A shudder jolted her back to the present, and she shoved the recollection down and cleared her throat. Old memories, just another reason to get away from here ASAP. Trying to sound normal, she asked, "Is that the top half of Harry's high school uniform you're wearing?"

Her mother absently plucked at the slippery fabric, the hem nearly reaching her knees. "It's comfortable."

"So's a shower curtain, Mom, but it's not a good look. What are you doing in here?"

"I . . ." Her mother shrugged, then made a vague gesture behind her. "Just, just . . ."

Bailey stepped inside the room to peer around her mother's newly skinny body. "You're eating in here?" A small saucepan, more than half full of mac and cheese, was on the bedspread behind her mother, a fork jammed in the middle. "You're eating out of the *pan*?"

Okay, Bailey ate out of pans often enough. Weren't Lean Cuisine microwave trays pans, after all? But her mother didn't eat out of them. And her mother didn't let people eat in bedrooms.

Bailey snatched up the food and tried catching her mother's eye. "Mom, we need to talk."

"Are you hungry?" Tracy asked, her own gaze wandering off. "It's not from a box. It's my recipe."

Her stomach growling, Bailey forked up a mouthful. "We need to talk about the store, about Dan, about what's going on." She retreated toward the room's windows and the desk that sat beneath them. Leaning her butt against the edge, she swallowed, then pierced some more pieces of macaroni. "Mom—"

"I don't want to talk about Dan." Tracy still didn't meet her eyes.

This wasn't good. Her mother didn't sound reasonable and willing to step back up to her responsibilities. "Mom—"

"And now you're here to take care of the store."

"Yes, but Mom—" Someone had upped the volume on his speakers, and "Joy to the World" blared its way into the room through the half-open window. Grimacing at the oh-so-inappropriate background music, Bailey clunked the pan onto Harry's desk. Then she twisted to shove shut the wooden sash.

The houses were so close together, she was peering right into Mrs. Jacobson's rear garden. There was a man there, a wide-shouldered man. She couldn't see his face, his back was turned to her, and he was carrying a Christmas tree through the kitchen door.

Her heart thumped. Her stomach clenched.

He could be anyone, her common sense told her. A handyman. Another neighbor. A generic good Samaritan spreading holiday cheer.

But that wasn't what her intuition said. Her intuition was cringing away from the glass and the soul-freezing knowledge of who was really moving through Mrs. Jacobson's back door.

She should ignore her silly intuition. She should

turn off those goofy internal warning bells and get back to real business. She should face her mother and insist they talk.

But her mouth was suddenly so dry, she couldn't find her own voice.

December 25 wasn't going to arrive soon enough, that was certain. Because Bailey had a very bad, very unignorable feeling that Scrooge and the Ghost of Christmas Past had both come home to Coronado for an untimely visit.

Bailey Sullivan's Vintage Christmas Facts & Fun Calendar

December 2

The word *Yule* comes from the Scandinavian word *Jol* which means festival. Though the festival often lasted twelve days, it was then not associated with the twelve days of Christmas.

Chapter 2

With the door shut behind that mysterious figure next door, Bailey had managed to put him from her mind to concentrate on talking with her mother about her recent separation and The Perfect Christmas. The effort hadn't gotten her anywhere, however. So she'd followed Tracy to an early bedtime and woke up early as well, to now find dark-rimmed eyes staring into hers.

Bailey jumped, pressing back against the pancake-flat pillow of her childhood, then relaxed again as she realized she was gazing at one of her old band posters and into Kurt Cobain's compelling—likely drug-addled—gaze. Even still, she felt a tug of attraction.

Once you jonesed for a bad boy, you always jonesed for bad boys.

But she wasn't going to think about bad boys, or mysterious strangers, or even the possibility that the mysterious stranger next door was Finn.

Even if it *was* Finn—*itwasn'tFinn itwasn'tFinn itwasn'tFinn*—this unlucky intersection of their lives didn't make it necessary for her to see or talk to him. Not that she couldn't! But surely it was natural to feel discomfort around an old—first— flame, wasn't it?

Especially as they hadn't parted on ideal terms. As a matter of fact, they were un-ideal enough to make her even more certain she should continue avoiding Finn just as she'd done for the past ten years.

With a last glance at that gorgeous, doomed Kurt, Bailey climbed out of bed and headed straight for the attached bathroom. The sooner she stopped thinking about old times and old flames, the sooner she could get on with her day. The sooner she got on with her day, the sooner she could tackle the chaos at the store and the renewed disorder in her mother's emotional life.

The sooner she could escape from all of it.

Despite her time in the shower, the whirr of the blow dryer, and then the rattle she made in the kitchen getting coffee and toast, neither mother nor even sound emerged from the master bedroom. Once dressed, complete with Christmas apron and striped stocking cap, Bailey let herself out the front door, resigned to the next resort of spending yet another day in sole charge of the store.

Her feet stuttered to a halt. The next resort would have to wait until she first made contact with the nitwit who'd left a refrigerator-sized wooden carton on the street, directly behind her Passat.

The folded invoice inside the plastic sleeve stapled to the pine slats confirmed her *un*luck was holding . . . the address was that of Mrs. Jacobson. If Bailey was going to do all that getting on and tackling she had planned, she first would have to knock on the one door she particularly didn't want to open.

Her feet dragged as she headed down the sidewalk and up the front walk of the other house. She might have excused herself that it was too early in the morning to disturb any occupants, but the unmistakable mingled scent of coffee and bacon had made its way to the front porch. Someone was up and cooking breakfast at the Jacobsons'.

Taking a breath, Bailey rapped on the wood. It didn't take long to hear the approach of footsteps on the other side. The door swung open.

Itwon'tbeFinn itwon'tbeFinn itwon'tbeFinn.

It . . . wasn't?

The T-shirt was the same, the broken-down

blue jeans, the battered motorcycle boots. But this wasn't a teenage juvenile delinquent. This looked more like an *adult* delinquent, someone who spent time on a chain gang, or bounced other bad guys out of rowdy bars, or ran security for Hell's Angels events.

He was certainly no boy and no angel himself, not with those wide, I-work-out shoulders, mussed black hair—sans the bleach overlay—and dark stubble. This man didn't wear her first lover's steel earrings, but instead a black eye patch covered one of his brown eyes.

Finn's eyes.

She took a step back.

A smile flitted over his face. *Finn's* smile. The uncovered eye didn't betray a flicker of emotion or familiarity, though. "Is it Girl Scout cookie season too?"

He didn't recognize her! The man who had been Finn, the pirate that was *this* Finn, didn't realize she was the grown-up girl next door. To him, apparently, ten years was distant history.

Okay.

That was good, easier, fine. She could at least pretend the same. It wouldn't be hard anyway, since he seemed so different than she expected.

Who was she kidding? Second only to prison convict, she'd have bet the farm that Finn would turn pirate.

She gestured behind her. "There's a package on

the street with this address," she said, in the tones of a polite stranger. "It's blocking my car."

His eyebrows shot up and he moved out the door and past her, leaving his scent in the air. The Finn she remembered had smelled like Irish Spring. This Finn smelled shower-fresh too, but with a subtler scent that tickled her nose. Following him out to the street, she rubbed it. As her hand came down, her fingers brushed the nametag pinned to her apron.

BAILEY
(Yes, like George!)

Damn Finn. He knew exactly who she was. Even if she didn't look exactly as she had at eighteen, he wouldn't have forgotten her *name*.

She snatched the dopey hat off her head and combed her fingers through her shoulder-length hair. He wasn't looking at her, though. Instead he strode straight to the carton, ripped the invoice from its plastic, and unfolded the thin sheet.

He cursed like a pirate too.

Then he glanced over at her. "Don't worry, I'll get this out of your way."

She smiled sweetly. "Don't worry, I'll get this out of your way, *Bailey*. The name's Bailey Sullivan."

His gaze flicked to her nametag, back to her eyes. "I can read."

But he couldn't remember?

She remembered *everything*.

The sullen expression on his thirteen-year-old face the first summer he'd been packed off to his grandmother's. The outrage that had replaced it when Bailey had accepted her best friend's dare and squirted him, long and cold, with the garden hose.

The summer she was fourteen and she cajoled him to the beach with her every afternoon. His kiss one July day—her first. She hadn't known to open her mouth for his tongue, and her skin had heated like sunburn when he whispered the instruction. Then his tongue had touched the tip of hers and he'd tasted like pretzels and Pepsi and salt water. Going dizzy, she'd clutched his bare shoulder, her fingertips grazing across gritty golden sand sprinkled on his damp tanned flesh.

Two years after that, the darkness of her backyard and the ghostly glow of the soccerball-sized hydrangeas. The fresh scent of night-blooming jasmine. The flinch of her stomach as his bony boy fingers touched her belly skin on their first, bold approach to her breast. The instant pebbling of her nipple beneath her neon bikini top and her naïve, desperate hope he wouldn't notice.

He had.

"Something wrong?" he asked now.

He'd always paid such close attention.

She tossed her hair back and crossed her arms.

"Nothing access to my car won't fix right up."

"Give me a sec."

She let herself watch him stride off, his long legs so familiar, the wide plane of his back and his heavy-muscled shoulders so not. What had he done to earn that beefcake physique? What had he done with his life? What had happened to his eye?

Did he ever hear "Smells Like Teen Spirit" and in his memory smell the fruity coconut-oil scent of suntan lotion? Would he then recall the way he rubbed it on her shoulders and then the small of her back, his fingertips sliding under her bikini bottoms to tease the round globes of her butt and then trace the half-hidden bumps of her tailbone?

He'd been such a bad boy.

Her bad boy.

But the bad boy had grown into a one-eyed stranger who was already back with a hammer and who didn't appear interested in talk.

Or interested in her.

So she clapped her mouth shut too and watched him break open the big crate.

Then felt her jaw drop as out of frothy curls of shredded paper he drew a shrink-wrapped gingerbread cookie. A life-sized, frosted-in-colorful-detail sheep. Followed by a calf, a chicken, two lambs. Then it was figures. A man, a woman, an angel, a baby in a cradle. Baby Jesus.

A whole, to-human-scale Nativity scene of gingerbread.

Bailey had to blink a few times to believe her eyes. "Someone has a Neiman Marcus catalog and a triple-platinum AmEx card," she said.

He said nothing. In silence he stacked the cookies on the lawn, shoved the packing material into a garbage bag, then finally broke down the wood carton, piling the pieces far enough away to create getaway space for her.

Getaway. Great. Perfect. All that she would have asked Santa for if she'd ever had the chance to believe in him.

But the craziness of the family business during December had prompted her parents to forgo the usual fantasy for their child. With Santa visits part of The Perfect Christmas's holiday schedule, instead it had made sense for them to explain that the man in the red suit who spent afternoons in their store was an out-of-work navy vet and that the character who supposedly left gifts on Christmas mornings for good little girls and boys was none other than their mommies and daddies.

But *shhh!* she had to keep the secret for everyone else.

So she was good at keeping quiet and she continued the practice as she ducked into her car, turned the key, then slipped it into reverse.

Not putting voice to her questions for Finn

didn't make them disappear, though. Just as wishing her memories of him to a cobwebbed shelf in the back corner of her brain didn't immediately send them there either.

But the fact that he didn't appear the least bit affected by her presence—or their past—should make the banishments not far off. Just, say, five minutes away.

Before that could happen, though, a knock on her driver's door window made her jump. The one-eyed pirate who was moments from being out of her mind forever was giving her another expressionless look from his one dark eye.

Bailey unrolled the window, trying to appear as if she'd already forgotten who he was and what they'd once meant to each other.

It certainly appeared as if *he* had.

"Yes?" she asked. "Did you want something?"

"Just checking."

She frowned at him. "Checking for what?"

"That you're still into skipping good-byes." And then he turned, leaving without another word.

She put the pedal to the metal and got out of there as quick as she could too.

Her palm smacked the steering wheel as she drove off. He had to do it, didn't he? Just when she was sure she could parlay *his* disinterest into her own, he had to make that little crack.

God, she hoped it was a wear-her-heels-down day at the store. Not just because they needed the business, but because without that, she was lost. Without a steady stream of spending customers, it was a damn certainty she wasn't going to be able to think of anything or anyone but Finn.

Finn Jacobson stalked back into his grandmother's kitchen, pissed off at himself for making that last remark—almost as pissed off as he was at Bailey. The fact that he was feeling anything toward her at all made his back teeth grind and the bones around his missing eye ache like a bitch.

On his way to the refrigerator, he kicked the leg of a wooden chair, shoving it toward the farm-house table. Then he jerked open the door to reach for a beer and had to swallow his curse as Gram nearly caught him at it when she came through the other door.

"Finn?" Her frail—too frail—hands stroked the velour of her holiday-red sweatsuit. Her lipstick matched, and with her white hair and white running shoes she looked like a sporty Mrs. Claus. Sporty, but not yet one hundred percent recuperated from the pneumonia that had hit her hard last month. She was on the road to recovery, though.

"Morning, Gram," Finn said, wrapping his fingers around the half-and-half instead. Then he poured her a cup of coffee and added a dollop of the cream, just as she liked it. Still, his actions were jerky, and he knew his brusque tone would only make her worry. "Wrong side of the bed."

From the corner of his one eye, he made sure she settled safely into her chair, then placed her cup in front of her. She smiled at him. "You spoil me."

"That's why I'm here." After she'd been released from the hospital last week, he'd packed up enough from his downtown San Diego loft to stay through Christmas. The field office had been ecstatic over short-tempered Finn using some of his pile of vacation hours—hell, they'd been this close to ordering him out anyway, even though it hadn't been long since his return from medical leave. His parents had been relieved to give over his grandmother's care to him. They were already at his sister's awaiting the birth of the first grandchild—a son.

Though Gram insisted she didn't need a keeper, the fact was, when he was a teenager *he* had needed one, and it was Gram who had volunteered for the job. He owed her—and maybe one other—for all that he'd become.

So he also owed it to her to plaster over that eleven-month-old crack in his soul and the simmering emotions it laid bare. Without finding a way to control his feelings, he'd end up killing himself by either drinking too much or driving too fast. Even if he managed to survive his sins, he owed his colleagues too. He couldn't return to his job unless he could return to his former professional, cool self.

"Did I hear someone at the door?"

"Mmm." He didn't want to rehash the visit with himself, let alone with his grandmother, so he ignored the question and tried de-growling his voice. "Mom called this morning. She reports she bought the prodigy-yet-to-be-born some sort of infant computer and educational software yesterday. Dad purchased a football, baseball mitt, and, his concession to the Midwest, an ice hockey stick."

His grandmother sipped at her coffee. "No drum set?"

God, she knew how to get to him. He almost found himself smiling. "Now how did you know that was what I sent for my nephew's first Christmas?"

"Your parents will be amused."

"You think?" Finn doubted it. They'd likely shudder at the bad memories the gift would evoke. The fact was, he'd caused his family buckets of anxiety as an adolescent hellion. At thirteen he'd started smoking cigarettes and hanging out with a new neighbor who had a band, a van, and a fake ID. Finn had been big for his age and the other guy had probably thought him nearer his grade than he actually was—or maybe the guy just appreciated Finn's talent with drums. He'd actually sucked . . . but then they all did, all of them who made up Corpses in Heaven.

At their wits' end that summer vacation, his parents had sent him from home in Northern

California to his grandmother's to get him away from his older friend and Finn's first brushes with the law. One dose hadn't cured him. By fifteen, along with the local cops, he'd considered himself a regular Bad Ass and his folks starting sending him to his grandmother's every summer *and* Christmas. They'd realized that even a Bad Ass had a soft spot, and Finn's was his gram. He was named for her husband, his Grandpa Finn, and though he barely remembered the man, Finn and Gram formed a two-member mutual admiration society.

His long bleached hair, his steel earrings, the skulls and other symbols he'd self-tattooed on his knuckles—she'd seemed amused by them. She was tolerant of him in every way except the cancer sticks. And because he hated upsetting her, during the weeks he spent at her house he would not only stop smoking but also try shedding his urban street image and begin fitting in with the Coronado sorta-suburban, sorta-surf-dude society—as well as anyone could, anyway, who had that scruffy hair, those steel earrings, the tattooed knuckles.

Then once Bailey Sullivan accepted him, the rest of the kids did too.

The name must have floated from his mind into Gram's. "I thought I heard Bailey's voice," she said. "It was like old times."

"It was her," he admitted, turning his back to reach for his own coffee cup when a beer still sounded so much better. Or whiskey. "I guess she's home for a visit too."

"Imagine that."

Yeah, imagine. He hadn't even bothered to consider it when he'd moved in at Walnut Street a few days ago. Just as he'd never imagined on that first visit at Bad Ass thirteen that he'd get tangled up with super-insider, super-perfect, Coronado's super It Girl Bailey Sullivan.

Teen tease. Ice princess. Girl next door. His first lover. His first love.

She been all these to him at one time or another.

Oh, yeah, and the first and only one to break his heart. But hell, what's youth for, anyway?

He should have let go of it by now, don't you think?

He'd never let go of it.

But that wasn't true. He'd done a damn fine job of letting go of Bailey and all the immature dreams he'd had at twenty years old when he'd come to Coronado that last time, only to find her gone. He'd moved forward with his life and surprised the hell out of his parents by becoming a son they boasted about.

Until eleven months ago.

He supposed they still boasted about him, but he didn't feel the same about himself. Certainly he'd never *be* the same.

He adjusted the strap of his eye patch, and the

sharp ache in his facial bones sank all the way to his gut.

Closing his one working eye, he sucked in a deep breath. For a second, over the coffee and the pain, he smelled Bailey again. He'd never pinpointed the name of her personal perfume, but it hadn't changed in a decade. Light, citrusy, with a layer of some flowery note on top. Then all wrapped up in bow of sex appeal.

One sniff this morning and, damn it all to hell, he'd been going hard and horny again.

Because that delicate blond prettiness of hers was still the same too. That sleek golden hair and gymnast figure that had made him feel both macho and clumsy when he was sixteen. That now just made him feel mean because despite himself it still pulled at him.

But who could blame him for reacting to all the memories between them? Innocent kisses. Not-so-innocent kisses. Her small breasts in his palms. The first time he'd touched the wetness between her thighs and how she'd buried her face against his neck in embarrassment.

The burn of her skin when he'd tasted that delicious wetness on his tongue.

As he said, who could blame him?

But hell, it only twisted the uncontrollable tension inside of him tighter. He was the Bad Ass again, feeling all edgy and penned-up and rebellious. Like then, just a razor's edge away from fucking up.

Oh, wait. He'd already done that eleven months ago.

But he was supposed to be getting past that. He was supposed to be icing over all the anger, the guilt, the sense of loss. During this "vacation" with Gram he was supposed to be unwinding eleven months of coiled emotions that had made him harder and meaner than ever before. And he couldn't—wouldn't—let the unwelcome return of Bailey Sullivan impede his objective.

December 3

Helen Keller said, "The only real blind person at Christmas time is he who has not Christmas in his heart."

Chapter 3

It was after midnight when Bailey left the shop and headed toward Walnut Street and the sleep she so desperately needed.

At the store's closing time, she'd been in no hurry to return to Christmas Central with its cacophony of holiday sound and emotional caterwauling of ancient memories, so she'd busied herself by restocking. The day's stream of customers had left gaping holes on the shelves and tables and under and on the half-dozen decorated trees inside The Perfect Christmas.

The last box she'd unpacked had contained St. Nicholas figurines from Germany. Dressed in old-fashioned robes of green, red, and white, they'd been frosted with a superfine glitter that she hadn't been able to completely wash off her hands. As she adjusted the Passat's rearview mirror, in the street-light she could see the stuff dusted across her nose and cheeks and clinging to the strands of hair surrounding her face. She rubbed at it with the back of her hand and tried finger-combing it out of her hair, but then gave up.

Glitter girl was going straight to bed, so what did it matter?

Except one block from 631 Walnut, she had second thoughts about sleep. As in, she didn't think she was going to get any right away. Maybe a teensy glass of Merlot and some crispy cheese straws would pull her overactive mind off its fixation with the past. And not just the past as in ten years ago, but also the past of sixteen hours ago. All day she'd been wondering what Finn had been doing with his life. She knew he hadn't been living with his grandmother all this time, though she didn't know anything else. For example, what was that eye patch all about?

And why did it give her the uneasy impression that he saw her clearer than ever? When he was a teenager, she'd catch him looking at her, sometimes with amusement, sometimes with bemusement, sometimes with a kind of heat that made her heart fall to her belly and throb there, low and hard. Though she'd tried to pretend that she managed all the dark, wild power in his bad-boy body, deep inside she'd known that he only let her feel that way.

A panther who tolerated the pretty girl riding him with ribbon reins.

Now he looked like a man who didn't have any patience for pretending.

The thought would be hard to fall asleep with.

So she turned left and headed for the grocery store a quarter mile away, gratified to see that it was open 24/7 as she'd expected. Grocery stores restocked in the off-hours too, and there was no sense not making a sale or two if they had to have employees in the store overnight anyway.

Though as she pulled into the lot, the number of cars surprised her. Late-night sales must be brisk because apparently she wasn't the only insomniac in town. Inside, the place was bustling with stockers and shoppers. Even with Bing warbling about snow and her wine and snacks quickly in hand, Bailey continued to wander around, in no hurry to return home to where the proximity of Finn was sure to plague her.

Here, at least, she could find some peace.

"Bailey? Bailey Sullivan?" said a female voice.

She swung around to find no one behind her, then adjusted her level gaze three inches lower to latch on to the gamine face of her oldest childhood friend. The only person who had ever made her feel tall. "Trin Tran?"

They let out identical squeals and rushed into

each other's arms, bumping and tangling plastic shopping carriers in the process. Laughing, they pulled back and went about disconnecting their baskets. Inside Trin's, Bailey glimpsed Cheerios, a box of pediatric cold medicine, and small jars of something the color of melted purple crayons.

She looked into her friend's almond eyes. "You're a mother?"

Trin nodded. "To Adam-sleeping-at-the-moment-but-with-a-cold-that-makes-him-cranky. He's not quite two years old. I've been married for three. My husband's Andrew Truehouse. Remember him from high school?"

"Of course I remember him from high school." A few years older than the two of them, he'd been student body president, as well as captain of the water polo and volleyball teams. Andrew Truehouse had been nicknamed "Drew So True." Bailey started to laugh. "Oh my God, that makes you Trin Tran True!"

The other woman scowled. "It was almost a deal-breaker, I'm telling you. But then we agreed I'd keep my maiden name and the wedding went forward. I would have sent you an invitation if you'd ever bothered to make contact during the last decade."

Regret and guilt gave Bailey dual hefty pinches. "I've made my visits home infrequent and extremely brief. Running from retail, you know?"

One of Trin's eyebrows rose. "Oh, I'm perfectly aware of who you were running from."

"I don't know—"

"And I just saw him on aisle three."

Bailey swallowed, trying to calm her suddenly rocking stomach. "Who . . . ?" Then she gave up all pretext and clutched Trin's forearm as if they were both still sixteen. "You saw Finn in here?"

"Mmm-hmm. He'll see you your bottle of wine and raise you a quart of whiskey."

Bailey searched the area around her, but there wasn't any sign of him. "Are you certain it was Finn?"

"Muscles? Eye patch? Big-boobied redhead hanging all over his wide manly chest?"

A redhead? A woman? But of course Finn had a woman. Did Bailey expect he'd mooned around for ten years, remembering some starry-eyed first love and finding nothing near as dazzling? "Well, um . . ."

Trin wasn't listening to her. "C'mon," she said, dragging Bailey around a corner. "Let's spy on him. It'll be like old times."

Of course Bailey would have never considered this on her own. She was too mature, too . . . uncaring about Finn and his probably fat redhead—the likely one with the equally plump wallet who had gifted him with that outrageous bake sale of a Nativity scene. But Trin, at barely five feet and maybe ninety-five pounds when wearing soaking wet winter clothes, was as strong as a freight train. She tugged Bailey behind a tall display of candy canes, red- and green-wrapped chocolate Kisses, and boxes of instant hot chocolate.

"There he is," Trin stage-whispered.

Bailey worked hard not to look his way. "Really, Trin. I'm not the least bit interested in . . ." But then she heard his deep laugh and it compelled her to take a peek.

The redhead did have big boobies. But despite her tiny waist, her hips were definitely fat. Hah. At thirty, Finn had developed a taste for tall fat women with hair the improbable color of a tequila sunrise. That was the problem with men—they never once considered that no real female had breasts that big or hair that red.

Or maybe the actual problem was that they didn't care.

Pigs.

The fake redhead had a loud voice too. "I know you must be a seal," she declared.

Fat, stupid woman. Pig, not seal.

"A one-eyed special ops?" Finn countered. "Guess again."

Oh. *Navy* SEAL. Since they trained at the nearby base, Bailey now could see where that guess came from. As if Finn would be in the military, though. She knew his rebel's soul better than that.

Bailey bent to Trin's ear. "What does he do, do you know?" At the other woman's measuring glance, she hastened to add, "Not that I care or anything."

But before her friend could reply, from the corner of her eye she saw that Finn had dis-octupied himself from Tequila Sunrise and was moving away from her. Moving in their direction. Bailey muffled a squeak of alarm and scurried away, this time with Trin in tow.

She took refuge in the feminine hygiene aisle, where the only masculine thing in sight was a display of condoms. A sudden memory seared her brain. Sitting in a car in a drugstore parking lot, trying to melt into the passenger seat as Finn went inside for the necessities. He'd come out, reached into the brown bag, and tossed an item into her lap, right there in front of God and everybody. She'd nearly cried in embarrassment.

Then looked down at the big bag of Reese's minis he'd purchased as well. "Never say I don't do foreplay," he'd said with a grin, settling beside her.

But his foreplay had been better than chocolate and peanut butter. Of course, they'd had years of foreplay before they'd actually had sex. First kiss to hours of kissing, to caresses over clothes, to caresses under clothes. Hours of that, too. Then all clothes off. He'd come to her more experienced in the kissing and touching department—certainly less shy about bodily responses to such—but she presumed they'd discovered the actual act together.

That first time had been on a blanket in her back garden, with the warm summer darkness draping over them. She'd been afraid and eager and then uncaring about whether it was right or wrong or the right or wrong time for them to become lovers. He'd already made himself familiar with that mysterious territory between her thighs, a frequent traveler of all the hills and valleys and every little bump in between. Before, he had always touched her there with his lean fingers, his eyes on her face, watching for her reaction.

And she, being a dumb girl, had thought it was important to show no reaction at all. Good girls— even good girls who played on the wild side with their bad-boy boyfriend—wouldn't gasp or cry out or show the pleasure that was shooting from his stroking fingers to run in rippling trails of tingling heat up her spine and down the backs of her legs. She wanted to arch into his hand, but wouldn't that look slutty? So she would close her eyes and bite her bottom lip, tensing her body against the tremors of bliss.

That night, he'd done more. He'd bent his head to touch her with his mouth. In half agony, half excitement, she'd screwed her eyes shut tighter. How could he? Why would he? It felt so incredible. So good! Don't let him know!

And so she'd yanked him up by the shoulders. The unexpected movement had caused him to collapse on top of her, his erection pressing against that wonderful wet place that he'd set to pulsing. He'd groaned—no concern about sluttishness from him, weren't boys so lucky?—and she'd loved the sound of it, and she'd so loved him, and she was so afraid of letting him know that she wanted his mouth back right *there*, that she'd whispered, "Oh, Finn," and shifted the tiny bit that took him to the entrance to her body.

And bad-boy Finn had surprised the heck out of her by practically leaping into the air. "Condom," he'd gasped and dived for his pants. That's when she'd figured out that like Boy Scouts, even bad boys were always prepared.

She was still pulsing, still loving, still battling her body and its responses so that when he'd come back to her, latex-protected, and uttered a breathy "Are you sure?"—that she was. In part to hide from Finn all that he could do to her with a simple touch.

"Earth to Bailey, Earth to Bailey."

Landing back in the present, she jerked her gaze down to Trin. "Sorry, I was drifting."

Trin snorted. Amazing how such an indelicate sound could come out of such a delicate-looking woman.

"What?"

"Dreaming, more like. I'd love to pursue what about, but I have to get going. Adam hasn't been sleeping more than a couple of hours without waking up, and he's due for another dose of kiddie cold stuff in twenty minutes. Sick babies make Drew panic."

Bailey frowned. "I thought I heard he was a pediatrician."

Her friend waved a slender hand. "Like I said, sick babies make Drew panic." She started up the aisle, hurrying in the direction of the checkout stands.

Hurrying off with the answers that could put all Bailey's questions to rest . . . and then maybe Bailey herself. It had to be close to one in the morning and she'd been up since before seven. With all these questions about Finn still clamoring in her mind, she'd never get any sleep. She trotted after her. "Trin, wait!"

The other woman turned around, but continued to pedal backward. "What?"

"Finn."

"Finn? What about Finn?"

The smile on Trin's face told Bailey she was enjoying making her beg. Some things never changed. "I'll tell Drew what you did on your seventeenth birthday," she threatened.

Trin had a dimple when she grinned and she was still moving toward the stands. "Unless what?"

Bailey hustled to keep up. "Unless you tell me everything. What he does, how long he's done it, who he's with, who he was with. The works, Trin."

"The 411 on the F-I-N-N?"

It was cruel to treat an old friend so. "Yes," Bailey hissed, then her voice rose. "I want to know what's up with his eye, and what he . . ."

Her voice trailed off as Trin's shoulder blades bumped into someone. Someone with muscles, an eye patch, and a wide manly chest. Trin squeaked, spun around, then shot Bailey an apologetic look.

"Hey there, Finn," she said. "What an, uh, coinky-dinky."

Coinky-dinky? Bailey stared at her friend.

Trin made a wild gesture in her direction, so wild that her arm whapped Bailey in the stomach. "Here's, uh, Bailey. You remember her. Bailey Sullivan."

Make that breathless Bailey. Speechless Bailey. But a Bailey who could still hear perfectly well. And see that cold stare that Finn leveled at her.

"If you're interested in knowing everything about me, GND," he said, "you're about ten years too late."

GND. If he wanted to slice her through with anything more than his chilly look and those flat words, then that was it. It was the nickname he'd given her before she'd left him, before they were lovers, before they'd ever even kissed. It reminded her that first he'd been the sulking boy she'd made smile and that once she'd been his pesky Girl Next Door.

The one who had grown older, fallen in love,

then run away from him. The one who was perfectly willing to run again, leaving behind the Merlot and the cheese straws, as well as her oldest best friend and her very first boyfriend.

Not to mention any chance she'd get a decent rest that night.

Ten minutes after his favorite bar closed and kicked his reluctant ass out, Finn pulled slowly up to his grandmother's. Thank God it was legal in California to drive with only one 20/20 eye. Losing his license after losing so much else would have flattened him. Gram had left the icicle lights on for him, and he checked over his surroundings in their silvery glow. It was dark next door, and Bailey's Passat looked as if it was as long asleep as the rest of the neighborhood.

With grocery bag in hand, he opened his door, climbed out of the SUV to come around the front of his car, then froze. In Finn's business, the goal was to thwart an assault before it ignited. To that end, the men and women he worked with talked openly about their sixth sense—that combination of instinct and training that made them aware when something was out of sync. Hours of drills coupled with innate self-confidence taught them to rely on their ability to foresee danger in order to take quick preventive action.

While Finn had good reason to doubt the

strength of his own sixth sense, he couldn't deny that it was screaming at him now. He gripped the bag tighter, but kept his back turned.

"What do you want, Bailey?" Every hair on the nape of his neck said she was standing directly behind him.

"Well . . . I . . ."

He was going to turn right, he decided, walking past her to head straight into the house. Trading old times with Bailey would be like pulling a thin scab off a new wound. Though the hurt she'd given him was ten years gone, he had recent injuries he was doing his damnedest to heal.

"I'm not—" he started, turning.

It was the glitter that did him in. With it dusted across her cheekbones and sparkling in her hair, she looked like something that had been dipped in the Milky Way before landing on the driveway beside him. That had always been the way of it between them. Finn with his feet in the gutter, Bailey looking as if she hovered above the ground.

With his willpower weakened by two whiskeys and a chaser of beer, how could he walk away?

Still, this was going to be her show. Drawing the liquor bottles in their brown paper wrapping closer to his side, he leaned his hips against the car and said nothing.

She didn't either, not at first. But he doubted she possessed the deep well of patience he'd developed over the years that he'd stood post.

To prove him right, she cracked in less that sixty seconds. "Hey, look," she said. "I'm sorry."

"For what?"

"For tonight, at the store, of course."

Well, of course. She wasn't apologizing for stamping her size sixes all over his heart and soul ten years ago, and he'd be dead before he let her know he cared about that. Before he let her know *anything*, damn it.

Be cool, Finn. Ice.

"I was naturally curious," Bailey went on. She'd put on a parka over her sweater and jeans, but the very tip of her nose was pink with the cold.

He lifted his free hand to his eye patch. "Everyone is."

"Oh." Her hand reached out, as if she would touch him, but then it dropped. "I'm sorry for that too."

The glitter in her hair framed her fine-etched features as she continued to study his face. She'd been petite as a child, and though she'd grown taller during adolescence, it hadn't been much. He'd been endlessly fascinated by all the femininity contained in that small body of hers. "I . . . lost the original and fake eyes aren't that comfortable," he heard himself offer.

Damn. He hadn't meant to volunteer a scrap.

Though instead of the pity he dreaded, his admission caused her to aim a cheeky little grin his way. It curved up the pink fullness of her baby-doll mouth. "Oh, be honest, Finn Jacobson. Admit you also like the whole Jack Sparrow pirate look-alike thing."

"I'm taller than Johnny Depp." And no one had been cheeky with Finn since his injury. Hell, since years before that.

"Oh yeah." She was still razzing him. "And you have lots more muscles too."

"What? So you ambushed me to issue compliments?"

Her teasing smile died, as did the sparkle in her eyes. "Finn . . ."

He wouldn't regret his refusal to play. "What is it you want, Bailey?"

She gave a shrug. "I'm trying to be sensible, okay? I'm guessing we're both here for the holidays."

He nodded.

"My mother said your grandmother's been sick."

Finn tightened his grip on the bottles again. "She's on the road to recovery. I'm here to see to that."

"My mom and Dan are having some . . . problems, so I'm working at the store for them until the twenty-fifth. Not a day later, but still I'm sure we'll be running into each other from time to time."

He nodded again, but offered nothing more.

Her mouth turned down. "Do you have to make this so hard?"

"What do you mean? I'm not doing anything."

"You are too!" She stepped closer, so that the toes of her soft suede boots were an inch away from his own scarred black leather.

"How?"

"Oh, please." Her small hand wrapped his flannel-covered sleeve, and his forearm went steely at the touch. "I know you, Finn Jacobson, and—"

"Do you?" Suddenly it was too much. Her unexpected return home, the glitter on her beautiful face, the way he couldn't ignore her touch. So much for ice.

He grabbed her wrist and pulled her hand off his arm, using the movement to yank her closer against him. The sides of her parka parted and the white sweater she wore underneath met the buttons of his shirt. "What the hell is it you think you know about me?"

Her eyes went wide and her pouty lips parted. He silently cursed himself for the loss of control, but he wasn't letting her loose. Though his sixth sense was screeching at him like a parrot now, because he was trained to prevent attacks, not initiate them, the Princess Next Door didn't have a clue who he'd become, and he needed to make that clear.

Maybe then she'd avoid him. Maybe then he'd find peace.

"What do you think you know, Bailey?"

She was breathing fast, and he could feel her

small breasts rising and falling against him. He pressed his hips against the cold metal of the car so that she wouldn't know what that small movement was doing to his cock. He hadn't been this close to a woman who wasn't a nurse in months, so it wasn't his damn fault, but he didn't want her to guess she was getting any more out of him than annoyance.

"What do you expect I do for a living?" he demanded.

She licked her lips, and he tried forgetting what they'd tasted like. "I don't know. Do you . . . work on cars? Motorcycles?"

He released a short laugh. "I work *around* cars and motorcycles, I'd guess you could say."

"Nice. Good."

The light glinted off her wet lips, and he couldn't look away from them. "Yeah. It would fit your expectations if I'm a dirt-under-his-fingernails grease monkey, wouldn't it? And that years ago I knocked up some chick and had to marry her."

She blinked. "You're married? You have a child?"

"Three. Their names are Cobain, Grohl, and Novoselic."

Her mouth pursed. "You named them after Nirvana band members? Now how come I don't believe you?"

"Which part are you suspicious of, Bailey?" Not the notion he changed oil for a living, he bet. She'd run away from him ten years ago because she thought he wasn't good enough for her.

"Make your point, Finn." She struggled to get free of the shackle of his fingers, but he didn't let go. "Tell me what you want to say and get it over with."

How could you fucking leave me? How could you walk away without a word and leave that raw, gaping hole in my chest behind?

It was hurting like it happened yesterday, but he knew that was because of Spencer. It was Spencer who had ripped him open again.

"I'm a Secret Service agent."

Bailey had been struggling to pull away again, but now she stilled. "What?"

"I went to college, got a degree in criminal justice, then joined the Secret Service." He gave a shake of his head. "Your obvious shock isn't flattering, GND."

"But . . . but . . ." Now she was shaking *her* head. "Rules, Finn. You were never good with rules."

"Still a struggle." Especially with the ones he made for himself. Regarding her. "However, I like the sense of purpose."

"But . . . the *Secret Service*?"

"It was Tanner Hart who introduced the idea to me." He didn't bother reminding her of the Hart family. There was a San Diego thoroughfare named after Walter Hart, Tanner's grandfather, who had been a World War II ace. Tanner's father and uncle had distinguished themselves in Vietnam, his brothers in Afghanistan and Iraq. A family peopled by famous military men. "Tanner and I met that summer I was twenty. Later, we entered the Secret Service Academy together."

"I didn't know . . . no one said."

If Finn had to guess, it would be that she'd never bothered to inquire. "Gram is quiet about it. The service likes us to keep a low profile. When asked I most often tell people I have a government job."

She stared as if seeing him for the very first time. He let her look, enjoying the idea that he'd knocked for a loop the girl who'd once knocked him on his ass and left him for dead.

"So, sweetheart, you don't know me so well after all, do you?"

She rubbed at her forehead with her free hand, and he realized he was still holding her other one. He couldn't seem to let it go. "Wait a minute," she said. "Tanner. Tanner was involved with—"

"Don't mention it if you see him." Finn dropped her wrist and shoved his fingers in his pocket. It was time they both went to bed.

But she was frowning now and rubbing her forehead as if coaxing a memory to the surface. "That assassination attempt."

Finn took a step around her. "As I said, don't mention it if you see him."

She caught his elbow in her own viselike grip and turned him toward her again. "Finn?"

Secret Service agents were known for their flat, cool stares. He could still do it one-eyed. "What now?"

Her gaze cataloged every feature of his expressionless face. Then her hand tightened on him as she spoke. "What did that have to do with you?"

"What are you talking about?"

"Oh, Finn," she whispered.

He didn't like that odd gleam in her eyes, or that she was touching his arm again, or the fact that he wanted to bury his face in her blond, glittering hair and lose himself in her scent. Damn those whiskeys!

"There's nothing more," he ground out, wrenching his arm from her grasp.

"There's more. I know you, Finn."

She didn't, goddamn it. No one knew him anymore, least of all himself. He'd been a damn fine agent, dedicated to the job, one who never wearied of the constant training and the constant stress of searching for that one face in the crowd. Cool and collected in his dark suit and his dark glasses. But his usual detachment was so damn hard to find and hold on to now.

"You were there," Bailey said. "Somehow. Somewhere. I'm trying to think . . . I've seen the video."

"The whole damn world has seen the video." Though the Secret Service had studied the tape over and over, it had also played for months on the news channels, the entertainment channels, *everywhere*.

"Until then I didn't know that the Secret Service had a Dignitary Protection Division."

Finn half turned, looking off down the dark street. "Besides the president and family and the vice-president and family, we're charged with protecting foreign dignitaries visiting the U.S. Prince al-Maddah was assigned some of our best agents."

"And the agents saved him."

Seeing red, he rounded on her. He couldn't help himself. "Is that all you remember?"

Her eyes went big again, but he couldn't bleed the bitterness from his voice. "An agent lost her life, Bailey. An agent on *my* detail."

"A woman," she said.

"Ayesha Spencer. She was twenty-five years old and her name was Ayesha Spencer. When the murderer took his first shot, she did exactly as she'd been trained to do—stood tall and made herself a target for the gunman—then took a bullet in the neck, above the protection of her Kevlar vest."

"Like I said, I've seen the video. She was a hero."

"But green as grass and wholesome as apple pie to boot," he couldn't stop himself from muttering, though he managed to stop the next words from rolling out. *Shouldn't I have sensed something was about to go down?*

Hell!

He was supposed to be icing all this emotion over, but the feelings continued boiling up inside him.

The Secret Service had an in-house team of shrinks who'd have happy hard-ons if only he'd let them out in a session, but that wasn't going to happen. He could take care of himself. Service training involved learning to discern warning signs of severe stress, and he'd self-diagnosed himself just fine, thank you very much.

He'd prescribed the cure too. These few weeks with Gram, getting her well again, and then he'd be as good as before too.

"So you were there," Bailey said. "Where, Finn?"

"You've watched the video," he answered, suddenly too tired to avoid talking about it any longer. "The Service kept my name out of the press, and it's mostly my torso caught on film. I'm the one you see shoving the prince into the limo. At the same time, I glanced over my shoulder to check if the enemy was closing in."

"Go on."

"Before a couple of other agents tackled him, the gunman got off his next bullet. It shattered my left orbital bone, destroying my eye in the process." He knew he sounded offhand about it. It made everyone more comfortable that way. "Hence your old friend Finn is now Finn the Fucked-up Pirate."

He watched her swallow, then again. Bailey,

obviously, finally, thankfully, silenced.

Tucking his whiskey and his wine under his arm, he at last turned from her and hurried off. He'd revealed more than he liked, damn it all, but at least it was something that shut her up long enough for him to make his escape.

┌-9999999999999999999┐
Bailey Sullivan's Vintage Christmas
Facts & Fun Calendar

December 4
In the sixteenth century, devout Germans brought decorated trees into their homes. If trees were hard to
come by, they built Christmas pyramids of wood and
decorated them with evergreens and candles. Not until
the mid-1800s, however, did Christmas trees become
popular in the U.S., thanks to the influence of Queen
Victoria and her German husband, Prince Albert.

Chapter 4

During hours lying in bed and hours
working in the store, Bailey had tried to
absorb what her bad-boy boyfriend had
made of his life. Finn Jacobson, college
graduate, Secret Service agent, man seriously
wounded in the line of duty. My God! Who would
have guessed?

She hadn't.

Not only was she embarrassed by her original
assumptions, she felt shaken by the truth. She'd

seen that video of the assassination attempt a number of times—it was one of the biggest news stories of the year, probably because it was so dramatically caught on tape.

The cameraman had won accolades for his work. Not only had he captured all the action, but he'd done a superb editing job as well. The version played by the networks always faded out on a pair of shattered sunglasses lying in a puddle of crimson. Those were Finn's, she now realized. Both the glasses and the blood.

Replaying it in her mind as she drove home from a fourth long day at The Perfect Christmas, Bailey felt yet another wave of nausea roll through her stomach. What had happened eleven months ago made her sick . . . and sad.

And more determined than ever to stay clear of Finn.

Sympathy over what had happened was normal, of course. But she was in downright danger of becoming sloppy over it. And long ago she'd made the choice not to be sloppy over any man.

Inching along behind the lookie-loos ogling Walnut Street's Christmas excess, Bailey knew that the permanent solution to avoiding the man living next door meant forcing another confrontation with her mother. This time, she told herself, she'd talk until her mother truly comprehended the predicament she and The Perfect Christmas were in.

Bailey was a sensible, rational person. Tracy

was an logical, reasonable woman. Surely some straight talk between the two of them would rouse her mother from her stupor or depression or whatever it was and get her behind back into the store.

And Bailey back to her Los Angeles life.

Ten minutes later, she let herself into the house. "Mom?"

"In here," came from the kitchen.

Squaring her shoulders, Bailey strode into the room. Surrounded by a plethora of vegetables, Tracy was tearing lettuce into tiny shreds and dropping them into a wooden salad bowl. In the last couple of days she'd abandoned the comfort of pasta foods and was going strictly rabbit. Just that was enough to depress anybody.

With a casual movement, Bailey set onto the counter the eleven-inch Christmas tree she'd brought home from the shop. The tiny pine needles looked real enough and it was decorated with firefly-sized lights as well as pine cones and glass ornaments no bigger than M&M's. She plugged it in without comment, though hoped it would remind her mother of what was waiting for her just a few blocks away.

"How was your day?" her mother asked without looking up, on obvious maternal autopilot. She appeared rumpled and drowsy, as if she'd slept the day away wearing yet another pair of ragged sweats.

Bailey glanced at the little tree, then took a

breath, preparing herself to hit the situation head-on. "It was *your* day, Mom, remember? I'm away from *my* life to run *your* store."

"It's the family store," Tracy replied, matter-of-fact.

Dead end there, Bailey thought. She tried another tack. "Okay, but Dan—"

"You saw him?" her mother interrupted, chin jerking up. "What did he want?" Color suddenly flagged her pale cheeks, and she seemed to find a surge of energy as she grabbed a carrot and began attacking it with a grater.

Bailey watched the violent process with dawning alarm. "No, I haven't seen him. Not yet. But Mom, face it. You can't hide here any longer taking your emotions out on defenseless vegetables. You need to talk to Dan."

The carrot was quickly decimated to the size of a mini gherkin as her mother's color faded and her mouth set in a stubborn line. "I don't see why." She picked up another innocent root and took it down to midget proportions too.

Bailey cooled her impatience. "Then at least you have to come back to the store."

"No," Tracy said.

"Mom—"

"I'm *not* going to talk with him and I'm *not* going to the store. Not if *he's* going to be there."

Frustrated, Bailey pinched the bridge of her

nose. "That's the problem, Mom. He's not there. You're not there."

"But you don't know that. He could walk in any time and then I'd have to see him and I might have to talk to him."

Bailey stared at her mother. Where was reason? Where was logic? She tried to keep her voice level. "The only one of the family there is *me*, and I made a three-year-old cry today because I said she was wrong and that there were only six reindeer not eight!"

That got Tracy's full attention again. She looked up, her brow furrowed. "Why would you say such a thing?"

"Because I couldn't remember all the names, okay? I had Dasher and Blitzen, Prancer and Donder, but then I blanked out and called one Disco and another Asteroid. I decided I better quit while I was ahead." The little girl's mother had whisked the tot out of the store, leaving her basket full of Christmas cheer behind—and unpaid for.

"Dasher, Dancer, Donder, Blitzen, Comet, Cupid, Prancer, Vixen. And then Rudolph, of course, for those nonpurists."

Bailey rolled her eyes. "See what I mean? You've got to come back."

"We've already gone over that."

"Then let's go over it again, and start at the beginning. Please." Bailey rescued the last carrot from her mother's brutal clutches, biting into it herself.

"It started right after we dropped Harry off at college."

Yesterday Bailey had called her brother and grilled him about the situation, but Harry was as mystified as she. Reluctant to put a damper on his first months away at college, big sister had promised him she would handle it—but that meant either getting to the bottom of the problem or getting through to her mother. "All right. You two dropped Harry off at college. Then a couple weeks later Dan left because . . . ?"

Tracy cleaved a cabbage in two. "Because I didn't notice his hair and his teeth."

Bailey had to cough up a chunk of carrot. "What?"

Her mother's knuckles went white on the knife. "He used something to get rid of the gray at his temples. *He bleached his teeth!*"

Okay. "That's not a capital offense."

"The capital offense was I didn't notice, according to him. He came home one day and stomped into Harry's room. I was sitting in there, just . . . just thinking . . . and he demanded that I look at him."

"And you didn't realize he'd gone George Hamilton on you?"

Tracy's knife clattered to the cutting board. "I'd been busy. I'd been preoccupied. So I didn't recognize the changes, okay? But Dan didn't give me a second chance. He packed up his things and left the house, right then and there."

Dan was an easygoing man. He'd married Tracy three years after her divorce and didn't seem the least bit ego-diminished by leaving his job at a big-time brokerage house to run his wife's family's store alongside her. Though Bailey had always kept a wall between herself and her stepfather, she knew that had been her choice, not his. Dan had never resented having a stepdaughter and he'd appeared to love the life he'd made with her mother and their son, Harry.

None of this was making sense.

"Is it . . ." Bailey cleared her throat. "Is it another woman?"

Tracy stared at the cutting board, unblinking. "I didn't see a gold chain around his neck, if that's what you mean."

A twinge of pain pierced Bailey's right temple. Gold chain, another woman. Another woman, gold chain. Was this some sort of code she didn't understand? A headache started blossoming, probably because the half of her brain that dealt with logic and reason was contorting like a pretzel trying to make sense of the irrational that had now become her family life.

Her calf itched and she flashed on that night she'd watched her mother sobbing in the dry bathtub. How could Tracy do this again? After

Bailey's father's defection, why had Tracy let another man get close enough to mess with her heart? Bailey could remember endless weeks of her mother crying in the middle of the night—had Tracy completely blocked that from her mind?

There were non-risky ways to negotiate the world, maybe even to have a man in your life, but none of them involved leaving the safe side of the emotion superhighway. It was up to Bailey to yank her mother back to the sidewalk.

"Look, Mom, think of the big picture. The store—"

"I can't go there." Tracy retrieved the knife and started killing the cabbage.

"Mom—"

"If Dan's going to go to the trouble of looking gorgeous, then I won't chance seeing him!" She reached over to whack an innocent green onion for good measure. "And that's final."

Not to mention completely crazy. Trying to think through her headache, Bailey grabbed some cellophane off the counter and moved to stuff it in the garbage beneath the sink. The bag was near full, so she tied it off and stomped toward the side yard and the big can left there, grateful to work off some of her frustration in the brisk night air.

Maybe it would clear her mind enough to allow her sensible, rational self to formulate a new strategy for dealing with the situation.

At this point in the property, a narrow, hip-high hedge divided their yard from the Jacobsons'. And wouldn't you know, Finn stood on the other side, beside his grandmother's own can. The combined strains of "Frosty the Snowman" and "Away in a Manger" must have masked the sounds of her leaving her house. He didn't seem to notice her presence as he broke down some boxes and stuffed them in the recycle bin.

Her frustration turned to something else as she looked her fill.

Wide shoulders, brawny arms, lean hips, long legs. As he moved, his T-shirt lifted, showing a brief slice of rippling ab muscles. She flashed back fourteen years, when he'd gone from the boy-she-loved-to-annoy to the boy-she-couldn't-ignore. The first day he'd arrived for that particular summer he'd gazed at her over that very hedge, finding her on her back steps where she was coloring a beat-up pair of white canvas sneakers with a pack of Sharpie pens.

"Hello, pest," he'd called out.

Her old bikinis had been tossed in the trash just that morning—the ones that had fit since she was eleven, but that didn't now that she was fourteen. The tops of her new swimsuits had actual cups, and she had actual breasts to put inside them. Her hair was long, past her back strap, and she'd turned it into golden ripples with a new crimping iron the night before.

That spring, she'd taken custody of her mother's Clinique Black Honey lip gloss, and loved the wet shine and darkened pink it gave to her mouth. About every twenty minutes she applied another layer, just as often as she took a brush to her gleaming length of hair.

She'd liked the Bailey she now saw in the mirror, and she admired that new Bailey's reflection on a regular basis. Even her little brother had teased her about checking herself out in the reflective chrome on the refrigerator door handle and in the side mirrors of any vehicle she happened to pass.

So that day when she glanced up at Finn's voice, she was ready for him to see that the "pest" had changed. She wasn't a whole lot taller, but she'd stood anyway, eager to give him his first glimpse of the works. Call her vain.

She had been.

But she wasn't prepared for Finn's changes. Maybe there weren't any. Maybe he'd looked just the same the previous Christmas, and it was Bailey's more mature eyes that now noticed the stretch of his T-shirt over his shoulders, the clean lines of his male face, the lean strength in his arms and legs.

The strange yet exciting expression in his dark eyes.

She'd prickled from her scalp to between her bare toes.

Half of her wanted to retreat. Half of her wanted

to flirt. That half won. She'd sauntered over to him, feeling shaky inside and hot everywhere else.

With eight feet still separating them, the urge to back away had coursed through her again, but she was pulled forward by that serious, mysterious expression in his ever-watchful eyes. "Oh shit," he'd whispered as she'd walked closer, her new hips swaying. "Oh *shit*."

Maybe he'd had a premonition.

Maybe he had one now, fourteen years later. Because without warning, he looked up, pinning her with his one good eye. She was caught red-handed, drinking him in.

It was still there, as if fourteen subsequent New Year's Eve balls had never fallen in Times Square. His dangerous male beauty, her attraction to it, that edgy sense of sex-in-the-offing that she hadn't been experienced enough to recognize as a naïve young teenager. At twenty-eight she knew what it was.

Had already experienced it again with Finn, of course. On his grandmother's front porch, at the grocery store, on the sidewalk, on each occasion she'd felt that fierce tug of physical awareness. It only ratcheted higher now, as without moving a muscle, without saying a word, his lashes swept down, his gaze running over her body.

Bailey froze as it seemed to strip her shirt from her shoulders, yank her jeans from her legs, burn away her bra and panties. With one look, making her naked for him. Again.

Her thigh muscles tightened. She crossed her free arm over her chest, reassured to feel cotton beneath her skin, but intent on hiding her tight, almost aching nipples.

"You scared to get too close, GND?" he taunted, a dark pirate with his eye patch and gleam of feral white teeth. "Surely you're not afraid of me."

She shook her head and forced her feet to venture closer. "Surely not." Sexual attraction didn't frighten her, a sensible, rational woman. What she was really afraid of she'd left behind ten years ago. Attraction wasn't the same as emotion.

So when you looked at it that way, approaching Finn was perfectly safe.

Finn didn't watch her toss the bag of garbage into the can and drop the lid. Instead he continued breaking down the boxes he'd dragged outside.

At the thump of plastic meeting plastic, he waited for her to walk away. Surely she'd be eager to distance herself from him and scurry back into her mother's house, still spooked by the scarred man who had silenced her outside Gram's. But her sand-colored boots stayed firmly fixed to the concrete on her side of the hedge.

Finn kept his mouth shut. Unlike the other night, when he'd visited a bar on his way home from the grocery store, now he was completely sober. No confessions, not even a little small talk, was going to spill from his trap tonight. Nothing off-limits was coming from his mouth this time.

"Am I seeing what I think I'm seeing?"

He glanced up. She was staring at the tallest, biggest box he'd yet to flatten. There was a photo on the outside of what it had contained—a five-foot-high chocolate fountain in the general shape of a Douglas fir.

"Is that thing for real?" she asked.

"Yeah."

"First the cookie Nativity scene, and now the Rockefeller Plaza of Christmas tree fountains. Someone must have a special admirer."

"Special's the word." He could clear up exactly how and why, but he didn't. Why shouldn't he keep her guessing? Not to mention she had this funny little curl to her lip that matched the one she'd had the summer he'd arrived in Coronado wearing a braided thread bracelet made by a girl from home.

He'd snipped it off that night, but he wasn't obligated to make things easy for Bailey any longer. Remember? He was a grown man now, not a half-tamed boy who wanted her more than another breath.

Though as she continued to stand there, he found he couldn't continue to ignore her either. Where the hell had he left his secret agent super patience? Was that suddenly gone forever too? "Is something the matter?" he asked.

"No." She glanced back at her mother's house

with a little grimace, then shrugged. "Just taking a moment to enjoy the strains of that new Christmas melody classic, 'The First Santa Claus Is Coming to O Little Town of Bethlehem.'"

He wanted to laugh. "Neighborhood celebration getting to you?"

Her sigh whispered beneath the clash of carols in the distance. "I hate Christmas."

A familiar refrain. He stuffed the last of the flattened fountain box into the recycle bin. "Tell me something about Bailey Sullivan I don't already know."

"Really?" Her eyes widened, all thick sexy lashes and unforgettable blue. "You want to talk?"

No.

Yet now that he'd thrown out the comment he couldn't play coward. Anyhow, turnabout was fair play, and last night he'd given her the CliffsNotes of his own life story.

"I just got to thinking . . . if I left the wild side and went straight, maybe you, on the other hand, went crooked." He looked over, curved his mouth in what he thought she might take as a smile. "You know, perhaps somewhere along the line little Miss Perfect fell off the great balance beam of life."

"I was never Miss Perfect." She was frowning.

"Could have fooled me." He rocked on his heels, staring her down with his one eye. "But then again . . . you did, didn't you?"

A shadow crossed her face and he dropped his

gaze to adjust the placement of Gram's cans. *Pull back, pull back,* he warned himself. *Don't get riled up, don't give her a chance to get to you.* Risking another look at her, he caught her watching him again.

Then she gave a little shrug. "Maybe I did change. Maybe I turned into someone with my own wild side."

He snorted. "Wild? You wouldn't know wild if it bit you on the butt."

Another frown pulled her brows together and she stamped closer to the hibiscus hedge between them. "That's what you did," she hissed. "Remember, Finn? You bit me on a lot of places, including my butt."

Hell. She had to remind him. There was no explaining away or excusing the primitive need teenage Finn had felt to mark Bailey's perfect skin. Her neck, the inside of her thigh, the high curve of her round, pretty ass, because it was one of the few places a hickey could be hidden by her itsy bitsy, teeny-weeny bikinis that drove him so crazy.

He cleared his throat. "That was a long time ago." He shifted the recycle bin two inches to the right. "We're no longer two adolescents hopped up on hormones."

"Is that what you'd call it?" She ran her forefinger over one of the yellow hibiscus flowers, its ruffles closed up tight for the night.

As if he'd confess to it ever being anything more. Not when he could also recall with perfect clarity the roadkill she'd made of his heart when he'd discovered she'd left for college early, despite their summer plans. At his autopsy, they'd find the four-chambered organ still flattened, without a skid mark in sight.

He ignored the old ache in his chest and went back to concentrating on gaining the advantage. "In any case, I'm more interested in this wild-thing Bailey you claim to be now."

She shrugged again. "Okay, maybe wild is an overstatement in comparison to your checkered past, but I live a pretty full life."

"Oh really?" He crossed his arms over his chest. "If I had to guess, I'd say you're a rigid, seventy-hour-a-week, all-work-no-play jobaholic."

"No—"

"And that even the balls-of-steel senior partner at the firm you run trembles when you call his name."

Her quick glance back at her house made it clear she supposed her mother had been filling him in. Then she put one hand on her hip. "Maybe he trembles for reasons you don't know about."

Oh yeah, like she was doing the horizontal tango with a white-haired lawyer who'd been married for fifty-three years. As if he'd believe *that* was a Bailey move. Finn gave her an appraising glance from the golden top of her head to her booted toes. "I bet your social life's lousy."

She exhaled an insulted huff and her other hand fisted on her other hip. "You think I can't get a man?"

This was too easy. Maybe it was mean of him to needle her, and he didn't know why it pleased him so much to make her mad, but he hadn't had this much fun in months. "I know you won't keep one."

She huffed again. "Who cares when L.A. is chock-full of eligible bachelors?"

"The bachelor you spend most of your leisure hours with lives in the condo below yours and is gay."

Her jaw dropped. "How—"

"Easy. The Secret Service's Office of Protective Research keeps extensive files on anyone who threatens the security of the president or the country."

A flush burned on her cheeks and her eyes sparked. "I have never threatened anyone or anything in my life!"

Finn lifted a hand. "Then, Bailey, so much for your claim of a bad-girl transformation."

"I'll show you a transformation."

Then she did. She did it so quickly that he couldn't leap away fast enough. One second she was glaring at him over the hedge and the next she'd grabbed him around the neck, yanked his head close, and sank her teeth into his bottom lip.

"That's what you get," she said, pulling back. "You wanted to take a bite out of me, so I took mine out of you."

She continued to glower at him, her breasts heaving against a fuzzy white sweater. "Though a garden hose might have been a better weapon."

"I'll say," Finn muttered, because he couldn't let her have the last word.

Or the last kiss.

He grabbed her shoulders and hauled her against the low, narrow hedge. He pressed close to it too, not even noticing the rattle of leaves and the dig of branches on his way to her lips. Her body was rigid beneath his hands, but her mouth was hot. Soft and hot, and he almost wished for that threatened cold blast from the garden hose because he was teenage-horny again, his cock going hard to fight the denim of his jeans.

He pushed his tongue between her lips. She made a sound, but he didn't care if it was a protest. She'd had her chance at punishment; this was his. The inside of her mouth was peppermint-sweet— as if she'd been sucking on a candy cane not long ago—and his eye closed at the intoxicating taste.

With her shoulders cupped by his palms and his tongue curling against the velvet of hers, time rewound. He was twenty again, nineteen, sixteen. The age he'd been that fateful day when he'd looked at her and the dark rebel inside him had recognized the golden girl who could be the calm to his hormonal storm. He'd cursed her, the world, fate, the moment he'd recognized it, but he'd been unable to take his feet off the path.

But it had never been so purely cerebral, he admitted, as he slanted his head, taking more of her mouth as he ran his hands over her sharp shoulder blades to the round globes of her ass. Not cerebral in the least. He'd been sixteen and he'd wanted sex too.

There were easier girls to get it from, he'd known that. Known them. It took time to persuade the good girls to put out, that was a given. It was going to take time to get Bailey to bed. But that hadn't stopped him from still wanting her. From wanting, wanting, wanting her.

Now nearing thirty-one, Finn didn't seem to have the patience of his teenage self. He found her waist and burrowed under the soft sweater to the sleek skin at the small of her back. Even that wasn't enough, and as he tracked his lips from her mouth to her warm cheek, his fingertips tucked under the waistband of her jeans.

At the same time that he found her lobe and bit down, he shoved his hands lower to fill his palms with the naked, curved globes of her ass. Bless thong underwear.

She jerked, her skin goose-bumped against his hands. He gentled his lips on her ear and rubbed his nose against her soft hair. Her familiar perfume filled his head.

Like that, it was a dozen years ago again. Leaves rattled as he tried moving closer. Like then, always needing more of her sweetness and the fire he wanted to find beyond it.

"Finn . . ." Bailey whispered, her throaty voice shivering down his spine.

"What?" He pressed a kiss to the rim of her ear. Still aching like sixteen, still as mesmerized.

"Finn?"

"Mmm?" His mouth found the satiny skin beneath her jaw.

"Finn?"

He froze, his tongue against Bailey's hot flesh. That wasn't her voice calling his name.

It was part of his sixteen-year-old world, though.

And his thirty-year-old world too.

Gram.

He broke free of Bailey. Then of her spell.

They stared at each other from opposite sides of the hedge, and he wondered how he'd gotten so stupid. Why had he let his mouth get him into trouble again? His lips were throbbing, the whole of him was aching for more kisses.

Such a damn dangerous ache.

At the same moment they turned from each other. The older dark rebel and the wiser golden girl beating hasty retreats from the traitorous, beguiling past.

On his end, cursing all the way. He could only hope it wasn't as it had been all those years ago . . . already too late.

Bailey Sullivan's Vintage Christmas Facts & Fun Calendar

December 5

In Italian legend, La Befana is an old woman who brings gifts to children on Epiphany Eve. It is said that the Wise Men visited her on the way to Bethlehem, but she was too busy cleaning house to accompany them when invited. Later, when she regretted the decision and set out to find them and the Baby Jesus, she could not. The story goes that she continues to wander, leaving gifts for the children she does come across.

Chapter 5

From the master bedroom, Tracy heard her daughter leave the house. That must mean it was morning.

She turned over in bed, drawing her knees to her chest. The orange sweat pants she wore had a hole in the knee, and she covered it with her palm, hunching her shoulders inside one of Harry's discarded T-shirts. If she remembered correctly, it advertised the basketball tournament his team had played in last spring. He'd come home after painting signs for some student function with long drips of blue paint on the front and banished the garment to the rag bin.

She'd rescued it in June, never realizing what comfort it might bring her come autumn.

Thanks to Dan.

At the thought of him, she bolted up. She'd call the SOB, she decided, temper flaring. Give him a piece of her mind. Better yet, she'd go find him at that sex-in-the-singles-complex that he now called home. His car would be easy enough to spot.

Her stomach clenched and heat shot up her spine to her neck. That's just what she'd do!

But then she remembered his newly brilliant teeth, his glossy hair, the tan he must be working on at the golf course now that he wasn't working at The Perfect Christmas. And she thought of the hole in her sweat pants, the paint on her shirt, the dull color of her hair and her complexion.

She fell back to the bed, despondence blanketing over the anger, and she burrowed under its safe, familiar weight too. Sleep beckoned again.

She could taste it, a sweet, syrupy lozenge on her tongue. So, so sweet. Tracy's limbs sank like anchors into the mattress while her mind drifted out on the calm morning tide. . . .

Bells were ringing.

Tracy woke at the noise, and without thinking stumbled from the bed to walk, zombielike, toward the front door. Her fingers found the knob, and the cold metal roused her to awareness. Who . . . ?

Through the sidelights, covered by gathered white sheer curtains, was the outline of a man. Short hair. Compact build.

Her heart jerked high, lodging in her throat. Dan. He'd come back to her.

When they'd first met, she'd hated men. Her divorce had blackened the edges of her heart forever, she'd thought, cauterizing it against any future mistakes. Then a friend of a friend introduced her to this lazy-smiling, easy-in-his-own-skin man at a party. She'd looked at him with instant suspicion, staring at the white wine he offered as if it were arsenic. But he'd worn her down, then won her over.

Twenty years later, he'd left her.

For that, she might have reverted to loathing all men again. Except when you had a son, she'd discovered, you lost your ability for nonspecific XY-chromosome hatred. So instead she just loathed Dan.

No! Her fingers tightened on the doorknob. She didn't loathe him. She didn't care that much. She wouldn't. Ever. Twenty years ago, she'd taken a second leap of trust only to fall flat on her face again, but Dan couldn't know that any part of her hurt.

Every part of her hurt.

Still, she steadied her breath, tightened down

the shell of her pride, then pulled open the door to face him.

It wasn't Dan.

The young man who it was, stared at her under yanked-high brows. "Uh . . . Mrs. Willis?"

Tracy swallowed the bitter pill of disappointment and put what little energy she had left into a smile. "Jeff." Jeff Gable, a high school classmate of her son, Harry. "It's good to see you."

Jeff shoved his hands in his pockets. "Is Harry home?" His glance danced away, as if it embarrassed him to look at her.

Tracy curled her bare toes against the foyer carpet, remembering her misshapen sweat pants and baggy T. Her hand went up to smooth her rumpled hair. "No. He won't be home from college until a few days before Christmas."

"Oh." Jeff shuffled back, as if to keep his distance from her. "I'm here for the month of December."

She tried to remember what school he attended. It had consumed her last year—not only Harry's college applications and essays, but all the tension and excitement of senior year and its effect on him and his friends. She'd been president of the Booster Club and secretary of the PTSA, and every week had been full of events to be attended, organized, or chaperoned.

She and Dan had adored every minute of it.

Maybe only she had adored it.

Jeff took another step away from her. "Are you sick?"

She blinked at him. Did she look sick? She thought of the orange sweat pants again. The hole in their knee. Of course she looked sick.

The boy grimaced. "I mean . . . you're usually at The Perfect Christmas this time of year. I didn't expect to see you at home."

"Oh. Bailey's at the store today. Harry's older sister." Guilt stepped forward, shouldering a place for itself among the other emotions crowding her chest. Bailey, who'd gone from five to forty in the space of a season. Tracy knew why, of course. As a little girl she'd borne witness to the end of her parents' marriage. Neither Tracy nor her ex-husband had tried to protect her from the ugliness.

Tracy had leaned on her little daughter—all big dry eyes and starched spine—then.

As she was doing now.

More guilt.

But then it was swept away as over Jeff's shoulder she glimpsed a familiar car cruising toward the house. Her heart jolted to her throat again and she grabbed Jeff's arm, dragged him inside, then slammed the door shut behind him.

The sweat pants. The T-shirt. The pillow-head hair. She couldn't let Dan see her like this.

She couldn't look at his face.

"We're not here, Jeff."

The heels of his sneakers thudded against the

hardwood floor as he backed away. "Wh-what?"

Tracy had said something similar before. *We're not here, Bailey.* She'd hidden from her ex, holing the two of them up in the house, locking the doors and telling her daughter to be quiet, quiet and good so that Tracy could avoid facing the man who was making her so miserable. *"Never give your heart away,"* she'd whispered to her daughter then.

Now she couldn't regret the advice.

"Mrs. Willis?" Jeff Gable's Adam's apple bobbed. "Do you, uh, need some help?"

Tracy sidestepped the young man to curl a finger around one of the window sheers and peek outside. The car was slowing, then it paused behind the one—presumably Jeff's—that was parked in the driveway.

"Mrs. Willis?"

The little-boy note in Jeff's voice got her attention. She glanced over at him, seeing the confusion on his face. Good God, what must he be thinking?

"I . . . um, wanted you to come in so I could send some Christmas treats home for your family." It was the first thing that popped into Tracy's mind, in case he was worried she was a serial killer or a Mrs. Robinson in the making.

And since she'd mentioned food, and he was a teenager, he grinned, relaxing. "That would be great."

Which meant she had to lead him toward the kitchen.

There, she stood on the cool floor between the sink and the tiled island and tried to think what she could possibly put together in the way of "Christmas treats." She found a paper plate first.

Then it was three crumb-dusted old Oreos from the bottom of the cookie jar. A handful of withered baby carrots. *For the reindeer,* she told herself. Two lonely martini olives from the test tube–like jar in the back of the fridge.

She found one foil-wrapped dinner mint mixed in with the pencils in the everything drawer. A lone freckled banana from the now-empty fruit bowl. Finally, a sprinkle of hardened raisins from the red box in the pantry.

To hide the pitiful sight, she covered it all with the last crumpled inches of the foil tube, then taped an even more pitiful smooshed red bow— also liberated from the everything drawer—on top.

The plate was just like her, she realized, blinking back a sudden sting of tears. Unkempt on the outside and a mix of old, lonely, and dried up on the inside.

How had this happened? Harry had gone, and no wonder Dan found nothing else to keep him at home.

She didn't even have the will or the energy to loathe him anymore.

"Here, Jeff."

He looked up from something he'd been fooling

with on the counter. A little Christmas tree. Jeff had plugged it in and the tiny lights twinkled in the shadowed kitchen. Tracy vaguely remembered Bailey setting it down last night and even more vaguely remembered ordering two dozen for the store last spring.

When she still had a son and husband at home. When she had a purpose. An identity.

"This is nice," Jeff said. "Maybe I'll get my mom one for Christmas. Do you think she'd like it?"

She shrugged. What did she know about the tastes of Jeff 's mom who was happily married, her home now complete with her son?

"Well, thanks for the plate," he said. "I guess I should be going now, Mrs. Willis."

"Of course," she said, following him to the front door. "Of course you should be going."

She waved to him as he drove off down the street. She knew she was feeling sorry for herself but couldn't seem to help it. "You all seem to do that."

"Where are those yummy little powdered sugar stars that are usually here?" Trin asked Bailey, frowning down at the hospitality table at the front of The Perfect Christmas. She rolled the stroller that held her sleeping son around to the other side. "And those tiny chocolate bells?"

"We're doing things a bit different today," Bailey answered, unpacking yet another box and hanging yet another angel on yet another tree.

"But nobody likes leftover Halloween candy at this time of year," Trin complained, her forefinger making waves in the candy corn and jack-o'-lantern-shaped lollipops Bailey had dumped on the gilt-edged Santa tray.

"It was all I could find in the drawer in the back office, okay?" Bailey snatched a piece of sugary corn and tossed it into her mouth. She detested the chalky stuff, but damned if she'd let anyone know it. "I didn't realize I had to put in a weekly order to get the usual from the baker and confectioner's down the street."

She wasn't going to feel bad about it.

There was already plenty of "feeling bad" to go around.

Last night. Finn. Kissing Finn. She felt really bad about that. He'd been needling her, she knew it, but hadn't been able to resist needling back. With her teeth.

And when she'd sunk them into his bottom lip, when she'd tasted him again after ten years . . .

She'd done it to prove a point, of course. To prove that she might have been a naïve teenager when they'd first kissed, but she was a grown-up now and could initiate whatever the hell she wanted. A kiss with teeth. With tongues.

When he'd touched hers last night she'd gone ready in one swift rush of wet heat.

And in that single moment he'd shown her he

still had the upper hand when it came to her body's responses.

Where that fit in with her sensible assertion that sexual attraction and emotional sloppiness were not one and the same she didn't want to think too hard about.

"Still, you should have better giveaways," Trin grumbled, continuing to dig through the candy. "Especially when I came all the way over here—"

"You live two blocks away."

"—to renew our friendship only to find you won't spill a sole small detail about what's going on between you and the Fabulous Finn."

His kiss *was* fabulous. And he was so strong. Stronger than she was. His grandmother had called his name and Bailey hadn't heard it at first, she'd heard nothing over the rumbling-train beat of her heart. But if she had, she would have ignored it, all to stay longer with Finn. To touch Finn more. To give Finn anything he asked.

What a weakling she was. First, surrendering to pressure to come back to Coronado. And second, surrendering to the sexual temptation of having one more taste of her first lover.

This time, it had taken Finn to break them apart.

"All set." The voice of Byron, the male half of her team of part-time sales kids, snagged her attention. Glancing over her shoulder, she saw him wrapping up a transaction at the counter. He slid the receipt into the store's trademark bag and gave the shopper his usual dreamy smile. "Like, have a cool Yule."

Trin's gaze caught Bailey's. *Cool Yule?* she mouthed, her dimple digging into her cheek.

"Now that you see what I have to deal with," Bailey whispered back, "maybe you'll stop whining about the quality of the free grub."

Byron, his shoulder-length blond hair cemented by salt water into tight corkscrews, drifted in the wake of the departing shopper, his flip-flops flap-flapping against the soles of his tanned feet. He sniffed the air as the door opened.

When it closed behind the customer, he swung toward Bailey. "I gotta leave a half hour early today, boss lady. Surf's up."

"What?"

"Brontë!" He raised his voice. "Surf's up!"

His female counterpart, down to the salt water–treated hair and the sandals, poked her head out of the back office. "Then you have to go home and get my wetsuit, By, I didn't bring it with me."

He nodded, and turned toward the front door. "Later, gators."

"Wait a minute," Bailey protested, stepping in front of him. There were browsers all over the store: gathered around the nearby tree that was dressed only in seashells, in the old kitchen where they kept the potpourri and holiday baking mixes, up the ornate staircase and in all the second-floor rooms, including the alcove devoted to Christmas dolls. "You can't go now. And you guys can't leave early."

Byron just looked at her.

"I'm serious." She narrowed her eyes and put the ice in her voice that made the two-hundred-dollar-a-billing-hour attorneys quake in their Prada loafers. "You and Brontë don't get off until six o'clock."

"But boss lady, it's Christmas time."

"Good, Byron," she praised, nodding. It wasn't clear to her if his brain was merely water-logged or if he was just plain dumb. "And we're a Christmas store, so that means we're busy and I need you to do your job."

Byron gave her his puppy-dog eyes. They'd worked on her during his first couple of shifts, but now she knew better. He didn't have a big paper due the next day or an important exam first thing in the morning. As far as she could tell, he wasn't even *enrolled* in any institution outside of the School of Surf Wax.

So she wasn't giving in again. She wasn't giving in to one more thing! Not to impulse, not to hormones, not to puppy-dog eyes, emergency requests, or guilt-tinged obligations. She was here, saving the family farm, and wasn't that enough?

The rattle of jingle bells drew her eyes to the door. An older man entered, just as "Santa Claus Is Coming to Town" piped through the store's speakers. *Oh right*, she muttered silently. *Santa Claus, my sorry behind.*

Instead of red felt and white fur, the man coming through the door wore a blue-and-gold cap that read "U.S. Navy Retired." And she doubted he was bringing her anything she wanted for Christmas. Yesterday this very gentleman had phoned to set up this afternoon's meeting, letting her know it was "imperative."

"Hey," Trin said, sotto voce. "Is it my imagination or what, but does that guy look like General Waverly from *White Christmas*? He's got the exact same military posture and military haircut."

Bailey looked over at her friend. "What are you talking about?"

"You know, the classic *White Christmas*. In the movie, there's that old World War II general who Bing Crosby and Danny Kaye put on that show for in Maine."

"Vermont."

"I think it's Maine."

"Trust me," Bailey said. "It's Vermont."

Trin scowled. "I thought you hate the holiday and everything that goes along with it."

Turning away from her friend, Bailey forced a welcoming smile, though instinct was telling her she should be anything but. "Captain Reed," she said with a little wave. "Or should I be calling you President?"

He strode toward her, chuckling. "Bailey, I'm

the president of the chamber of commerce, not the United States, as you very well know."

"Your orders sounded mighty presidential over the phone yesterday." But when she'd asked him why they had to meet, he'd held out his reasons for the face-to-face.

"I like to do these things in person when I can," he said, still smiling.

These things? That didn't sound good. "Well, I don't have much time, we're busy here, and"—she broke off as she realized that Byron had slipped out after the newcomer's arrival—"we're short-handed."

Next chance she got, she was going to smear suntan oil on the surface of Byron's old-school longboard. It was a surfer's prank guaranteed to give him a cold dunking when he tried to stand on his first wave of the day. She hadn't grown up half Gidget for nothing.

The captain drew out a folded piece of paper from the breast pocket of his sport coat. "Don't worry, I won't take up much of your time."

Bailey eyed the paper. "What do you have there?"

"First off, I just want to extend the chamber's appreciation for stepping forward, Bailey. We understand you have your own job, but this is important too. To your family and the community at large."

She didn't bother wondering how he knew so much about the circumstances. Coronado comprised a mere seventy-five hundred households—and due to the military presence, that meant significantly fewer were full-time civilians. Those civilians were the kind of people who reveled in the small-town atmosphere that included plenty of small-town gossip.

"We knew we could count on you, Bailey. We're all glad you didn't turn your back on The Perfect Christmas. It's a landmark."

"An institution." She should have turned her back on it. That would have been the easier path. But the weight of tradition and her innate first-born perfectionism had rendered her genetically incapable of allowing the decades-old family business to fail on her watch. She'd had to at least *try* to make it better.

"I'm doing my best until the twenty-fifth," she said, making clear she had her limits, though. "After that . . ."

The captain beamed through her warning. Bailey supposed she was glad someone still felt like smiling. She could barely breathe for the weight of the albatross.

Which only got heavier as he held out the paper in his hand.

"What's this?" she asked, afraid to take it.

He still wore his charming smile as he forced the sheet into her hands. "The chamber events scheduled for the store."

"Events? What events are those?" she asked, but

slowly opened the paper. It outlined the next days until Christmas.

Santa Storytelling Hours.

Christmas Movie Nights. Which apparently included dessert.

Tea for the walking tours on Saturday mornings.

Her head shot up. "We can't possibly do this. I don't have the time or the extra employees necessary."

She'd pressed Byron and his twin, Brontë, to find her additional help, but they were more interested in the state of the surf than the state of the store's staff. "I'm sorry, but The Perfect Christmas will have to back out of these events this year."

He was already shaking his head. "I know it might be difficult, but the flyers have been posted all over town for weeks. Concierges in the big hotels have organized groups of interested guests to attend together. We can't disappoint the tourists. It's our livelihood."

Behind her, Trin was whispering in appalled tones. "Bailey, he's a veteran! You can't let the general down. Who'll bring snow to Maine?"

Vermont.

Albatross.

She tried picturing Byron in the dry-cleaner-wrapped St. Nick costume hanging in the back office. *Yo, dude. Have yourself a cool Yule.*

Bailey groaned. On her watch it was going to be

the Big Kahuna playing the Big Claus. Terrific.

But despite that, with Trin whispering behind her and the chamber's representative wearing an expectant smile in front of her, she discovered she couldn't say no to the gen— *captain*. President. Whatever.

Whatever was wrong with her?

She still didn't have the answer to that question at 11:58 P.M. that night. Back from the store but unable to sleep, she was wide awake when the phone rang in her old room. Channeling her inner teenager, she automatically picked up the receiver on the little table beside her bed.

Her spine jerked straight against her skinny pillow when she heard the voice on the other end.

And she couldn't say no to that person either.

December 6

In 1843, British businessman Sir Henry Cole asked artist John Calcott Horsley to print some Christmas cards. One thousand cards were printed in black and white and then colored by hand. The cards, which depicted a happy family raising a toast, were criticized by some for promoting drunkenness.

Chapter 6

Bailey had showered after coming home from work and scrunched her hair dry, but she had to shimmy out of her flannel sleep pants and cotton-knit tank top. Considering the circumstances, she yanked on her black jeans, her stiletto-heeled black boots, then pulled over her head a tight black camisole followed by a looser, see-through silk one of midnight blue with black sequins sewn along the edge of the vee neckline.

Without billy club or badge, but with two layers

of brown-black mascara and plum-rose lip gloss, it was the best rescue uniform she could come up with on short notice. It said, "I'm a kick-ass babe and I'm in charge."

Or so she thought until she strode into the unfamiliar bar on the nontourist side of town. Simply named Hart's it was located at the far corner of a small strip mall, next to a darkened nail salon. She'd gone through the single-wide, dinged-metal door with confidence.

But as she stepped into the low-lit room that smelled of beer and loud aftershave, rocked by the noise and the vibration of a pumping bass line beneath the soles of her boots, her bravado drained right out of her.

Had she ever walked into a bar by herself?

Certainly not one like this.

Though women accented the room here and there, it was mostly filled with men. Young men with shorn hair and muscular bodies. Military men, she deduced, who liked their beer and their raucous music. In one dark corner a few couples moved on a scarred dance floor. In another, dueling pool tables glowed green under drop lights.

When a knot of tough-looking men turned to check her out, she almost backed through the door.

But she'd promised Mrs. Jacobson to retrieve Finn and bring him back safely. How could she fail an eighty-something-year-old lady who had crocheted the receiving blanket she'd been bundled into for her trip home from the hospital?

Then there was Finn himself, of course. She couldn't help but be concerned about him after his grandmother said he'd called, clearly inebriated. She didn't want him driving himself home. The elderly woman swore she'd have gone after him herself, but she'd recently given up her license.

Bailey didn't want Finn driving himself home either. She owed him that, at least. After all, it was Finn who'd held her hair off her face and out of the gutter when she'd puked up wine coolers until her belly button hurt.

Seventeen and stupid.

Now she was twenty-eight and on a rescue mission.

Except she didn't see Finn anywhere.

Then a man blocked her view. He was huge, one of those shaved-head, biceps-like-hams types, who looked as if he spent Sunday afternoons wearing blue face paint and yellow San Diego Chargers bolts on his cheeks. His voice was hoarse, as if still recovering from screaming for the team. "Can I get you something?"

When she felt for the doorknob behind her, a little smile played over his mouth. It made him look almost like a human being. "The manicure place is next door, hon. They won't open again until nine in the morning, though."

Somehow it was a relief to know he didn't believe she belonged here either.

Another man walked up to the first. "Troy—" he started, breaking off as he glanced her way. "Bailey? Bailey Sullivan?"

She knew who this was, though it had been a decade since she'd seen Tanner Hart in person. There was no mistaking his blue eyes, his golden-haired, movie-star good looks. Six months ago he'd become a media sensation, though then he'd been clean-shaven and his blond hair cut tight to his head. Now it was reaching his shoulders and the gold stubble on his chin hadn't seen a razor in a couple of days.

Obviously Tanner had changed his life since the incident that had caused Finn to warn: "*Don't mention it if you see him.*" So she stuck to general niceties.

"Hey, Tanner. Fancy, uh, meeting you here."

"This is where I work." He jerked his thumb at the Mr. Clean look-alike who'd first spoken to her. "This is my brother, the bar's owner, Troy Hart. Troy, this is Bailey Sullivan."

Her hand disappeared inside Troy's huge paw, as she recalled what she knew about him. Heroism was a Hart family tradition. He'd won more than his share of medals in Afghanistan.

When her fingers were returned to her, surprisingly unscathed, she looked over at Tanner. "I'm here for Finn. His grandmother sent me to bring him home."

"Sent *you*?" Tanner echoed.

"I live right next door, if you remember. I promised I'd rescue him, since he's apparently pretty, um, intoxicated. Is he here? Have you seen him?"

Tanner and Troy exchanged a glance. It must have spoken volumes, because Troy backed off with a little wave while Tanner crowded her toward the door. "Don't worry about it. I'll make sure I confiscate his keys. He'll, uh, stay the night with me. Or, uh, something."

"So you've seen him?" She rose on tiptoe to peer over his shoulder. "He's here?"

"You bet. Sure. And he's fine." Tanner kept moving her backward. "I'll take care of it. Make sure he comes out okay. You have my word. Scout's honor. Cross my heart."

Bailey's eyes narrowed. She didn't manage a law firm peopled by a bunch of motor-mouth attorneys without learning a thing or two about what a bunch of fast talk could really mean. Planting her feet on the sticky floor, she crossed her arms over her chest. "What aren't you telling me? I'm not leaving until I know he's okay. I promised his grandmother, Tanner. I won't go until I at least see him."

He rubbed his hand over his stubbled chin.

"Listen, Bailey. Finn . . . Finn hits the bottle kinda hard, now and then. When he does, I watch out for him. He's not going to get into any real trouble."

Her stomach clenched. Not any "real" trouble. What did Tanner mean by that? She pictured a broken nose, bloody lips. Finn picking bar fights. Or worse, Finn stumbling around in the dark, half blind and prey to criminals, pickpockets. Maybe even terrorists. Remember, he was a federal agent.

She clutched Tanner's arm, even as she realized she might be overreacting just a tad. "Take me to him. I'll get him home right now."

"Bailey—"

"Tanner, I'm not leaving until I at least see him for myself."

The guy who'd been the lead story on more than one infotainment television program groaned. "You don't—"

"I certainly *do.*"

Shaking his head, Tanner turned. "My life sucks," he muttered. Then he pulled her by the wrist, leading her left to a part of the bar she'd missed before. Jutting off from the main area was a smaller room, filled with more tables and chairs, another couple of pool tables, and in one corner . . . Santa.

Santa *Finn,* with a bevy of giggling beauties lined up before him, all ready to sit on his lap and tell the pirate what they wanted for Christmas.

A red-and-white fleece hat perched sloppily on his dark head. Candy canes poked from the pocket of his shirt. And after each woman whispered her secrets in his oh-so-eager ear, he gave her a piece of candy . . . and a lingering kiss.

Something told her Finn Jacobson wouldn't relish her rescue.

Which was exactly why she took her place at the back of the line.

The women shuffled forward slowly, since Finn took his sweet time with each lady. It gave Bailey plenty of minutes to work up a good mad. Oh, he was going to cringe when she got through with him.

Because he gave each woman his full attention (not to mention a swat on the butt as she left his knee), he didn't see her coming until she was right in front of him. Even then he wasn't fully aware of the trouble he was in because he was checking out his stash of candy sticks as he automatically curved an arm around her waist and drew her nearer.

"Have you been a good little girl?" he asked absently, still looking down as he pulled her onto his lap.

She landed with unnecessary force. He *oomphed*.

Bailey smiled with satisfaction. "I don't know,

Santa," she said, pitching her voice to bad-girl sultry. "I thought you had a list."

Finn's head came up. He looked stunned.

Good.

She waited for embarrassment or remorse or shame to overtake his surprised expression.

Instead, he smiled. Slow. Sexy. His arm tightened around her as his gaze dropped to her breasts. "Oh, sweetheart, Santa has a list all right, and you're at the very top."

She was going to kill him! Of course, she should have known he wouldn't cooperate and feel the least bit of guilt for . . . for . . .

Well, of course she didn't care if he kissed a hundred other women in front of her. It was none of her business.

Digging her stiletto heels into the linoleum floor, she jerked off his knee. "Your grandmother was worried about you. But obviously you're in fine form. Tanner will take you home, though you look like your usual capable self to me. Good-bye, Finn." She started off.

"Whoa. Wait." He stood to make a grab for her. His arm swung wild, and his body followed it, half turning him so that he stumbled into the chair he'd been sitting on. It toppled with a crash. The women who'd been in line behind her scattered.

Finn spun a full circle, his momentum taking

him forward and into Bailey. She grabbed his arms to steady him.

"You *are* drunk."

He grinned at her. Still unrepentant. Still sexy as all get-out. "Not so you'd know."

Rolling her eyes, she pulled him toward the main room with a plan to deposit him in Tanner's care. "Just keep telling yourself that, handsome."

But neither Tanner nor his brother Troy was in immediate sight. And Finn wouldn't stay under her control. With her hands still trying to hold him back, he lurched to the bar. "Gimme another," he told the guy on the other side. He yanked the Santa hat off his head, stuffed its puffy top into his front pocket, then hitched one hip onto an empty stool. "And white wine for the GND."

"*Finn . . .*"

He handed over the wine with exaggerated care. "Now don't be like that." His fingers, damp from the sweating glass, trailed down her cheek. "Not when you're looking so pretty. So pretty and so hot."

Despite herself, a pleased flush prickled up her neck. He'd only seen her in bulky sweaters and her store apron before this, and she had actually grown a cup size since leaving home at eighteen.

He smiled again, then palmed her hips to pull her between his legs. Studying her face, he downed the shot of liquor he'd been served in one quick swallow. Then he shook his head, that smile still glinting in his one eye.

"Bailey Sullivan, still slaying me."

She smelled the liquor on his breath, but it wasn't unpleasant. Nor was the heat of his hands seeping through her black jeans. The Christmas following her and Finn's first summer kiss, Trin had given Bailey an old-fashioned muff made out of fake mink and matching ear warmers.

She'd worn them on an under-cover-of-darkness walk to the beach with Finn. He'd laughed at the warmers, but after he'd built a bonfire of pallets and newspapers in one of the cement rings set in the sand, he'd pocketed his lighter and pulled out a flask in its place.

He'd put it to his mouth, and in the light of the flames she'd watched him grimace as he swallowed it down. Her bad boy. Then he'd sat toe-to-toe with her, their legs bent. Reaching around her knees, he'd shoved his cold hands and the cold flask in the warm nest of the muff. His fingers had slid between hers, and just like that her inner thigh muscles had pulled tight. The place between them had started to pulse.

At the tangy smell of tequila in the air between her and Finn, the same thing happened now.

And as then, it spooked the hell out of her.

It shouldn't be this fast!

Perhaps he was reliving the past too, because in the dim light he shook his head again. "Bailey.

Whatever made you put up with a guy like me?"

"Did I have a choice?" she replied, surprising herself by being honest with them both. "It never felt that way."

His fingers tightened on her hips for an instant. "Not for me either." He looked away. "But I could have corrupted you . . . hell, I did."

Because of the sex? But she couldn't ask that out loud. It had never felt like corruption, not even close.

And sex had never again felt like what it had with Finn.

But of course it wouldn't, she assured herself, before the thought could begin to worry her. *Because everything was a first with Finn.*

"I was riding the edge, GND," he went on. "When I was home, I'd think to myself how I wouldn't be able to see you if they locked me up in juvie."

"So you'd avoid crime?" The notion pleased her. "Because of me?"

A corner of his mouth kicked up. "Nah, I just got better at not getting caught at it."

"Oh." Instead of laughing, she whacked his chest with her free hand.

Even drunk, his reflexes—or his luck—made him able to catch it, and he flattened her fingers over his heart.

"I was riding the edge," he muttered again.

As he was now too, she could tell, and she

wondered why. With that niggle of curiosity in her head and his hard bone and the beat of his blood beneath her hand, Bailey realized she was riding a dangerous edge as well.

She'd come to rescue Finn, but if she didn't get out of here, that life-of-its-own sexual attraction might overcome her again. There wasn't one good reason for her to indulge a second time.

She drew her fingers away. "I have to go."

"Bailey—"

His protest didn't stop her from resorting to her usual MO. She ran out on him.

This time though, he caught her. He wouldn't have, but she was fumbling with an unfamiliar set of keys in the dark parking lot.

He grabbed the bristling ring out of her hand. "You're driving Gram's T-bird?"

"She insisted." It was a 1969, silver-blue with a white landau top, not-quite-classic Thunderbird. Bailey snatched back the keys. "Because I was doing her a favor by rescuing you."

This time she managed to get the door open, but before she could get herself safely ensconced within the three bazillion tons of steel and white-wall tires, Finn stepped around her and ducked inside to slide along the bench seat.

His grin was wide and toothy in the overhead light. Drunk. Reckless. Sexy. "Okay. Rescue away."

Not now! Not now when he was so damn attractive and she was so easily lured back to memories of the past. When she was an adult, yet still so stupidly tempted into wanting to make those memories new.

" 'Fraidy cat?" he said softly.

And as if she was eleven and he was thirteen all over again, she responded to the taunt and flounced into the driver's seat. Then hedged her bets by not looking at him as she started the car and drove toward safety.

Not fast enough. Because Finn reached out and drew a fingertip down her bare arm. "Aren't you cold?"

"No."

"Because I can keep you warm." He started to slide closer, but she held him off with her hand.

"All I want for Christmas is for you to keep your distance."

She heard the smile in his voice. "That's right, Santa didn't get to hear your confession."

You're too close. Too attractive. You're making it too easy for me to—

—forget all those other women lining up to have a taste of you.

That thought cleared her head and put the spotlight on her good intentions, but it was still a relief when she pulled into the Jacobson driveway. "Here we are," she sang out.

He put his hand on her forearm as she made to open her door. "Just a sec," he said. "I'm a little dizzy."

He'd gone so quiet on the short ride, she'd almost forgotten he'd been drinking. With a sympathetic pang, she remembered that woozy wine cooler incident. The tender way he'd cared for her. "Finn, you shouldn't have had so much to drink," she scolded. "Let me open your window."

With a scoot, she was free of the steering wheel and able to lean across him. Too late she remembered the T-bird had power windows.

Too late because Finn pulled her over him and onto his lap, bringing them face-to-face. She was kneeling on either side of his thighs, held there by his hands at her waist.

Her wiggles didn't get her free of his grip. "What are you doing?"

"I'm dizzy." He nuzzled her throat. "You and all this pretty bare skin makes me dizzy. Pretty Bailey. Pretty, bare Bailey."

She put her hands on his head, to push him away. "You're drunk."

"Mmm-hmm." It was an agreeable sound he hummed against her neck, then he licked the notch of her collarbone.

Goose bumps rushed like holiday shoppers across her skin. Her fingers tightened in his hair, and the strap of his eye patch pressed into her right palm. "Finn . . ."

His lips were hot as they roamed higher. They found the angle of her jaw as it curved toward her ear, and he bit down. Those holiday shoppers were in a frenzy now. Sizzling nerve endings were racing them to the bargain tables. Her hands curled into fists and her head fell back.

"This is such a bad idea," she whispered.

"Yeah." Agreeable again as his hands cupped her head and tilted it forward. His mouth found hers.

Hot. Then it was wet.

She opened her lips to him and he made it wild.

His tongue plunged deep, sliding along hers with a velvet thrust. Then a second time. She held her moan back but couldn't help herself from falling against him as he thrust again.

His chest was hot against hers. His erection hard against the juncture of her thighs. He kept kissing her, tasting every surface of her mouth as his hands slid down her shoulders, her arms. Then he was pressing his palms hard against her thighs and pushing his hips up into the cradle of her body.

The delicious pleasure made her squirm, but he held her firm, the heavy placket of his jeans and the heaviness of his body beneath them nudging her right where it felt just fine.

But nudging wasn't enough.

As it had been dozens of times before, as it had

always been with Finn, she was wet and ready and pulsing so fast. So needy, it was embarrassing. Undignified.

Beyond her control.

Her body tried to circle, move, get the rhythm and the pressure she couldn't stop herself from craving, but Finn—as he always had—played her, toyed with her, strung her along.

She could beg, but she'd always tried to keep some decorum when it came to sex. When it came to Finn.

With one forearm across her thighs, holding her steady, he angled his head to take her mouth even more deeply. His other hand brushed the spaghetti straps of her over-camisole off her shoulders. As they fell to her elbows, he broke from her mouth to trail kisses over her chin, down her neck, along the neckline of the second, clingy camisole and up one of its thin straps.

He caught it between his teeth to lower the Lycra fabric. Hot shivers rolled over her skin as quarter inch by quarter inch, one breast was revealed. Her breath backed up in her lungs, and she trembled as the stretchy fabric caught on her nipple. She gasped as it popped free.

Groaning, Finn caught the other spaghetti strap with a hand and yanked the clothing beneath both breasts. Then he dipped his head, his mouth latching on to her flesh. His tongue washed her nipple, then he sucked, strong.

Hard enough to hurt so good.

Pleasure paralyzed her. Her muscles clenched, everywhere, inside, outside, her fingers digging into his shoulders.

Rubbing his nose along her flesh, breathing deeply as he moved across her cleavage, he found her other nipple. He flattened his tongue against the hard nub, pushing the point into the yielding flesh surrounding it. Her hands jerked to his head, buried in his hair. He opened his mouth around the nipple and she shuddered, pressing her cheek against the silky coolness of his hair.

It took everything she had not to cry out.

As if he knew, as if he wanted her to give in, he used the edge of his teeth. Delicate, then harder. The stinging heat arrowed from her breast to her womb. His hand went to the snap riding low on her belly.

Her skin jittered as two fingertips tucked beneath the waistband to the first knuckle. Paused. For permission? Or anticipation?

Bailey's blood boiled hot. It was always like this with Finn. Had only been like this with Finn. She opened her mouth to tell him, then remembered.

Four words.

Nothing flocked can stay.

Four simple words that acted like an icy snowball to cool the heat of her desire.

Nothing flocked can stay.

She threw herself off Finn's lap and onto the

seat beside him. Breathing hard, she dug her nails into her palms.

"Finn." She had to clear her throat, start again. "We need to slow down . . . or think . . . or something. Give me a minute here."

"Yeah." His voice was harsh. "Fuck. Okay."

Christmas Central was dark and quiet—it was nearing two A.M.—and she wished she could feel so peaceful inside. What was going on? How could she have fallen so quickly back into his arms?

How come she wanted to be back there so very badly right now?

Stress.

Old memories.

Hormones.

Take your pick. She hadn't dated in months. Hadn't bedded in much longer than that. She hadn't wanted anyone.

Now she wanted Finn. Again.

A reckless, crazy thought popped into her brain. Well, why not? Sex didn't have to be sloppy or emotional. Or even pretend to be permanent.

Maybe a release was her reward. Good girl comes back to save the farm and gets to take the neighboring rancher for a ride.

Okay, fine, it was silliness talking—and desire—but God help her, she found herself willing to listen. It was the gift-giving season, and this interlude with Finn could be her gift to herself. When was the last time she'd gotten herself such a very nice present?

Her heart was still racing, her breasts were still bare, her nipples still wet from his mouth.

Why not?

"Finn." Surrendering to impulse, she whipped toward him. "Call me nuts, but okay, let's—"

The rest died in her mouth. Her almost offer evaporated in the air that felt suddenly chilly. Lonely.

He was asleep. Make that passed out. Slumped down on his grandmother's tucked-and-rolled leather upholstery, Finn was dead to the sober world.

She probably should be relieved, but instead she was pissed at him all over again. Here she was, ready, willing, hot for his body, and he'd gone beyond disinterested.

It took her only a second to find her purse, lying alongside his stupid Santa hat on the floor of the T-bird. She started to toss it into his lap, but then hesitated, staring down at the fleece.

After a moment, she propped it on top of his head. Then she wrote a note, and used a safety pin to fasten her message to his flannel shirt. Finally she grabbed the keys and eased out the car.

Tiptoeing toward the mailbox on his grandmother's front porch, she tripped over a large box.

The top flew off and she stared at the contents. Three dozen—count 'em—long-stemmed roses. Dipped in gold.

Real gold?

Thinking of the over-the-top Nativity scene and the Bunyan-sized chocolate fountain, Bailey would bet the family farm on it.

That made her grimace as she put the car keys in the Jacobson mailbox, but she didn't take a last look at the Thunderbird and the one-eyed idiot inside, sleeping it off.

His gift giver could worry about him. Whoever was delivering those outrageous presents could rescue the Secret Service agent next time.

But as Bailey slipped between her cool sheets, they abraded her still hypersensitive skin and she couldn't help but worry. When it came to Finn, she hoped she didn't need something or someone to rescue *her*.

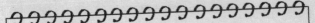
December 7

Charles Dickens wrote, "Happy, happy Christmas, that can win us back to the delusions of our childhood days, recall to the old man the pleasures of his youth, and transport the traveler back to his own fireside and quiet home!"

Chapter 7

"Finn, you know I love you, but watching you pace is like watching Wimbledon," Gram said, sitting at the kitchen table with coffee, the newspaper, and her plastic, compartmentalized pill container. "I'm getting neck strain."

He forced himself to halt, and swiped his own mug off the counter to take a swallow. "Sorry. Just restless, I guess."

"You should be at work then, not babysitting me."

He didn't want to tell her the agent in charge had practically locked him out of the office. It wasn't a secret to the Secret Service that to be half the agent he'd been in the past, Finn needed to get his head together.

And speaking of heads . . . The aspirin bottle sat beside the sink and he reached for it. Twenty-four hours and his hangover was still pinned into his brain by what felt like two ice picks. He'd woken up the morning before in Gram's T-bird with a tongue the size and consistency of a dried kitchen sponge, a piercing headache, and a sheet of paper pinned on his shirt.

Sliding his hand in his pocket, he touched it. *U O Me.* Bailey's handwriting was quite clear.

But what exactly he owed her, he wasn't sure. A thank-you for bringing him back from Troy's? More days of avoiding her like yesterday? A follow-through on what they'd started in the dark confines of the car?

That wasn't a wise move. Getting mixed up with the GND wasn't on his holiday agenda.

However, a hazy recollection—or was it wishful thinking?—continued to tickle the outer edges of his memory as it had since he'd woken up with the ancestor of all hangovers. After Bailey took the safe and sane path and climbed off his lap, *had* she turned back to him? Had she really said, "Finn . . . let's . . ." implying she'd changed her mind?

If it was true, he'd been too drunk to swim free of his tequila stupor and take her up on the offer. If she'd made it at all.

But there was no mistaking she'd told him he owed her, and he still couldn't decide what to do about that.

Stifling a groan, he promised himself for the dozenth time since being released from the hospital that he wasn't going to drink like that ever again. Each time, he meant it. God, the queasy stomach, the sponge tongue, and the rotisseried brain made it a hell of an easy vow to make.

But then something would set him off. A talk with Gram's doctor. A phone call.

"Ayesha Spencer's parents called," he said, staring down at the bottle of aspirin in his hand. It was nearly full, but there weren't enough tablets in the world to ease this pain. "They'll be in San Diego next week and want to have dinner with me."

Gram's voice was quiet. "It might make you feel better."

Ah, but *feel* was the important word. He couldn't afford to *feel*, damn it. Every agent knew that. Every agent knew it was death to sleep, maybe even sanity, if he started letting the worry and the stress of the near misses, and in his case, the real tragedy, take root inside him.

Except he couldn't forget Ayesha's crumpled body and the responsibility he bore for it.

Finn's hands started to tremble, and the aspirins

danced inside their plastic. He dropped the bottle back to the counter to halt the telltale rattle.

"Finn?"

"Hmm?" He white-knuckled the edge of the countertop and worked at pasting something he hoped was a smile on his face.

"Are you all right?"

He chanced a look at his grandmother, for the first time noting the new shadows under her eyes and then her pale hands fumbling with her pill container. With a silent curse for his distracted self, he strode to the table.

"We should be talking about you and how you feel," he told her. Impatient with himself, he used unnecessary force to pop the top marked *Th* for Thursday. Medications tumbled to the tabletop, and he had to corral them with his palms before they hit the floor.

This time he didn't keep the curses silent as he scooped the pills in front of Gram. Then he spun toward the sink. "I'll get you water," he said, his voice tight.

Calm down, he reminded himself. Cool it. *Ice over all the emotion.*

He managed to fill a glass and set it in front of her without a spill. Calming down. Cooling it.

His grandmother touched his wrist. "You can't stop the seasons," she said. "There's death and there's birth. There's a reason we celebrate Christmas at the darkest time of the year, Finn. To remind us that hope and light will always arrive."

Finn closed his eyes. He loved the messenger but the message wasn't something he wanted to hear. So he let his mind skip from seasons and Christmas to The Perfect Christmas and Bailey. His hand slid into his pocket again. Touched Bailey's note.

U O Me.

What the hell had she meant by that? But his sixth sense was clamoring again, warning him against any investigation.

December, and there were bikinis poolside. Even though Dan Willis had been a Coronado resident for the last twenty years, the juxtaposition of Santa decorations and suntan lotion still startled him. But it was one of those postcard days, near eighty, that fueled the jealousy of New Yorkers and Chicagoans. He'd been each himself at one time, so he knew.

All that "land of fruits and nuts" and "Hollywood elite" trash talk was just an outlet for envy. So you couldn't get a real bagel or a true, bone-jittering wind in SoCal—he'd settle for Baja fish tacos and kids in shorts on skateboards any day. Though Dan wasn't a native Californian, he admitted to embracing their inner smugness. It had taken him a few years to detect it, but there came a point when he realized that every time someone denigrated the Golden State, the natives clammed up. No defensiveness. No pleas for un-derstanding.

Just a hidden smile and the inner fervent hope that the naysayer would stay in his own—sunless and/or sea-less—part of the world. Sure there was enough sunshine to go around, but Californians didn't mind soaking it all up themselves.

Twenty years and Dan didn't see himself leaving the place, even though he'd changed addresses from his comfortable suburbanesque single-family home to the caffeinated lifestyle of a modern con-dominium complex. He let the wrought-iron gate that surrounded the aquamarine pool and pebbled deck clang shut behind him. Women glanced up from their fashion magazines. One of the condo complex's very few male residents opened his eyes, then dismissed him.

At the two-hundred-unit Crown Palms, men were at a premium, he'd found. And so attracted more than their fair share of attention.

"Dan!" As if to prove that last thought, a pretty, thirty-something brunette waved at him from her spot near the shallow end. "Just the person I hoped to see."

"Is that right?" He settled in the lounge chair beside hers, his ego puffing like a balloon. This morning he'd been with a bright, blue-eyed blond, and it looked as if this afternoon he'd be busy too.

These women needed him. Appreciated him. Even if Tracy didn't.

He shut his estranged wife out of his mind and turned on his hip to give Brenda—the brunette—his full attention. His smile was for her alone, in gratitude for all the ways she'd distracted since he'd moved and set upon his single life.

Her dimple dug deep into her right cheek. "You're looking good, Dan. Sleeping better now?"

When he'd first moved to the complex, his biggest complaint—besides the ache in his heart—was insomnia. He'd taken to whiling away the late-night hours in the weight room, and it was there he'd met Brenda. And Lynn. And Cherry.

If he called them his little harem in the privacy of his thoughts, it didn't offend anyone.

Leaning on his elbow, he propped his head on his fist. "I'm working out in the mornings now. How 'bout you?"

"Not getting into the gym as much as I'd like." She shrugged, shifting the oiled curves of her breasts in the tiny turquoise triangles trying to contain them.

While he didn't ogle, Dan let his gaze sweep over the feminine flesh laid out on the other lounge. He thought it was expected of him. Even appreciated. "Whatever you're doing looks fine from here."

Brenda gave him another of her smiles. It did seem grateful. "You always know the right thing to say."

Not to Tracy. One September afternoon it had

hit him hard. She didn't see him. She didn't hear him. Though they worked together every day and went to bed in the same room every night, he'd become a piece of furniture. No different from a chair. The computer. Not a man. Not her lover.

Panic had sent him to the mirror. It had shocked the hell out of him. In his mind's eye he'd seen himself as young and fit as his eighteen-year-old son, Harry, but in the impersonal reflection of the mirror there was a middle-aged guy with too much gray, going soft around the middle.

No wonder Tracy looked past him, he'd thought.

But all that he'd done—his personal *Extreme Makeover* episode—hadn't changed a thing. She hadn't even noticed.

Crushed by her disinterest, he'd moved out.

"You're going sad on me, Dan."

He wrenched his attention back to the younger woman. "I'm not." Sad was how he'd felt each time Tracy looked through him. He lowered his voice and sent Brenda his new, six-hundred-dollar, blinding-white smile. "But I'm hoping you were happy to see me for a reason."

She nodded. "I need you, Dan. You're the only man I know who's been able to make it . . . I don't know what you'd call it exactly. Hum?"

He pushed down his sunglasses to look at her over them in disbelief. "I'm the only one?"

She nodded. "No kidding. It's been four years

that I've struggled. Then one hour with you and . . ."

"Hum."

"Yeah."

They smiled at each other. While his time with Brenda—and Lynn, and Cherry—didn't completely obliterate the pain of his messed-up marriage, it soothed some rough edges, filled some empty hours. *They* thought he was good for something. Almost fifty years old and maybe he *did* know a thing or two that other men did not.

"Well, whenever you're ready I'm prepared to make my magic," he said. A few more tricks and maybe he'd have Tracy out of his mind forever.

Brenda swung her legs off the lounger. "I don't want to wait a minute longer."

They stopped off at his place for protection. A few minutes later they were in Brenda's cream-and-apricot condo and ready for action.

"The real trick is in how you put it in," he instructed. "Careful. Gentle. Then you move it gently too."

"Gentle," she repeated, her breath warm against his neck.

"If you get another man here, tell him not to shove it in or push too hard. Tease it."

He put his hands over hers to show her exactly what he meant. They worked it together for a few minutes, playing with the pressure. "Easy," he murmured. "Not too hard. Take it easy."

Then, suddenly, the tension broke.

"There," Brenda breathed. She was still for a moment, then she smiled up at him. "Thank you, God. Thank you, Dan."

Withdrawing his pole, Dan grinned down at her. "You're more than welcome." He reached over to flip the switch.

The garbage disposal—instead of being frozen—hummed.

They both drew off their protective safety goggles and listened to the happy sound.

Satisfied it was in good working order again, he turned it off. "Do you want my special tool?"

She laughed at him. "Someone could take that wrong, you know."

"I *meant* my special sawed-off broomstick." The complex's garbage disposals were notoriously finicky. One too many lemon peels or celery tops and they went from happy hum to high-pitched whine. That's when you knew the blades weren't turning.

Once he'd shared his solution with one woman, word had gotten around. This morning he'd fixed Lynn's, the blue-eyed blond. Now Brenda's. Cherry's wouldn't be far behind, he supposed, and he was always glad for the chance to *do* something.

"Cold drink?" Brenda asked.

"Sure."

They settled into matching wicker chairs on her small patio. Over a tall hedge of jasmine was the sweeping curve of the Coronado Bridge that linked the island to San Diego. After a few minutes of comfortable silence, the younger woman tossed him a little glance. "You'd make someone a fine husband, Dan."

And just like that Tracy was in his mind again. He wished he could see himself as someone else's anything. But so far, it seemed he was a one-woman dog.

He'd caught sight of Tracy a couple of days before when he couldn't stop himself from driving past the house like a teenager with a crush. But he didn't need that glimpse to remind him of what she looked like. He had a dozen images of her stored in his memory. A hundred.

Windblown hair, her nose sunburned, one hand holding a little girl's, the other gripping a plastic pail of sand. Their first date.

Smooth ponytail, little white suit, roses trembling in her grasp as they told the judge, "I do."

Happy tears, sweaty bangs, the perfect curve of her arms as she held their newborn son.

Tracy with a pencil behind her ear. With a fire in her stride as she went toward the neighborhood bully who'd pushed Bailey off her bike. With her fingers trembling as she brushed imaginary lint off Harry's comforter after making his college bed.

He saw again the flinch of her body, then the

distant, almost vacant look in her eyes when he'd told her he was leaving.

"I couldn't believe she married me in the first place," he heard himself say. "She'd been hurt by her ex."

Brenda gave an understanding nod. "Been there. Done that. Have worn the hair shirt."

"I was persistent." It had taken time, but he'd won Tracy over. Not Bailey, though. As much as he'd tried, as much as he regretted the failure, he knew he'd never quite cracked that hard shell she'd built after her father left. And it was as if Tracy had retreated behind that very same barrier now too.

He shook his head. "The garbage disposals aren't going to do it, are they? And not the sticky doors or broken cabinet hinges?"

Brenda looked into his eyes, then away. "I don't think I'm going to do it for you either, Dan. Not me, or Lynn, or Cherry. At least not now."

Not ever, Dan corrected.

He let the truth of that sink deep. It pierced his heart and fell like an anchor into his churning gut.

Moving away couldn't move his wife out of his mind, his thoughts, his emotions.

His soul.

But no! He couldn't let that be a certainty. They'd had happy, but not ever after, and he couldn't, *wouldn't* let himself be miserable without Tracy for the rest of his life.

* * *

Finn went on a long walk that afternoon to relieve his fidgety legs and restless memory. Head down, hands in his pockets, he didn't realize the path his feet had taken him until he heard a familiar voice hail his name.

He looked up, then down, into the amused eyes of tiny Trin Tran, pushing a stroller so laden with shopping bags and drooling toddler that it had to weigh more than she did.

"Come by to check on your old flame?" she asked, a saucy smile on her lips.

Uh oh. Finn was standing in front of The Perfect Christmas.

He resisted the urge to duck down in case Bailey was looking out the windows. *U O Me.* He still didn't know what the hell she wanted from him. He still didn't want to know.

"How are you, Trin?" Finn said, warding off a Bailey discussion. "And how is your, uh . . ." The child was dressed in a one-piece thing of nubby brown fabric, complete with an antler-topped hood.

"Raindid," the kid said, a trail of drool running over its bottom lip. A little plump hand waved overhead. "Raindid."

"That's right, baby. You're so smart." Trin, whom he'd always considered a logical, reasonable human being, gazed at the drooler with fanatical pride. Christ, his sister and parents were going to go nuts when his nephew was born. "He's telling you he's a reindeer."

"Yeah? Uh, impressive." That river of drool was pretty amazing too.

The kid was staring up at Finn now. A finger pointed at his face. "Pie-did."

"Pie-deer?" Finn guessed. "Is that some new species?" They were just miles from the world-famous San Diego Zoo. Maybe the kid was a zoologist in the making.

Trin's gaze cut toward him, a frown between her brows. "Something wrong with your hearing? That's *pirate.*"

"Sorry." Touching his eye patch, he grimaced. "I'm not real familiar with little kids."

"Oh, *really*?" Trin fiddled with the collar of her white shirt. There was a piece of "jewelry" pinned to it, a one-by-two-inch LED screen that flashed NAUGHTY? NICE? at three-second intervals. "We—*I* was wondering if you had any little Finns wandering around the world. We—*I* didn't know if there was a woman in your life in the recent past, or the now, or the near future."

"We pie-dids like to keep a little mystery going," he replied, unwilling to play criminal to her cop.

At the narrowing of Trin's eyes, he hastened to divert the topic again. "So," he said, pointing to the bags hanging off the stroller. "Getting started on your Christmas shopping already?"

She made a weird little sound. Something between a hoot and a screech. Frankly, it was frightening. Even the raindid looked up at his mom, with wide eyes and the Schweitzer Falls roaring over his bottom lip.

" 'Started'?" she repeated slowly. " 'Already'? Have you seen any Go-Go Toaster trains in the stores? Any Flash It–Paste It–Post It software programs? What about the Demons Behind the Wheel video game?"

"Uh, no?" Seemed a safe answer.

"That's right. It's because they've not been available since the day after Thanksgiving."

"Oh."

She talked right over him. "I bet you're just like my husband. I bet you don't believe people are out shopping at five in the morning on the Friday after Turkey Day. But let me assure you they are. This year you could get Howard Stern or Nemo to give you a wake-up call at four A.M."

Finn didn't know who Nemo was, but he sure as hell wasn't going to confess it to Trin.

"And for your information, people shop early on December twenty-sixth too—for the *next* year!"

Good God. With the exception of this Christmas because of the whole nephew-in-the-oven thing, Finn shopped on the twenty-fourth . . . twenty-third if he was at loose ends. It boggled his mind to imagine a world as Trin described. Lucky for him, it appeared the incensed woman didn't expect a response as her voice rose in obvious passion.

"So good-bye, pie-did. I have to go home now and see if the elves baked the fifteen plates of cookies for my husband's office party tomorrow night. And maybe they've planned the menus for our holiday get-together, Christmas Eve, and Christmas Day, and done the three-stop grocery shopping trip too. Perhaps they've been nice enough to wrap all the family presents, the gifts for the baby-sitter, the gardener, the mail carrier, and my hairdresser, not to mention the hostess thank-yous I picked out for the seven parties we're invited to between now and New Year's." Rushing past him, she ran over his foot.

He yelped. "You're scaring me, Trin."

That gave her pause. She turned, shooting him an unreadable look. "And I'm a woman who *likes* Christmas. Think about the kind of mood the elf in there is in." She jerked her thumb toward the store's front door, then went on her way.

What elf?

Duh. He knew what elf.

But he wasn't going in. Except, though he couldn't swear to it, he thought Trin's pin had suddenly stuck on NAUGHTY NAUGHTY NAUGHTY. Was that supposed to be a clue to Bailey's mood?

What red-blooded American man would think that . . . and think about the feel of her under his hands in the car the other night, then walk away?

So he pushed the door open, wincing at the telltale clatter of jingle bells. His plan was an anonymous little peek at the anti-Christmas elf, just . . . just because he couldn't stop himself.

As the door swung shut behind him, the scent inside the store rushed into his lungs, triggering an instant, intense olfactory memory. It was so damn real he could watch it play out on the blank screen of his missing eye. His hand still squeezing the doorknob, he closed his working one so he could see it even better.

Nineteen. Christmas vacation. Gram had baked oatmeal-raisin cookies to welcome him back, and he'd taken a plateful with him when he'd gone to meet Bailey at The Perfect Christmas.

The bells had jingled then too, and he'd breathed in the store's spicy scent, the cookies in his hands adding a second layer of sweetness. And then more sweetness as Bailey flew into his arms—he hadn't seen her since Labor Day. She'd looked like a celebration in a tiny red skirt, tight green sweater, black boots that hit just below her knees.

They'd kissed, Finn gripping that plate between them so that he wouldn't hold her as hard as he wanted to. So hard that she'd melt into his bones.

At closing time they'd shooed everyone else out, then locked the doors and dimmed the lights. She'd tugged him to the farthest corner of the farthest room and they'd made a place for themselves beneath a tree twinkling with multicolored lights. White fake fur circled its base, and she'd lain back on it like a child, gleeful in the snow.

"Come here," she'd whispered, smiling, but he'd resisted, his blood pumping so hard and hot in his veins that he'd only trusted himself to look at all her angelic prettiness.

"Come here," she'd insisted, a wayward angel now, who drew one heel toward the other knee, shifting the hem of her little red skirt higher on her bare, opening thighs.

Weakened by the sight, he'd leaned over, propping himself on one elbow to feed her a fragrant cookie.

Crumbs had dusted her green sweater and he'd made a big show of brushing them away, drawing the side of his hand back and forth against her hardening nipples. The nape of his neck had burned and his cock had been ready for more long before he let his tattooed knuckles sneak under her sweater to stroke her bare midriff.

The skin there goose-bumped beneath his fingertips and he'd stared, fascinated by the matching ones that rushed down her inner thighs. Desperate, he'd sucked in air that was sweet, so sweet, a dizzying combination of the smell of the store, the cookie on Bailey's breath, her perfume.

Pushing her sweater toward her breasts, he'd kissed her navel, close enough now to inhale a creamier scent that he wanted to think was proof that she desired him too. As usual, her face surrendered nothing. With her lashes brushing her cheeks, he couldn't see the expression in her eyes.

Her baby-doll mouth was plump, but pursed. Silent.

So he could only hope, wish, then finally believe once he touched her thighs, tracing those goose bumps in reverse, and curled his forefinger beneath the elastic of her panties.

As he touched the wetness waiting for him, he didn't think she breathed.

It paralyzed him.

"What do you want, Finn?" she'd asked, her eyes shut tight.

Everything. Every day.

He wanted her joy in seeing him. To her, he wasn't the screw-up son, the delinquent teenager, the failure one arrest away from jail.

He wanted her mind. The brains that made her number three in her high school class. The intelligence that could write a paper on *The Sun Also Rises* that not only he could understand, but that also made him want to read the book.

Finn, the fuck-up, wanting to *read*.

As much—more, hell, he'd only been nineteen, for God's sake—he'd wanted her body. Every lithe line, every feminine curve, every small moan that he could manage to wring from her. He wanted to rub his face against her belly, the small of her back, the hills of her pretty ass.

"Finn?"

She'd faint if he told her the truth—that he wanted to dip a cookie in that sweet, delicious cream between her thighs and then gobble it down.

"*Finn?*"

Her voice had lost its breathiness. It sounded surprised.

Or annoyed.

His eye popped open.

And there she was. Not sweet or tremulous or laid out for him like a Christmas banquet. Instead she looked harried, her elf hat askew, her eyes fatigued. As if she'd spent the day searching for the last Go-Go Toaster train in Southern California. A passel of kids were gathered around her, the littlest ones with her work apron clutched in their fists. A gooey-looking, child-sized candy cane was stuck in the ends of her hair.

He didn't mean to laugh. But it was funny— the joke on him—that he'd been dreaming of the seventeen-year-old princess who ruled his body and then been rudely awakened by this grown-up, hassled-looking woman who gazed at him like he was a frog instead of a god.

Then the joke really *was* on him, because she glanced down at the kiddie squad. "Hey, everybody, remember how I couldn't promise we'd have Santa to read you stories tomorrow? Because Santa was probably planning on riding the uh, big surf?"

Disgruntled nods all around.

"I was wrong. I'm certain our AWOL Santa will be here!"

The motley crew cheered. Bailey grinned at their enthusiasm.

Then she looked over at him. Her forefinger aimed at his chest.

U

Her hand curved into a circle.

O

Her thumb jutted backward, her lips formed the word.

Me.

Too late, Finn remembered he hadn't wanted to know what exactly she meant by that.

♀♀♀♀♀♀♀♀♀♀♀♀♀♀♀♀♀♀♀♀

Bailey Sullivan's Vintage Christmas
Facts & Fun Calendar

December 8
In medieval England, people attended church at Christmas wearing Halloween-type masks and costumes. They'd sing rowdy songs and even roll dice on the altar.

Chapter 8

"You're supposed to be nice to Santa," Finn hissed, the words twitching the silvery beard and mustache strapped to his head beneath the plush red-and-white hat.

"Only if Santa has something in his bag I want," Bailey retorted in a hushed voice, shoving a storybook into his hand. She looked down at the dozen or so little ones who were cross-legged on the floor in the front room of The Perfect Christmas for story hour. Their moms were either hovering at the edge of their semicircle or—better yet—edging away to look over merchandise and check price tags. "Now stop yapping and get ready to read."

"I only asked for a glass of water."

"No time," she said, for his ears only. "The kiddies are here and we said we'd start at eleven on the dot. This is a business, Finn, and I don't have time to hold your hand."

She wished back the comment the minute she said it. It *was* all business at The Perfect Christmas, no matter that she'd dragged her old flame—a man whose hand she used to love to hold and also a man whom she'd had to admit to herself she was once again out-of-control attracted to—into playing Santa. But that had been a business decision too!

He'd been standing there yesterday afternoon, just as she'd finished an exhaustive hour doing the Pied Piper thing for a passel of sugar-buzzed, Christmas-crazed, two-legged little rats. The idea of having to read Christmas stories to a similar group the next day had made her want to run, screaming, for the Hollywood Hills.

With the surf up and her sales dude Byron heading beachside, she'd desperately needed a Santa more than she needed distance from Finn. Plus, he owed her, and he seemed to accept that fact.

Now if only his piratical take on St. Nick wouldn't scare the kiddies or do any lasting psychological damage. It looked as if *Sesame Street* and those weird Wiggles (the store stocked both their Christmas CDs) had actually taught the kids to accept differences, however. Only one munchkin at Finn's feet had made note of his patch—and then only to ask if he'd been poked in the eye by an antler. Finn had murmured something under his breath about a Red Ryder BB gun, and one of the younger mothers laughed. She was still there, cozying up to the kiddie circle.

Bailey checked the clock. "Go," she said.

He glanced up at her.

A sharp pang pierced her, somewhere between her stomach and her throat. A bullet had wounded Finn, she thought, and not for the first time. It had taken one of his eyes.

He could have died.

Somehow she was suddenly holding his hand after all.

Frowning, he squeezed her fingers. "Bailey . . ."

She whipped her hand away. *Business!* "The book," she said. "Start reading."

With a little shrug, he turned away from her and opened the storybook in his hands.

With a lot of relief, she moved away from him and toward the cash register on the other side of the room. For several minutes her hands occupied themselves with organizing the pen cup and tidying the checks in the drawer even as her ears took in Finn's low voice. She stole a look at him. It was kind of cute, really, to see the baddest boy she knew dressed up like the nicest man in the world, telling children a story.

Made you think about him as a dad some day—

No. It did not make Bailey think of him as a dad. No damn way. God, the sentimental glop The Perfect Christmas sold by way of merchandise and atmosphere was trying to wear off on her.

Turning her back on the storytime tableau, she thought about her *real* office, where people dressed in suits the colors of stone and dirt and ash. Her *real* work, where the kind of business conducted was just right for a hard-hearted, hard-headed realist like herself.

A place where people bled money, not red.

She found her gaze on Finn again, and she wrenched it away as the front door opened. Through it came the general—no, *Captain* Reed, the president of the chamber of commerce. With him was a woman with the battleship bustline and helmet hair of her elementary school principal. Bailey narrowed her eyes. It *was* her elementary school principal.

Both newcomers paused to watch Santa and his little buddies for several minutes, then made their way over to Bailey at the register.

The captain beamed. "I knew you would take care of things," he said. Then he gestured to his buxom companion. "Do you remember Peggy Mohn?"

"Of course I do." She nodded. "Principal Mohn."

The older woman shot out her hand and squeezed Bailey's fingers like she used to squeeze the upper arms of little kids who couldn't stand still in the lunch line. "Bailey. Good to see you back home. I've left education and I'm now in medical equipment sales."

Education was better off for the defection, Bailey thought, but she pitied the bedpans.

"Peggy's also the VP of the chamber," the captain added. "She's an idea person, I'll tell you. It was she who coordinated all these Christmas events among the local businesses."

"Oh . . . nice." Though thanks to the old battle-ax Bailey was within spitting distance of the first male she'd ever shared spit with—and whom she wanted to share spit with again.

"It's been a great success," Peggy put in. "Though I had a few bad moments when I heard The Perfect Christmas wouldn't stand by its obligations."

Her disapproving tone set Bailey's neck hairs on fire. Not only had the old biddy tried to squelch every childish joy at Crown Elementary—she'd had the swings removed and there'd been a no-running rule on the *playground*—but Bailey didn't like her intimations about shirking responsibility. While *she* might assert that her mother would have to wake up soon and smell the single-woman java, it wasn't up to Peggy Mohn to stand in judgment. The older woman didn't understand the hell her mother had gone through during her divorce from Bailey's father. *She* did. The memory of the misery and the tears could still scratch like fingernails against the chalkboard of her mind.

Bailey's voice sounded stiff. "Look . . ."

"But now you've taken over," Peggy went on. Even she was beaming now. "I remember your attendance awards, citizenship medals, the recess and lunch peacekeeper program you started in sixth grade."

"Pretty easy to keep the peace when there were rules against play," she murmured under her breath.

"So I know we can count on you," Peggy finished.

Bailey felt a cold chill put out that still-burning fire on the back of her neck. "Count on me for what, exactly?"

"The Valentine's Weekend celebrations we have in mind." The older woman was ticking them off on her fingers. "The coordinated events we're planning for St. Patrick's Day, Memorial Day, Fourth of July, Labor Day, Thanksgiving."

"I'm not . . . I won't . . ." Bailey fumbled for words, as she felt heavy chains draping over her, cold links twisting around her waist, her wrists, locking her to the store, to Coronado, to—

"Bailey, I'm having some trouble here."

Finn, it was Finn, plucking at the patent leather

belt around his waist. She realized that storytime was over. The children had joined their mothers and were crowded around the display of books she'd conveniently set up behind the Santa chair.

"Let me help you with that," she offered, coming around the register. "Excuse me," she told the chamber of commerce people, "but I have to get back to work."

They both were smiling again. "That's just what I like to hear," Peggy said.

Bailey ignored her and dragged Finn in the direction of the stock room in the back, signaling Brontë toward the front register. "Don't take the costume off while you're in sight of the kids," she scolded Santa in a fierce whisper, half because Peggy pissed her off and half because even a pirate—especially a pirate—should realize he was playing a role here.

With the door shut to screen them from the rest of the store, while he removed his hat and luxurious facial hair, she went after his belt. The mechanism was stiff and stubborn, and she grunted in exasperation.

Finn's voice sounded amused. "Never in a million years did I think I'd have you working so hard to open my pants again."

"It's your *jacket*, as if you didn't know." In any case, her face prickled with embarrassed heat. She gave the belt's leather tongue an impatient yank, which sent him stumbling back. A tall stack of boxes tumbled.

"Damn. Now look what you've done." She pushed him aside to reright the packages.

"You're so very welcome," Finn said, sarcasm dripping from the polite words, as he stripped off the Santa suit so that he stood once again in a white T-shirt and seen-better-days jeans. "I was glad to extend my services."

She flushed. "This is new stock that I haven't put out yet. I don't want any of it damaged."

He picked up one of the boxes, stacked it, stacked another. "You're getting this stuff from all over the country. And lots of the addresses are handwritten."

Bailey bit her bottom lip, then cast a glance at the closed door. "Here's the thing. Due to the upheaval caused by my folks' separation, there's a bit of a . . . a hole in the stock. So I've bought a few things—okay, more than a few things—off eBay and some other sites. Older pieces. I'm going to turn the smallest room upstairs into something called Grandma's Attic." She believed the idea was brilliant herself, but she wasn't sure what anyone else would think.

So it was good to talk about it out loud. To talk about it with Finn, for some odd reason. "To be honest, I hope to make a killing on vintage decorations."

Finn placed the last carton on top of the stack. "Markup?"

She could hardly hide her smile. Then she gave up trying. "In a tourist setting like this? With vacation dollars burning holes in their Bermuda pockets? Grandiose."

Finn laughed. "Now there's the creative little business wonk I know. Remember that lemonade stand you ran one summer? Way before Starbucks opened its doors, you were the first fast-food service person I knew to keep a tip jar by the cash box." For some reason she couldn't imagine, he linked his arms around her waist. It was a friendly gesture, she supposed, wondering if that was how he saw her now.

She stared at the pulse beating in his throat and realized hers was pounding much, much faster. It wasn't exactly "friendly" feelings on this side of the aisle, damn it.

His voice lowered. His head did too. "You know what, GND?"

She could smell him again. That scent that wasn't Irish Spring, but that was Secret Service Finn. Man Finn. Still sexy Finn. "What?"

"I have a sneaking suspicion you're happy in this place."

Bailey couldn't deny it fast enough. "It's just business."

His long fingers caressed the small of her back,

and a little shiver ran up her spine. She remembered his lips on hers in the T-bird. His teeth scraping against the skin of her shoulder. The wet suction of his mouth on her nipple. God, that had been so *good*.

He smiled as if he was reading her mind. "The Perfect Christmas is a business you just happen to love."

The words paralyzed her. "You're wrong. None of this is what I want," she said, her voice hoarse.

He ran a soothing hand along her back. "Bailey—"

Jolting back, she jerked free of his touch. *"None of it."*

His arms fell to his side. His expression hardened. "That's right. It's only business. *All* business. That's why you rushed home when you heard the store was in trouble. That's why you coerced me into playing Santa. I'm sure you'll say that's why I had your tongue in my mouth and why I had my mouth on your breasts the other night too."

Digging her nails into her palms, she turned away from him. What was she supposed to say? "Do you have a better reason?"

"No." He laughed again, without amusement. "Fuck no. I wouldn't be that stupid, now that I'm a college-educated man and all."

She didn't know how to respond to that either.

So she stuck to practicalities. "We'll have to sneak you out the back door so none of the kids see you. I think they'd recognize the eye patch and we don't want to blow your Santa cover."

"Yeah. Fine. Whatever."

With her hand on the door, though, he halted her, his fingers over hers. "Tell the tall brunette at the front of the store where to find me, will you? The one with the twins? We're going out for coffee."

She stared at him over her shoulder. "You made a date with a mother while you were wearing a Santa suit?"

He smiled, that ol' bad-boy smile she was so familiar with. "What can I say, sweetheart? I'm good. And for your information, she's a nanny. She's off at noon and doesn't have to watch the rug-rats again until tomorrow morning."

Just another good reason to keep her mind off him and on business.

Fifteen minutes later, Bailey realized she'd been doing such a good job at that—all her attention on the customers lined up at the cash register—that she'd forgotten to tell the beanpole brunette nanny where she could find Finn. Oh darn.

Thirty minutes after that, from her perch on a stepladder in a small room on the second floor, she caught sight of the couple strolling down the Coronado street. The beanpole carried an iced latte with two straws. Bailey dropped the vintage heart-shaped glass ornament she was in the process of hanging. It broke into five sharp pieces.

Figured. There went $32.50. See, self? Finn was bad for business.

Tracy sat perched on the bed in Harry's dark room, trying to figure out her future and what to do about Dan. Instead, though, her gaze kept returning to her son's empty chair and the open space on the desk where his laptop used to sit. In her mind's eye she could see his wide but bony shoulders, his shaggy hair, the arpeggio of his fingers flying over the keys. She and Dan used to shake their heads, Tracy wondering if their straight-A son was really plotting to take over the world from that computer since he would always switch the screen to something else when they walked by the open door.

Dan would elbow her and whisper "Porn," the rat, because that would set her to worrying. She'd pause about fifteen times in the making of sloppy joes, or tacos, or tuna-noodle casserole—all favorites of the starving teenager-slash-global dictator upstairs—to look at Dan and say, "Do you think?"

And he'd laugh and say, "Of course I think," and she'd throw a dishtowel at him and he'd duck, then grab her around the waist and whisper they'd be looking at naked bodies together later too. When the starving teenager-slash-global dictator-slash-possible deviant came downstairs for dinner, the three of them would sit around the table and she'd have to avoid Dan's eyes so that she wouldn't laugh or blush or both.

After dinner, Tracy would have to run out to a meeting or type up some meeting minutes, or be making phone calls regarding some upcoming meeting and then it would be late. She would be tired and Harry would still be up, fingers tap-tap-tapping on that keyboard, so that when Dan turned off his computer or *CSI: Akron* or *Tucson* or whatever the latest iteration was and turned to her in their bedroom for that naked-body viewing— her naked body and his—she would be too tired and feel too constrained by the idea of their son awake and alert across the hall. "Not tonight," she would say.

And Dan would turn away and she would turn away and somewhere between then and the teeth whitening her husband was gone.

"Mom!" Downstairs, the front door slammed and Bailey stomped into the house. "Just answer me this," she yelled out. "Whose nifty idea was it to subsidize the electric company this season?"

Tracy's knees creaked as she pushed off Harry's bed and moved to the top of the stairs to look down at her daughter. "What are you talking about?"

Bailey's annoyed expression was a duplicate of the one she'd worn as a child, when she couldn't get her little brother or her best friend, Trin, to listen to "reason"—Bailey's version, that is. "The corner house has a helicopter hovering with an inflatable Santa inside holding an American flag. I don't even know what that's supposed to mean."

"We live in a military town? It's Christmas?"

Bailey shook her head, then her eyes narrowed. "You know what's wrong?"

"I've no doubt you're going to tell me."

"We both look pasty," her daughter declared. "We need roses in our cheeks and highlights in our hair."

"What?"

"We're not making the most out of our natural coloring. Brunettes won't stand a chance against us after a little foil and peroxide."

"Didn't you mention 'natural'?"

Bailey waved an impatient hand. "Don't get technical on me. Let's go."

Tracy didn't want to go anywhere, but her daughter had been stubborn since babyhood. After making a research phone call to Trin, Bailey dragged Tracy through the front door.

She glanced over her shoulder as she was pulled toward Bailey's car. "Is that a wreath on the front door?" It was fresh, with a pretty gold ribbon threaded through it and a tiny glass hummingbird sitting right on top.

"Mmm," Bailey said, pushing her into the passenger seat. Once she was behind the wheel, she handed over a pair of sunglasses, even though it was full dark. "Sorry, but I don't have earplugs."

The decorations on the block *were* outrageous.

Bailey shielded her eyes with her hand and muttered in complaint as they crawled behind other cars cruising the scene.

Tracy smiled, not only at her daughter's typical Christmas-curmudgeon-ness, but because the ostentation lifted her heart a little. There were so many sad times, so many tragedies in a year and in a life, why shouldn't people feel free to go over the top on occasion? There should be no shame or sin in lighting up their lives with every bright bauble that the season offered, not because there weren't dark times, but because there *were*.

It was the spirit with which The Perfect Christmas was built.

A pang of longing took aim at Tracy's heart. For a moment she wanted to be back in the store—dusting the Victorian villages, adjusting the positions of the Santa figurines in the front window, straightening the pinafores of the angelic Christmas dolls. Then she thought of Dan and the longing dried to dust.

She'd told Bailey she couldn't go into The Perfect Christmas because she didn't want to see her husband there. But the fact was, worse than facing him within the confines of the store would be facing the truth that he wasn't in the store at all.

If Dan wasn't busy in the back room making coffee, if he wasn't inspecting the track of the North Pole Express that ran along the ceiling of the bottom floor, if he wasn't greeting the children who came into the store with wondering eyes as big as lollipops, then the place would only feel lonely and bitter.

Oh no, that was she.

Tracy and Bailey finally made it to the hair salon that Trin had recommended. The windows were painted with a colorful winter theme. A surfing snowman in red and green boardshorts held a sign that proclaimed they stayed open late and welcomed walk-ins. When Tracy demurred as they entered, concerned about submitting to an unknown stylist, Bailey just issued orders.

"Sit."

"Stay."

To the first available hairdresser. "Dump my mom's gray. Brighten the blond."

Half an hour later, they were in side-by-side chairs, their hair in leaflike layers of tinfoil. It created a sort of silvery, sci-fi Afro effect.

"Do you do this often?" Tracy asked. Frankly, she thought the look more than a little scary. "If men saw women like this, maybe they wouldn't cause us so much trouble."

Bailey made a snorting sound that communicated something between "Fat chance" and "Men are dogs."

Oh no, that was Tracy's thought.

She tried distancing herself from it. "So, uh, how did it go at the store today?" she asked.

Bailey's eyes were closed. "Byron was off on

another of his searches for endless summer. Finn played Santa."

"Finn?"

Bailey tensed but didn't open her eyes. "I told you he was living next door for the holidays. I told you that I'd run into him."

You didn't tell me you were letting him get close to you again. Interesting.

Bailey's eyes popped open. Scowling, she skewered Tracy with her gaze. "You knew what kind of boy he was, Mom. You couldn't miss that crazy hair, the earrings, those tattoos all over his hands. Why the *heck* did you let me start dating him?"

Tracy stared at her beautiful daughter. She'd made many mistakes with her, particularly during the ugly divorce. Some of that experience, she supposed, was responsible for creating the determined, you-won't-knock-me-down attitude of her older child. But there were other parts of Bailey she'd been born with.

Things she'd been born to. From the moment that dangerous, sullen-looking teenage boy had shown up next door, her stubborn perfectionist was determined to bring him to heel. Perhaps, though, all the moves between Bailey and Finn had yet to be played out.

"Mom?" Bailey looked impatient for her answer.

Tracy thought about trying to explain it to her. But then she shrugged. Sometimes it was better to just get out of the way.

Her firstborn, naturally, wasn't going to let it go. "Mom? Come on. Why did you let me date him?"

"Oh, sweetie." Tracy sighed. "I didn't think I had a choice."

Bailey stayed silent for a moment. Then she closed her eyes again. "Funny, I said something like that to Finn."

Definitely some moves left between them, Tracy decided. But then another thought congealed like a cold lump in her stomach. Maybe, maybe when it came to her and Dan, the moves were over.

The game all played out.

December 9

In 1939, Robert L. May created Rudolph the Red-Nosed Reindeer for a storybook given away by the Montgomery Ward department store. As a boy, May had been teased about his small size, so he developed a character with a physical quirk. May's boss was concerned the shiny red nose might be associated with drunkenness, but after seeing sketches of the reindeer, the company was won over.

Chapter 9

Perhaps it was the highlights in her hair that brightened Tracy's outlook. The new cut that fluffed around her face to end in soft wisps at her jawline. Or maybe it was the sunshine streaming through the downstairs window and the promise of another seventy-something-degree day. For whatever reason, she found herself with her hand on the front door. For the first time in weeks, she walked out into the sunlight. She even dressed up for the occasion, dumping the sweats and taking a pair of Bailey's jeans from the pile of clean clothes on the dryer.

She was wearing a lot less gray hair and a dozen fewer pounds. The "divorce diet," she supposed, recalling a phrase coined by one of her friends.

Outside, warmth bathed her face. She sucked in a deep breath and smelled heated green—the combination of the grass and the hibiscus hedge and the leaves from the jacaranda tree growing in the front corner of the yard. Her mother and father had been late-in-life parents, and she'd lived here since birth. It had always given her a sense of comfort and security, until Dan had left.

Last night she'd decided they were probably done, but maybe she could find peace again. Alone, in the house built by her parents, she could become one of those women who found contentment in work and a safety net in a caring circle of other single females.

Who needed a man? What were they good for?

Still savoring the warm air, she strolled to the mailbox nailed to a post at the bottom of the front walk, noticing someone had decorated it with a lush bow of red ribbon. Tracy ran her forefinger over its velvety surface. Even though the season was always hectic because of the store, she'd still managed little holiday touches like this once she and Dan married and the children were young.

But now with Bailey only an occasional visitor to her life and Harry's hectic presence off to college, there was no reason to put forth the effort. She wasn't someone's mother anymore, she realized with a wrench.

Worse, she wasn't sure who she was without that.

The metal mailbox was almost hot to touch, so she pried the door open with a fingernail, then pulled out the pile of envelopes stacked inside. She scanned the names on them.

Mr. and Mrs. Daniel Willis.

Mrs. Daniel Willis.

The couple was dissolved. That woman didn't exist anymore.

A burn rose from her suddenly clenched stomach. Damn Dan! How could he take this away from her! How could he take *herself* away?

No, no. She slammed the mailbox shut, and the violent clang shut off the anger rising inside her. The new woman she wanted to be wasn't going to *feel* like this. The new Tracy would choose her emotions just as she chose her identity.

She was going to be a serene person, she decided. One of those types who floated over the highs and lows of life.

As she turned back to the house, a car coming down the street caught her eye. Her hand tightened on the mail, creasing the cable bill. *Serene,* she told herself. *Tranquil. Peaceful.*

It was her footsteps that rushed in a panic up the front walk. Inside, she was a calm sea.

The calm sea didn't make it through the entry before Dan was out of his car. "Tracy?"

She shut the door when he was on the sidewalk. Locked it as he mounted the porch steps.

Then, her heart clattering in her chest, she slid down against the painted wood, her legs no longer able to hold her steady. She rested her forehead on her upraised knees, fighting for breath.

It was still a struggle when she heard the scratch of a key in the lock. Her head jerked up, and she scrambled to her feet. She just managed to move away before the door hit her in the butt.

Then he was framed in the doorway. Her husband.

Her *estranged* husband.

"What the *hell* are you doing?" Her heart jumped again, astonished by the curse—she *never* cursed—and *The Exorcist* rasp of her voice.

"I have a key. My name's on the deed. Why wouldn't I enter my own home?" His dark hair was longer than she'd ever seen it. It swung over his brow like a boy's—like Harry's—and she could see the faint whiteness of the crows' feet at the corners of his watchful eyes.

He *was* tan, damn him. No hiding out in dark rooms for the SOB who'd walked out on her.

Anger rose like bile again, but Tracy managed to swallow it down as she turned her back and strode off toward the kitchen. "Get what you came for, and then leave," she said over her shoulder.

God, she was good. That had sounded somewhat sane. Poised, even. As if she were in control of her emotions and not the other way around.

She could carry off this serenity thing. Be it, even. She could.

Until she felt Dan's hand on her elbow. "Tracy—"

She whirled with a screech, as if he'd burned her. "Get your hands off me."

He lifted them, surrender style. "I just want to talk."

"No." She backed away.

He stalked forward.

Her heart hammered against her breastbone as she retreated down the hall. "Come back some other time."

"Now is the time." His voice was hard, his gaze intent on her face. It had been years since she was aware of how strong he was. Though he wasn't a particularly tall man, his build was powerful, thanks to solid shoulders, lean hips, sturdy legs. He'd been working out, that was obvious.

Bastard. Probably bench pressing bunnies at that Sodom and Gomorrah he called home.

No, he'd just called *here* home. Anger shot through her bloodstream like a drug. She started to tremble under its all-consuming influence.

"Tracy." Her gaze dropped from his face to the

sinews in his arm as he held out a hand to her. "Now."

"No."

He took a step forward, and she whirled again. Ran.

Get away. Get free. Panting already, she sprinted down the hall, hearing his heavy footsteps behind her.

"Damn it, Tracy!"

No. Damn *him*. Damn him for making her miserable. Angry. Alone.

Catching the baluster at the bottom of the stairs in her hand, she swung herself around and took off up the steps. Yesterday her knees had been creaking. Today she felt supple, strong. A gazelle. A lioness.

A woman running from heartache and all the other emotions that were trying to catch up with her.

Her pulse was pounding in her ears as she gained the upper hall. Dan was still behind her, determined.

To bow her. Break her. Make her cry.

Never. Never never never.

Her first husband had torn her skin off her bones on his way to shattering her heart. She wouldn't be so vulnerable again.

The master bedroom doorway was in sight. The double doors locked and there wasn't a key to open them. Dan was too civilized, surely, to break them down.

Just three . . . more . . . steps.

She flew through the doorway even as Dan's big hand clamped down on her shoulder. With a wrench she yanked away from his touch.

But it was too late to lock him out of the bedroom.

Her gaze trained on his face, she backed off again, putting the king-sized mattress between them while he stood, unmoving, at the entrance to the room.

Her chest heaved, her breath stuttered in and out of her lungs.

The tension in the room stretched like taffy between them, but it was nothing so sweet. Tracy licked her suddenly dry lips.

And Dan's gaze shifted from her face to focus on her mouth.

Heat skittered up her spine. Tracy's glance darted to the right, catching a glimpse of herself in the mirror over her dresser.

We need roses in our cheeks and highlights in our hair.

Her face was flushed from her race, and it had disheveled the wispy ends of her new haircut. The way her breasts were moving against the T-shirt she wore—tight, another item borrowed from Bailey—made her look like a woman who was less angry than . . . wanting.

From somewhere, a thought burst in her brain. She looked like a woman ready for sex.

Her gaze jumped back to Dan. There was a new tightness across his cheekbones, a new kind of watchfulness in his eyes.

A new quality to the tension in the room.

Who needs a man? What are they good for?

All at once, Tracy remembered.

He took a measured step into the room. Another.

She clutched one corner of the four-poster bed, her knuckles going white. "What do you think you're doing?"

His hands went to the hem of his polo shirt and in one swift movement, he stripped it off.

Definitely working out. His shoulders were smooth, round hills of muscles that led to his tan chest that tapered to the flat skin of his belly. Tracy swallowed as his hands pulled at the buttons on his 501s.

Don't retreat, she told herself. *Don't give him the satisfaction.*

"I don't know what you think is going to happen here."

"You know exactly what I think is going to happen." The dark, hard thread in his voice sent a hot shiver down her back. "Take off your clothes, Tracy."

In broad daylight? The neighbors, their son—

But he was away at college and she wasn't a

mother first and foremost any longer. She was . . .

"Take them off, Trace."

At Dan's command, a brand-new, sexual flame inside her leaped. The heat running down her spine spread, burning every inch of her skin, making it feel tight and too small for what she was trying to hold inside.

Excitement. Arousal.

He was naked now. This man—this stranger in her bedroom—drew closer, his penis jutting toward her with the same aggressive attitude she could see on his face and hear in his voice. Her knees went rubbery again.

Reaching out, he caught the end of her T-shirt in his fist. Then he yanked her close to his nakedness, his other hand biting into the skin at her waist as he jerked her shirt over her head.

"I want you."

His eyes widened.

She realized the words were hers.

"Then unhook your bra. I want to see your breasts."

Her fingers trembled as they found the hooks behind her back. Dan's gaze didn't move off her face until her bra dropped to the Oriental carpet with an almost silent plop. Then he palmed her shoulders with his hands, squeezing a moment before slowly moving them down her torso to cover her breasts.

Making a cup of his hands, he plumped them for his inspection.

Between her legs she felt swollen, aching, *empty*.

His thumbs rasped across her nipples and she gasped. Her eyes closed.

"Look at me," he ordered, his voice harsh.

Her lashes flew open and instinct made her try to move back. His hands tightened their hold on her breasts.

"You're not going anywhere. You're not looking at anything but me. You will see me. Know me." His nostrils flared. "Fuck me."

Tracy's heart slammed against her breastbone. He'd never said that word to her before. Never called what they did together a four-letter word.

It excited her, she realized. Maybe she'd found someone else to be instead of Mother! Someone sexual. Excited. Exciting.

Dan rubbed her nipples again. "Take off your pants."

He didn't stop touching her breasts as she obeyed. Once nude, she had a moment of doubt. The divorce diet had turned her bony in some areas and saggy in others.

But he was focused on her mouth again, and he leaned over to kiss her, the first thrust of his tongue as strong and sure as she'd always thought her marriage. He shifted his hands to her hips and drew her flush against his body. His chest hair abraded her nipples, his erection pressed hard against her belly.

He still desired her.

His hands cupped her bottom and the angle of his head changed to take her mouth deeper. Heat flashed over her again and that swollen place between her legs throbbed in time with her pumping heart. *Oh God.*

Her panting breaths rubbed her nipples against his chest and his smooth penis still kissed her abdomen. But it wasn't enough.

Not enough closeness.

Not enough sensation.

She pushed closer, and his leg slid between hers. His tongue pushed deep as his knee lifted, pressed steadily against the empty place between her thighs. Groaning, she ground herself against it, without regard for daylight or heartbreak or maturity. Did middle-aged women desire like this?

"Do me," she whispered against his lips, astonished at the raunchiness of her words. A little pleased. She lifted her mouth. "Do me now."

His eyes narrowed. "Then get on the bed."

Out of a thousand years' habit, she half turned to pull back the covers.

"I didn't tell you to do anything but get on the bed."

Tracy froze, then glanced over her shoulder at him. "But . . ." But this was a stranger in her bedroom and he looked determined to have his way.

She slowly climbed onto the bed, letting him have a full-on view of her butt, even as she thought, *Who is this woman?* She could see her in the dresser mirror, blond hair wild, color high on her cheeks, mouth and nipples the same red. A sexual being. A start to a new woman.

"Hurry up." Dan put his big hand on the curve of her waist, flipping her to her back and then coming between her legs. "I want to get inside of you."

His knees pushed her legs wide. His penis took aim, headed in.

"Wait." Tracy placed her palm on his chest, keeping him at bay. "Protection."

The man blinked. "What? Protection?"

"Condoms. I don't know where you've been sleeping."

His jaw tensed. "Tracy—"

"No condom, no come." She was pretty pleased with the pithy phrase, even though her blood was screaming to get on with it, for him to get on *her*.

"Where the hell do you expect me—?"

"My son's bathroom." At least he wasn't carrying them in his pockets. Or at least he pretended he wasn't. "Right across the hall."

He didn't say he knew where Harry's bathroom was. He didn't protest about the protection any longer. Instead he vaulted off the bed and then returned in a flash, foil packets spread like a poker hand in his fingers.

"Feeling lucky?" she asked.

"No. But I feel like screwing." His head lowered. His body lowered. His latex-covered erection felt like heaven against her wetness. "I feel like screwing you."

They didn't use each other's names.

They didn't say much of anything.

Instead, palm to palm, fingers gripping hard, they tumbled on the bed, trembled in each other's arms, worked hard for release.

Tracy—still not recognizing herself or her lust—turned her head and bit the pillow to keep from screaming when she came.

Dan bit her shoulder as he finished.

Then they were on their backs, side-by-side, not touching. Separate again.

A familiar position.

When he turned to his side to look at her, she kept her gaze on the ceiling.

"We haven't—"

"No." They hadn't fixed anything.

"I won't apologize."

"Don't." Amazingly, she'd wanted it as much as he.

He rolled off the bed, then reached for his clothes. She watched the newly firm curve of his butt until it was hidden behind his jeans. He pulled his key ring from his front pocket.

There were keys on it she didn't recognize.

Just as she didn't recognize herself.

She hated him all over again.

But she curled into a C to keep the anger inside her and bit back her crone shriek as he let himself out of what had once been their house.

December 10

Santa Claus's history traces back to a fourth-century bishop named St. Nicholas. He was credited with bringing three boys back to life, and thus became the patron saint of children.

Chapter 10

Finn watched Tanner slide a cup of coffee onto the bar in front of him, lining it up with the Coke, 7-Up, and glass of iced virgin Bloody Mary already waiting there. He'd been too restless to sit around Gram's house all evening, but he'd made himself a promise to avoid hitting the alcohol. Two binges a month were his limit.

Not to mention the trouble he'd gotten into last time he was drunk. Tonight he was determined to keep himself jam-free.

Maybe a bar wasn't the best destination for him, but after Gram had gone to bed, within minutes he'd been sick of his own company and the replays of past and recent life experiences that continued to run through his brain. The only relief he'd come up with was to leave the house in search of safe, like-minded company.

Tanner was the other most messed-up man he knew.

Finn cupped his palms around the hot ceramic mug. "The Mad Gift Giver struck again."

Tanner shook back his newly long, pretty-boy blond hair. "What now?"

"Late Friday afternoon, when Gram and I came back from her doctor's appointment—"

"Anything new there?"

Finn focused on his coffee, edging it closer to the Coke so that there was equal distance between his beverages. "No. I told you. She's on the road to recovery. As I was saying though, when we came home from her doctor's appointment, there was a set of knight's armor waiting for me on the porch."

"Need I ask? Real knight's armor?"

"Your guess is as good as mine, though it looks museum quality to my admittedly untrained eye. It's life-sized and filled with Tootsie Rolls from metal heels to metal helmet."

Tanner swigged down half a glass of ice water. "Good candy choice, at least."

"She must be nervous about coming by the bar because there was also something left for you."

The other man carefully set the glass down. "Don't tell me what it is."

Finn couldn't help his grin. It had been a good idea to come to the bar and hang with his buddy. "One of those big, five-pound—"

"I said don't tell me!"

"—candy Kisses."

"Shit." Tanner rubbed his hand over his face, jostling all that Hollywood hair. "You had to do it. You had to tell me. My life sucks."

Finn could only shake his head. Eleven months ago they'd been on the same diplomatic protective detail. But while Finn had been outside the fund raiser when the assassin had fired at the prince, Tanner had been stuck inside. Tanner Hart, the youngest member of the famous, multigenerational family of Hart military heroes, had become infamous for the big ol' wet one the prince's daughter had laid on him while all hell was breaking loose outside. Cameras had caught both ends of the action.

Tanner had been guilty of nothing more than following the plan and sticking close to the spoiled young woman who was the product of a brief marriage between the Middle Eastern prince and an American model. One look at the tabloid photos published all over the globe, however, and he had resigned from the Secret Service. It hadn't cooled the international gossip for an instant.

Tanner had yet to get his head screwed on

straight about his lack of culpability regarding the tragic results of that night, but Finn was giving him time. If something didn't happen soon, though, he'd make it his New Year's resolution to fix his friend.

One of them had to get back to normal.

"That woman is the devil," Tanner muttered.

At that moment, his brother Troy passed by. "Who?"

Tanner busied himself with a bar rag. "That damn Desirée."

"She might be a pain in the ass, but you have to admit she's a looker," Troy said.

The younger Hart froze. "When have you seen her?"

Troy shrugged, a mountain of shaved-head macho marine. "What do you mean? The photos, of course."

His brother's blue eyes narrowed. Like Finn, he'd been trained to discern the smallest thing out of place. There was an odd twitch along Troy's jaw.

"Tell me she hasn't been by here," Tanner demanded.

"She hasn't."

Tanner groaned. "Well she will. And I'm warning you, Troy. Don't even let her in the door. She's trouble with a fucking, capital T."

"Little bro, what is she, like fourteen or something?"

"She's over twenty-one. And though she might

look all innocent with those big eyes and long hair, I tell you, she's the devil. Just wait, you'll find out. I dare you to try kicking her out when she comes in and you'll see just how pigheaded she is."

Troy waved his brother's warning away. "I'm a marine. I can handle one little half princess."

Tanner groaned again. "Trouble, I'm telling you. With a capital T."

Finn couldn't help but silently laugh at the note of concern in Tanner's voice and the ill-fated confidence in Troy's. Poor guys. The things that a woman could do to a man.

Then a feminine voice sounded in his ear. "I hope Tanner doesn't mean me."

Finn's head whipped left. His amusement died. She'd come up on his blind side. Bailey—his own personal devil—Sullivan.

"Whoops. Gotta go," he said, starting to slip off the bar stool. He'd left Gram's because it made him edgy being so close to the Girl Next Door. Getting snarled with her had already proved to be too damn easy, and being her bar buddy would only make it easier.

She grabbed his wrist. "Finn . . ." Her voice trailed off and she frowned at his hand. "I just realized. Where are your tattoos?"

He flexed his fingers. They were bare of embellishment, except for the heavy signet ring he wore on his left pinkie. In the old days, his knuckles had been perma-inked with skulls, dots, and cryptic messages, most of which only made sense if you were young, stupid, and drinking beer.

"I had them lasered off before I applied to the Secret Service."

"Ouch." Bailey winced. "So they're all gone?"

"Mmm." Pulling his hand free of hers, he stood. "Now I really do have to go."

"A date with Fran?"

"Huh?"

"You know, *The Nanny*."

He looked into Bailey's upturned face and noted the sleek fall of her blond hair, the darkened lashes, the kiss-me color of her mouth. His gaze dropped. Since she'd returned to Coronado, he'd yet to see her in anything beside pants and jeans.

Now here she was, in a red sweater and a short black skirt that exposed plenty of her slender legs, one crossed over the other. Swinging back and forth was one small foot encased in a dominatrix shoe that was all tall stacked heel and B&D black straps.

His eyes narrowed. "What do you want, GND?" Despite her second appearance at Hart's, he didn't think she'd come for the ambience, unless the sound of clacking billiard balls was suddenly a Bailey turn-on.

"Well . . ." She leaned her elbow on the bar, and her tongue swiped the gloss on her lower lip.

His blood rushed south, as well as the intelligent instinct to run. He rubbed his palms on his jeans, but that didn't erase the tactile memory of the silky softness of her bare legs. Making love with Bailey had always begun with slow, heated kisses. The kind of kisses he never tried to rush, even though his teenage hormones were screaming, *In! In! In!*

Once her mouth was red and swollen, her lips trying to follow his as he lifted them away, he'd allow himself to touch her body. A hand over her breast or his fingers sliding along the damp small of her back. More kissing. When he'd finally move to bare her, she would squeeze shut her eyes, tight enough to make sunburst lines at their far corners.

He'd unbutton her shirt. Unhook her bra. Catch the elastic edges of her panties and draw them down her legs. And because Bailey was still flying blind, he found he could deliberately run his palms up her legs and spread them without her protest or any sort of modest resistance. Maybe she pretended it was happening to someone else. Maybe she avoided embarrassment that way.

Whatever the reason, his heart would be slamming against his chest and his blood would be rushing in his ears as he pushed against the silky skin of her inner thighs ... and then looked his fill. He supposed she didn't know how his heart would stop, his air back up in his lungs as he traced with his eyes the blond curls and the petaled wetness of her sex.

Then he'd reach out a finger—one of his rough fingers with its even rougher-looking black tattoos—and bathe the tip in her arousal so he could paint her folds with it. One finger became two and he didn't think she ever knew that he would always suck her taste from them before donning a condom and beginning the slow slide inside her heated body.

Then her eyes would fly open, but only for a moment. As if reassured that it was her bad boy covering her, she'd release a little sigh and he'd complete the journey. The *In! In! In!* screamers inside him would sigh too, and settle.

Inside Bailey, they'd say, as if all was right with the world. *Inside Bailey.*

"You were so . . . cute with the little kids the other day at The Perfect Christmas," this open-eyed Bailey now said. "I should have thanked you more. Several people have stopped in to comment on what an excellent job you did."

The *kids* had been cute, not Finn, and she knew it. He sighed, even more wary. "Back to the original question. What do you want, Bailey?"

She made another swipe of her mouth with her tongue. Witch. "Would you consider a reprise of your role as Santa?"

"No."

Tanner had quit arguing with his brother and turned his attention to them. He was smirking. "Finn? Santa?"

"Ho ho ho," he answered. "But I'm not doing it again."

"Please, Finn." She put her hand on his forearm. "I didn't want to have to ask, but Byron's surfing at Swami's Beach tomorrow, so I'm desperate. It's either you or me, or . . ." Her head turned so that her gaze included Tanner.

Finn stood. It wasn't that it bothered him she was looking farther afield. It was that it released him from looking at her anymore: her mouth, that skirt, those legs. So "See you later," he said, and made for the exit.

Damn if Gram's T-Bird wouldn't start. He'd taken it instead of his SUV because its battery needed the workout, but now it *heh-heh-heh*ed like a barking seal instead of catching with its usual powerful *vroom*. Rather than sticking around to coax it to life, he decided to leave it in case Bailey struck out with Tanner and went for Finn again.

And if she didn't, if she found her knight in Santa's clothing within Hart's bar, then Finn wouldn't have to know anything about it.

There wasn't a reason in the world he couldn't make the less-than-a-mile home on foot. Lucky him, he was wearing his running shoes.

He took off at an easy jog. A turn or two and there weren't a lot of streetlights to go by, but he continued at a decent pace. At the hospital, he'd been taught to move his head slightly from side to side to compensate for the loss of peripheral vision on his left. The first attempts at walking briskly or running outdoors had freaked him—in the same way as weird vibes could creep up on him while snorkeling. In the ocean, there was that foreboding awareness of great depth and darkness lurking somewhere ahead. Without one eye he would perceive a similar shadowy looming well to his left.

Picking up speed, he shoved the uneasiness away by congratulating himself on his escape from Bailey. Then a slow-cruising car approached him from the rear. It wouldn't be . . . it couldn't be . . .

He glanced over his right shoulder, groaned.

She must have spotted him. He increased his pace, but she accelerated to get even with him. Then her window rolled down. He kept his gaze focused ahead.

"Hey, Finn," she called out.

He pretended deafness.

She tooted her horn.

And scared something out of the darkness on his left. He heard its rustle, but he didn't see it— cat—until its path bisected the visual field of his remaining eye. Too late to avoid the tangle.

Too late to avoid the tumble.

He went down on his knees, hands, and elbows, hard. He kept the position for a few minutes, to catch his breath and to curse black cats, black shadows, blindness, Bailey.

"Finn!" Her high heels clattered on the sidewalk. "Are you okay?"

Yeah, but of course he had to accept her apologetic offer of a ride back to Gram's—unless he wanted to look even more like a graceless idiot. Then he let her talk him into allowing her to play nurse.

Trailing him through Gram's house toward the kitchen, she spared a single glance for the set of medieval armor with the wide gold bow tied around its chest that he'd propped up against a wall in the living room. There really was no sane way to explain it, so he didn't bother.

First aid supplies had always resided in the narrow cupboard to the right of the sink. He settled into a kitchen chair, holding a paper towel against the worst wound on his left elbow to staunch the bleeding. When Bailey approached, a box of bandages in one hand and a bottle of hydrogen peroxide in the other, he drew back in his chair.

"I just remembered," he said, eyeing the brown bottle with distaste. "You used to enjoy this kind of thing."

She laughed. "*I'm* not the one into self-tattooing."

"They're all gone now." The ring on his left hand squeezed his finger. "And that was a long time ago."

Her citrusy-flowery smell filled his head as she neared. He watched her saturate a cotton ball with the peroxide, and then she pushed his palm toward his shoulder and pulled the paper towel away from his elbow.

Finn focused on the kitchen faucet and waited for the first sting.

It didn't come.

He glanced up at pseudo-Nurse Sullivan. She was staring at the wound on his arm, sticky with blood. A single tear ran down her cheek.

"Bailey?"

She blinked, then rubbed her face with the heel of her hand. "I'm okay." Another tear spilled over.

"GND? What's the matter?"

Shaking her head, she swiped at her cheek again, then under her nose. "Lost . . ." With a little cough, she cleared her throat. "Lost my clinical detachment for a moment, I guess."

Finn frowned. "It's not that bad. Really."

Nodding, she sank to her dominatrix heels and made quick work of cleaning, then bandaging his elbow. Without looking at his face, she moved on to his hand, then his other elbow. His right palm, the least injured, she saved for last, dabbing it with peroxide on a clean cotton ball.

He stared at her bent head, bemused by her odd mood and uncharacteristic silence. She threw the used cotton onto the table but kept hold of his hand, studying it as if she was reading his fortune.

Weird, he thought, frowning again. "Bailey?"

She made a choked sound and pressed her face to his fingers. More tears.

"God, Bailey." His pulse jacked up and he

touched her hair with his free hand. "What's going on? Did something happen?"

Her voice was thick. "Something happened to you."

Now he felt even more like a graceless ass. "It's just a little case of road rash."

"You could have died, Finn."

"Not even cl—"

"Not t-tonight. Then."

Oh. She was crying about, thinking about, talking about, the assassination attempt.

Sometimes he wondered if maybe he should have died. Maybe it would have been easier than to live with the screwed-up mess the assassination attempt had made of his life and his future. At least it would have saved him from the damn agony of feeling Bailey's hot tears and not knowing what the hell to do about them.

"But I'm okay," he said. "I'm okay."

Tears continued to drip between his fingers. Hating this helpless feeling, he pulled her up and onto his lap. She buried her face against his neck, whether for comfort or out of embarrassment, he didn't know.

"Shhh," he said, stroking her soft hair again. "I'm right here."

Her shoulders continued to shake, and a sick sense of panic rose inside him. He couldn't remember ever seeing her cry. She'd never been that kind of girl.

He cupped the back of her head, trying to curb his anxiety. "What can I do to make it better?"

"Nothing." Her mouth moved against his wet skin. "I'm sorry, and I f-feel so d-dumb. I'm not usually sloppy. I'm tired, I g-guess. J-just really tired."

"You've been working too hard," he said, relief calming his heartbeat. He could fix *tired*! Anything to stop this emotion leaking all over his shirt. "Tell you what, I'll do that Santa gig for you."

When she didn't immediately respond, he promised more. "I'll do that Santa gig and anything else you want from me at The Perfect Christmas."

"What?" Her voice was still muffled against his shirt.

"I'll help you out at the store. Whatever you need."

Her head lifted. His nose touched her pink one. Her lashes were wet and spiky, and he thought he could execute an Acapulco cliff dive into the drenched blue of her eyes.

Her forefinger reached out to trace the outline of his eye patch. Her pretty mouth turned down. "You don't want to do that."

He wanted her to stop looking at him with something that looked suspiciously like pity. He pinched her chin between his thumb and forefinger and adjusted her head so she was looking at him, and not at the stupid patch. "I offered, didn't I? I'll help you with The Perfect Christmas."

It was as if the sun had come out. A smile broke over her face. "Oh Finn. Oh *Finn.*"

Oh fuck.

Too late, he realized he'd held out a noose and offered to tie it around his own stupid neck. It was crazy to tangle himself up with Bailey again! He thought of that damn knight suit in the next room and wondered if he could blame it for his rescuer impulse. Or . . . had she planned this herself?

Damn it.

In years past, she'd had plenty of practice getting him right where she wanted him.

"Finn?" Her nose wrinkled. Smelling the renege in the air.

But going back on his promise would be stupid too. That would show weakness. To both of them. There was another way to handle this.

"Yeah, I'll do it," he decided, pushing her off his lap so they were both standing. But he'd do it for a price. *His* price. "In return, you'll go on a date with me Tuesday night *and* you'll tell me exactly why you ran out on me ten years ago."

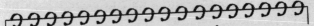

December 11

The original "White Christmas" had an opening verse about a shining sun and swaying palm trees, as writer Irving Berlin was in Southern California when he wrote the immortal song that became a holiday standard.

Chapter 11

Dan found the woman of his dreams standing in the afternoon sunlight on a sidewalk corner diagonal from The Perfect Christmas. She looked like his Tracy, in khaki pants that hung low on her hips, a thin white shirt that was rolled to the elbows, bare feet shoved into two-tone loafers. Dark glasses and a baseball cap almost hiding her short blond hair lent her a celebrity-on-the-lam air.

He watched a passing couple give her a second glance. The silver-haired husband half gave her a third. Checking out her ass.

It was enough to make him hurry forward to stake his claim. "Hey."

The woman turned dark lenses his way. He couldn't tell what the hell she was thinking.

"What are you doing here?" she asked.

"Same as you, I suppose." He nodded toward the store across the street. "Making sure it's still standing."

Tracy returned her gaze to the two-story Victorian that had been her parents' livelihood, her livelihood, and then theirs. In silence, they watched the steady stream of traffic going in and out of the white-on-blue front door. Eight out of ten people leaving carried the store's signature bag— Christmas stripes around a centered watercolor version of the storefront.

"Bailey's holding her own," his wife finally said.

It had been Dan's biggest gamble—walking away from the store as well as the house. He'd thought it would wake up Tracy that much quicker, shock her into seeing him, seeing *them*, when she tried managing the place on her own. Instead, she'd let the cavalry take over.

He'd considered returning to work at that point, but that would have been caving in. If they were going to make their marriage work, they had to forge something independent of The Perfect Christmas. He had to find a way for her to know him again, as a man outside of father and business partner.

"Bailey's persuaded Finn to play Santa Claus for Story Hour and Christmas Movie Nights."

Dan's gaze jolted toward Tracy again. "What?"

A smile quivered at the corners of her mouth. "Alice has been ill and he's living with her for a while. Didn't take long for magnet Bailey and magnet Finn to find each other all over again."

That sidetracked Dan for a moment. Finn had been a father's—albeit stepfather's—worst nightmare from the look of him. Sullen at thirteen, dangerous at sixteen, obviously head-over-motorcycle boots in love with Tracy's daughter, who looked too perfect for one of the delinquent rebel's tattooed fingers to touch.

But now he could feel almost sorry for the other man. Dan had spoken with Finn on occasion, and noted that he'd grown up into someone with a different kind of hard edge. Bailey, on the other hand, pretended she didn't have a soft bone in her body. He could imagine all the sparks that were going to fly if—when—they clashed.

Dan shook his head. "I always thought . . ."

Tracy had been reading his mind for almost two decades. ". . . she threw what they had away too easily."

Like her mother?

"I heard that," she murmured.

It almost made him grin. "Trace—"

"Harry said he's getting two Bs and an A. He thinks he can bring up at least one of the Bs with the final exam."

Dan shrugged. "He's always been an optimist."

"Like you used to be."

"Trace—"

"He also says he has a girlfriend."

"Shelley. I heard about her." Dan wanted to make clear that he kept in contact with their son too. "Harry's a fast worker, wouldn't you say?"

"Like you?"

An insult? A rebuke? "Trace—"

"I have to go."

His hand caught hers.

In a blink, his mind flashed back to the scene in their house two days ago. To the incredible, hot sex. His first glimpse of her as he drove up to the house had clawed at his heart. She'd looked so great, so familiar, so his. He'd hated that she'd run from him.

They were both angry once he'd caught up with her, and then that anger transmuted into something else entirely—lust. The bedroom had been smoky with it.

He hadn't thought about what he was saying or doing. He was compelled to act . . . taking off his clothes, telling her to take off hers. The only pause . . . protection! *What the hell?!* he'd thought.

But at that point he hadn't wanted to go into long explanations or even short recriminations.

He'd wanted Tracy. So he'd dashed for the damn things and then struggled some putting one on—condom coverage was *not* like riding a bike—and then it had been over and he was over her and they'd had that mind-blowing sex. Fingers entangled, bodies driving, pleasure so good.

It hadn't fixed anything between them, they'd both known that right away, no words necessary. Then, as now, he could read her mind and she could read his. He hadn't cared.

He cared now.

He needed to find a way to fix things between them.

Losing, losing Tracy, was no longer an option.

She tugged at his hand and he clutched it harder. Glancing down at her, he could see nothing but his reflection in those sunglass lenses and the expressionless set to her face. She was shut away from him now, he realized. Before, he'd been invisible to her. Now, she looked as if she was trying to keep herself invisible to him.

He swallowed, then gambled again. "So, come here often?"

"What are you talking about?"

"Coronado. I haven't been here long. I could use a local guide."

Tracy stilled. "I seem to have heard this before."

It was close to the first thing he'd said to her at the party where they'd been introduced. Somehow he'd wangled it into an invitation to meet her on the beach the next day. Seven-year-old Bailey as chaperone. Sandcastle building as activity.

If he could get Tracy's feet on that sand again, she'd open that door she was hiding behind. He was sure of it. Hopeful, anyway.

"C'mon," he urged, giving her hand another small squeeze and then letting go so as not to spook her. "It's a beautiful afternoon. We're still playing hooky. Go for a walk on the beach with me?"

The bill of her cap ducked toward her chest, completely obscuring her face. "I'm not—"

"It's just a walk, Trace."

"I'm not interested in it being anything else." There was that door again, slamming right in his face.

He'd been patient before, though, and he could be patient again. Once she got the feel of the sand between her toes, she'd let go. A little. Please.

They strolled the short blocks toward Central Beach, crossing Ocean Boulevard, which was lined with extravagant homes and mansions to reach more than a mile's length of a wide swathe of sugary sand. He offered his hand to Tracy to climb over the tumbled boulders and rubbery ice plant that was the last barrier to the beach itself. She ignored it to scramble over them on her own.

They weren't alone. Though the beach was

wide enough—and the water cool enough in December—to prevent it from looking like a remake of an Annette and Frankie *Beach Blanket Bingo* movie, there were still plenty of people taking advantage of the postcard-come-to-life day.

Little kids braved the winter-chilled water, their white chubby tummies and plastic blow-up rafts screaming "tourist" even louder than a four-door sedan with Enterprise stickers. Local preteens in wetsuits, flippers, and boogie boards showed off their gymnastic skill, SoCal-style. Others with skim boards scattered the pipers and gulls as they threw the thin pieces of wood down on the wet sand and rode the retreating white water.

Young men played football. Girls in bikini bottoms and sweatshirts wiggled their toes to the beat of their iPods. Young moms toted toddlers on one hip and mesh bags of sand toys on the other. Retired couples in L. L. Bean windbreakers lifted binoculars, training them toward the Pacific's commuter lanes, where migrating whales could be spotted heading to Mexico for the winter.

Something odd struck him. He looked over at Tracy. "There's no one our age."

"What?"

"Out here." He gestured toward the clean sweep of sand around them. "Our age group is missing."

"No . . ." But Tracy's voice trailed off as she

scanned the beach. Then she shrugged. "All at work, I guess."

"Busy putting kids through college, I suppose."

"Or busy making money for those cutesy new wives and the new families they plan to make with them." There was a hot, bitter snap to her words. She shoved her hands in her front pockets. "Now the old wives, they're off looking for their decimated pride and shattered expectations while scrambling to figure out how they're going to support themselves and their children on a single income."

He blinked, startled into stopping. "Tracy—"

"I'm sorry." Her voice cooled as quick as it had snapped. "That was uncalled for."

She drew her hands from her pockets and crossed her arms over her chest, closing up again like a sea anemone touched by a painful finger. Pivoting south, she started trudging down the beach in the direction of the red-peaked roofs of the Hotel del Coronado, the wind blowing the tails of her shirt around her hips.

Dan hurried to catch up. "Is that—"

"By the way, I was thinking about Christmas gifts. Bailey's taken care of and I've ordered a few for Harry off the Internet. A college sweatshirt, some gift cards, but if you—"

"I don't want to talk about Harry."

"I found this funny battery-operated fly-zapper shaped like a tennis racket for Bailey. I'm going to put it in her stocking, though I have a feeling the first annoyance she'll use it on is Finn."

The old wives, they're off looking for their decimated pride and shattered expectations while scrambling to figure out how they're going to support themselves and their children on a single income.

Dan couldn't get the words out of his head as he trailed behind her. The wind changed direction, flattening her shirt to her back, her shoulder blades looking suddenly so fragile. When they'd met, she'd been working at the store full-time, but he knew she'd upped her part-time hours after her first husband left.

Because it was a family business, because she'd been almost fully running it with minimal help from her parents when they'd met, Dan had assumed it wasn't a career she'd "scrambled" to put together, but a perfect opportunity for a newly single mother.

"Did you not want to work at The Perfect Christmas?" he asked. "Was there something else you wanted to do with your life?"

Continuing to churn through the sand, she glanced over at him. "What about you? You're the one who left a big-shot stockbroker job to join me at the store."

But that had been easy for him. When it came to choosing between a stress-full or a Tracy-full life, taking on comanagement of The Perfect Christmas after her parents' death had been an obvious decision. "I get more satisfaction out of the store's customers than any of those whose portfolios I used to fatten."

He didn't comment on his use of the present tense. Before she might have, a Frisbee landed at her feet.

Tracy stopped, stooped, and peeled the plastic disc off the sand. Without a word, she handed it over to him.

Without a word, he took it. She couldn't throw a beanbag, and they both knew it. He swallowed a bittersweet smile as he took aim at the shirtless young man standing downwind. What would kill him was to lose moments just like this, when two people's shared domestic intelligence made an everyday occurrence a ritual that strengthened the relationship's bonds.

Except for all that domestic inside dope, he *didn't* know everything he should about his wife. "*Is* there something you'd rather have been doing all these years?"

She'd turned to study the surf. Two more waves rushed in before she spoke. "Sometimes I think about the places where we get the items for the store. Remember those cranberry candles we had last year, the ones shaped like old-fashioned Santas? They were from Michigan. Sometimes I think about Michigan and its lakes that have waves like our ocean."

For their honeymoon, they'd spent a week in

San Francisco. But between the demands of the store and the kids, the fact that he'd moved like crazy growing up, and finally that they lived in a premier vacation destination, travel had never occurred to him. "Anyplace else?"

"Those little sugary-looking cottage ornaments are imported from Switzerland," Tracy said. "I think about going there. And I can smell the history and the burning sun on the clay piñatas that we import from Mexico City."

Dan shook his head. She had places she wanted to see that she'd never shared with him. Feelings too? *Decimated pride and shattered expectations.*

Digging into her first marriage and subsequent divorce had never been on his agenda. He'd thought she felt fairly neutral toward the other man. He'd told himself she was entitled to her privacy. Now he wondered if he'd been ducking her pain.

Was there some good way to bring it up?

He couldn't think of one. "Tracy, about Kevin . . ." Though he watched closely, she didn't even flinch.

"Why would you mention him?"

"He's Bailey's father." Lame, but the best he could do. "When she was living at home, he would show up at the house on occasion—"

"On the occasion he felt bored," she said, the words spitting like ice cubes onto the sand, "or some pang of guilt managed to bore its way through his unfeeling hide."

Oh-kay. Not neutral. Definitely not neutral. Dan took a breath and plunged on. "It was obvious that Bailey was, uh, conflicted when it came to him, but how about you?"

Tracy turned her face toward him. A strand of windblown hair stuck to the corner of her mouth, and she drew it away with a finger. "How about me, what?"

"How . . . how did the divorce affect you?"

In the ensuing silence, his gut churned in nervous anticipation.

"You know those carved jewelry boxes we have at the store? The ones that require opening a dozen latched and hidden doors to get to the prize inside?"

Dan nodded, wondering for a moment what country they came from and if that was another of Tracy's dream destinations. "You have to know the secret to get to the center."

"Right. Well, after the divorce was at last final, that's where I put my feelings about it. Locked and hidden away behind a dozen secret doors."

With a password that she would never share with him, he realized in dismay.

For some reason, he remembered again her trembling hand on Harry's college comforter. Their son had already been making jokes with his roommate, helping set up the other boy's computer as his mother blurred around the edges in front of their eyes.

Had that been Dan's mistake too? Had he been laughing, joking, hooking up computer wires when the connection he should have been making at that moment was with his wife?

Shit. He wanted to shout, to scream, to shake her. Because while he'd definitely found out more about this woman, this love of his life, he felt as if she was farther away than ever before.

December 12

In 1955, a newspaper misprint directed children who wanted to call Santa Claus to the Continental Air Defense Command instead. Realizing the error, the Director of Operations had his staff check the radar data in order to provide children with updates on Santa's position in the skies throughout Christmas Eve.

Chapter 12

Propped against the headboard, Trin lay on Bailey's bed, studying Kurt Cobain's face on the poster pinned to the opposite wall. "I think Finn used to wear black eyeliner like our grunge-band buddy here. I remember his eyes always seemed to smolder."

Still smoldered, Bailey thought, as she rummaged through her closet for something to wear on their date. "It's the thick eyelashes," she said, glancing over at the other woman. "It's unfair that I got puny blond ones and his are so dark."

Trin crossed her ankles. "So what's the occasion of this dinner of yours?"

"Heck if I know." Was it only to ensure they could have a private chat without interruption? She wasn't certain. In his grandmother's kitchen, Finn had set the night, she'd agreed, and then been ecstatically happy that he'd left it at that and let her leave the house without fulfilling the other part of their bargain: that she'd tell him why she'd run ten years ago.

And that embarrassing, sloppily emotional interlude in the Jacobson kitchen was something she'd been trying to distance herself from too. It had started with watching Finn fall on the dark street. Then only gotten worse at the sight of his torn skin. He'd assured her it was nothing, but it was enough to give her perfect recall of the infamous assassination attempt video. Though his face was never shown, and his name kept secret by the government agency that employed him, now she knew it was he who had taken the second bullet. She knew it was his shattered sunglasses, his puddle of blood.

Finn who could have died.

Once again, the thought gave her that weird, weightless feeling in her stomach and she pressed against it hard. *He's okay*, she reminded herself. *Just fine.*

She knew that for a fact, because that day and the day before he'd shown up at The Perfect

Christmas as promised. With little direction on her part, he'd reorganized the back room, replenished stock, donned the Santa suit at the appropriate hour. With the additional, very capable help, she'd been able to relax a little.

A surprised Byron had caught her humming to the store's background music. And, funny, she'd been recalling old memories of The Perfect Christmas when he'd pointed it out. Not the chaos of the post-Christmas sale or the endless summer shifts she'd spent at the cash register as a restless teen. These memories were of quiet afternoons when she'd stood on a stepladder to help her grandmother rearrange the Christmas villages on the shelves. Of poring over product catalogs with her grandfather, Bailey on his lap, the warmth of his chest at her back. He'd had a special fountain pen that he'd let her use to circle pretty things that caught her eye.

Then her parents had divorced and everything changed, including her feelings toward The Perfect Christmas.

Refocusing on the issue at hand, Bailey slid some hangers along the closet pole. A dress for a dinner date. A dinner date during which it was unlikely she'd be able to duck the question of why she'd run away a decade ago.

Not that she couldn't answer. It wasn't such a big deal, was it? But still it felt as if looking back with Finn would let him see other things she didn't want him to know.

Like how strong she was pulled toward the man he had become.

Like how much she had once loved the young man he had been.

Like how hard it had been to turn her back on him then.

"We were just kids, right?" she said aloud. "Nobody expects those kinds of feelings to last forever."

"Hmm." Trin palmed the head of her sleeping son, who was sprawled over his mother's body in toddler abandon. "Are you trying to convince me or yourself?"

Flushing at what she'd revealed, Bailey shoved a blouse farther down the pole. "Did I invite you over here?" she muttered. "Because I forget."

"You walked away from me too, Bay," Trin said, her voice quiet. "All those years growing up, you were the yin to my yang."

Bailey swallowed a sudden lump in her throat. "Wouldn't that be the trang to your trin?"

"See, that cleverness is just one of the many reasons why we got along so well together. You were my best friend since preschool. There have been times over the years I've needed you. Times I could have helped you too."

Bailey's hand, lingering on a blue sleeve, moved

to a black one, her mood sliding toward funereal. After she'd left early for college that summer, she'd never spent another night in her childhood home until now. "I had to make a clean break," she tried to explain. "As clean as I could, anyway."

She heard Trin sigh, then listened to the other woman roll off the bed to stand behind her. "Not that dress. You look lousy in black."

Bailey turned to face her friend. Baby Adam's head rested on Trin's shoulder, his body limp. She reached out to stroke the little boy's back, surprised by its sweet warmth. In breaking from her past, she'd lost out on reunions, weddings, births, all the many ceremonies that connected someone to her community.

In L.A. she had acquaintances, colleagues, fellow condo dwellers. But no one who knew where she used to hide her love letters, how she could sneak out of her house with the help of an open window and a trash bin, why she hated the smell of Chanel No. 5.

At eighteen, she'd been so afraid that one part of her life would blow up in her face, that she'd walked away from the rest of it . . . and lost so much.

"I'm sorry, Trin." Tears pricked the corners of Bailey's eyes and she stroked Adam again. "I've missed you."

Trin sniffed. "Stop it. We both look ugly in tears."

Bailey smiled at that. "Remember when we

hoped we were one of those girls who look pretty when they cry?"

"Yeah. And so we rented the old *Romeo and Juliet* to check it out."

"Your nose turns an icky red," Bailey said.

"You get splotchy. From your forehead to your neck."

"Oh, Trin." How had Bailey managed the last ten years without her?

Her friend's nose was turning crimson. "Don't be a stranger anymore. Deal?"

"Deal." Even when Bailey went back to her current life on the twenty-fifth, she had to acknowledge she'd reforged some connections here. Tenuous ones to The Perfect Christmas, oddly enough. Rock-solid ones to Trin, thank God.

But that didn't mean Bailey was reforging anything with Finn. There was no more future in any sort of relationship between them now than there had been then. Even if Finn had gone straight and become a downright hero who could wreak havoc with her hormones. Because Bailey knew that inside her chest her heart was crooked—if it was in one piece at all.

The fading photograph of a twenty-year-old in a rented tuxedo was no match for a grown man wearing black slacks, a black, open-necked shirt, and a nickel-colored sport coat. Bailey met Finn in her mother's foyer and tried not to register how handsome he looked in the glow of the lighted dried-fruit-and-fir garland she'd brought home from the store and wound around the stairway handrails in her latest effort to remind her mother of the season and the store waiting for her just a few blocks away.

But there was no denying he looked good. Strong, solid. Over the past couple of days she'd had to back out of the storeroom when she found him working inside. It was too small. The first afternoon, he'd turned when she'd walked in. One glimpse of his five o'clock shadow had surfaced another memory. He'd always had a heavier beard than any boy she knew, and when they were making out on the beach or in a car, he would rub it against her, tickling the bare skin of her neck with his whiskery cheeks.

When they had more privacy and her bra was off, he'd rub his stubbled chin back and forth against her nipples, turning them stiff and rosy-pink. She would sneak a peek at his dark head and her hands would itch to hold him against her, to demand a harder touch, a wet, sucking mouth, a soft tongue, but she'd press fingernail half-moons against her palms instead of the sleek feel of his hair.

She'd been careful never to ask for more than he offered.

From the first, skirting rejection.

But when he'd looked at her across those few

feet of floor space in the storeroom yesterday, it wasn't rejection in his dark stare, in the suddenly heavy, too-warm air, in the arrow of desire that shot between them to trail like a fingertip from her throat to her belly.

The same fingertip she could feel tracing her flesh right now, as Finn stood, his hand gripping the doorjamb. His gaze ran over her, from her dress—a midnight-blue, tight-fitting wrap with elbow-length sleeves, a self-fabric belt, and a skirt that ended above her knees to display a deep flounce of black lace—to her black pumps topped with small organza bows.

But his face remained expressionless even when his gaze traveled back to the evening-amount of cleavage the dress exposed, tickling Bailey's bare skin with more imaginary touches. Making her knees weak.

Clearing her throat, she picked up her evening bag and tried to appear businesslike instead of nearly breathless. "Ready to go?"

"Yeah." To her surprise, he did the whole date thing, holding doors for her, helping her into his SUV with a touch to her elbow, shutting the door for her firmly.

In the time that it took him to get around to the driver's door she worked on assembling a strategy to handle the inevitable. Okay, she told herself. During dinner he was going to insist on knowing why she'd run and she was going to give him her explanation. Now that they were older, he'd un-derstand.

Probably thank her for it.

And then they'd finish their meal and return to their respective beds, the past and then them-selves finally put to rest.

Because sweeping clean memory lane would likely sweep away their present physical chemis-try as well. That was something to welcome too.

He seated himself, but didn't start the car right way. His hands squeezed the wheel and she heard him take a deep breath. He didn't look at her.

She braced for it. The Question. Apparently he wasn't going to wait until they'd ordered.

"Bailey . . ." He opened one hand and rubbed it along the leather covering the wheel, his gaze trained out the dark windshield. "I should tell you . . ." He cleared his throat, started again. "I should tell you . . ."

His hesitation set off warning bells. "What? Tell me what?"

"We're not going to be alone for dinner."

She blinked. "We're not?" Here she'd been imag-ining an awkward confrontation, just the two of them, and now that wasn't going to happen? Well, heck. Forget the humming, she just might start singing. "Who else is going to be there?"

"Another couple." He went silent again, then turned the key, still without looking at her. "Some people I know through work."

"Oh." This was good. She didn't have any trouble talking to strangers, and people he knew from work—Secret Service people, obviously—had to have some entertaining tidbits to share. With a little relieved bounce, she settled back in her seat. "I'll bet we'll have fun."

Theirs wasn't the only vehicle heading across the graceful arc of the Coronado Bridge toward downtown San Diego. But it was only a little over two miles in length, and even with traffic, the travel time was hardly long enough to become concerned by the heavy silence on Finn's side of the SUV.

Maybe he was tired after today's Santa gig. Maybe the never-ending Christmas hoopla was getting to him as much as it always got to her.

Apparently it was a busy time of year in the Gaslamp Quarter, the revitalized section of the city now devoted to restaurants, bars, and other entertainment. Red brake lights were doing their part to add to the holiday atmosphere as cars crept along the streets. Bailey craned her neck to take in all the new construction. "I heard that downtown was becoming a popular place to live too, but I had no idea."

"I have a penthouse loft down here myself." They were the first words he'd said since hitting the bridge.

"Yeah? You rob a bank or is there something about government salaries I'm not aware of?"

A smile ghosted over his mouth. "I'm not sure you know, but my dad's in investments. When I went straight and then into the Secret Service, I got smart too, and gave him a big chunk of my money every month. I didn't need much, because I used to spend most of my time traveling. For a few years I was on the presidential detail."

She stared at him. "Get out!"

"Two words even the president of the United States rarely says to his agents."

"I'm impressed," she confessed, as he whipped into a corner parking lot.

He sent her an enigmatic look as he turned off the car. "Hold that thought."

Then he did the whole date thing again, coming around to her side, helping her out, taking her hand as they started off down the sidewalk. In her heels on the pebbly pavement, she was grateful.

His fingers suddenly squeezed hers. "Bailey . . ." There was that odd hesitation again. "I should tell you . . ."

All right, now the warning bells were clanging. "What? *What?*"

"The other couple is Ayesha Spencer's parents."

It took her a minute to put the pieces together. Ayesha Spencer was the Secret Service agent who'd been killed during the assassination attempt eleven months before. The young woman on Finn's team. "I don't belong here then," she said.

"Bailey—" He fell silent, his gaze dropping to their joined hands.

No. No, no, no, no, no. She could have revisited their past. Gone through the awkwardness, the explanations, the possible recriminations. But that was *their* past. This situation was something that was Finn's alone. She pulled her fingers free from his. "You've got to see that it's not my place."

Grieving parents, upset Finn. His body language was telling the whole story. She realized now that beneath that lack of expression and leaden silence she'd noted earlier was a wealth of tension. He was stiff with it.

"I'll take a cab back home," she said. A passerby bumped her, and she stumbled closer to Finn. Her palm landed on his shirtfront for balance and she felt the jerky beat of his heart against her hand. Her gaze jumped to his face. "Are you all right?"

"No." His good eye squeezed shut. "I can't do it, Bailey." The words were low, hard. "I don't think I can do it alone."

She stared up at him, the bad boy whom she once thought she'd tamed, now the strong man who risked his life protecting others. This morning he'd made breakfast for his recuperating grandmother. This afternoon he'd read *The Polar Express* to half-a-dozen children. Tonight . . . tonight a dark pain etched his face.

He didn't come straight out and ask for help,

though. He didn't touch her again. Still, her pulse
synced with his erratic heartbeat and her mouth
went dry with sympathetic distress. Despite how
reckless she knew it was of her, how unlike her
usual keep-your-distance self, she allowed his
unspoken need to find its way inside her.

Oh God.

It was so risky to care like this.

But she couldn't seem to help herself.

"All right," she heard herself whisper. Her hand
reached from his heart to cup his cheek. "I'll be
there with you."

He turned his face to press a swift kiss on her
palm. "I had no right . . ."

She tried to rub his burning kiss away on her
thigh. "Damn straight, you didn't," she agreed,
doing her best to sound brisk instead of broken-
down as she tugged him in the direction they'd
been going. "But let's get it over with."

He waited until they were hailed by an older
couple in the waiting area of a trendy steak-and-
seafood place to drop the next bombshell.

His mouth touched her ear.

Goose bumps raced down her neck.

"I meant," Finn said, his breath hot and smelling faintly of cinnamon. "I had no right to tell
them you're my fiancée."

Later she would kill him, she decided. Later
when she didn't notice that his entire body had
turned to steel and that the grimacelike smile he

gave to Ayesha Spencer's parents looked as if it would crack open his face.

Her mother, a beautiful black woman with skin as supple as a teenager's, touched the temple beside Finn's eye patch and blinked away tears. Her father, a tall, spare man with red hair going gray and pale blue eyes, hung onto Finn's outstretched hand as if it could rescue him from dangerous, deep waters.

Then they turned to Bailey. She was hugged by them both. Exclaimed over as a "beauty" with "such a lovely smile." Ayesha's parents were effusively glad to know that Finn had found someone "new."

That was her first hint.

Throughout the rest of the meal other clues couldn't be ignored. They shared with her pictures of their daughter, and Bailey realized among the photographs Mrs. Spencer carried in her wallet was one of Finn and Ayesha. It looked to be a picnic setting and they were in swimsuits, his arm around her shoulders, her face turned up to his.

The older couple told Finn in detail about the marble headstone they'd placed on her grave and the memorial scholarship they'd set up at Ayesha's high school. From his jacket pocket, Mr. Spencer pulled out a folded Orioles baseball cap.

"It was hers," he said, fondling it as he would a child's hair. "I thought you might like to have it, but not if . . ." His gaze moved from Finn's face to Bailey's.

Her "fiancé" took the hat, mumbled something, and signaled the waiter for another round.

None of them ate very much. Finn drank.

Three-quarters through the saddest evening of her life, Bailey got desperate enough to redirect the conversation and start talking about The Perfect Christmas. They actually ended up the evening laughing—well, she laughed and so did Ayesha's parents—when she told them about the surf-crazy sales help, this year's piratical Santa, her Retired Citizen Service Patrol buddy who met her at the door of the shop when she closed each night and walked her to her car, watching her drive away only after he checked her for parking infractions with his official measuring stick.

It was closing in on midnight when the two couples went through a round of fragile hugs on the sidewalk. Then Bailey and Finn headed off in the opposite direction from the Spencers.

Nothing was said between them. After a few minutes, she took a peek at him, trying to gauge his sobriety. Throughout the evening he'd been drinking steadily, but tonight there was none of the sloppy-drunk St. Nick in the Finn that was keeping pace beside her.

Tension continued to radiate from him. His hands in his pockets, he walked with his head down, apparently oblivious to the other people on the crowded sidewalk. They gave him a wide berth, his dark mood sending out clear warning beacons. A young guy traveling in the opposite direction tapped Bailey's shoulder as he passed, and Finn snarled at him, shooting out a hand to pull her close to his side.

Her stomach jumped at the viselike grip of his hand on her upper arm. He left it there, keeping her near as he towed her along, his knuckles pressing into the soft side of her breast. She tried pulling away, but he drew her close again, his fingers just that much tighter.

And then, despite every reason why not, her nipples reacted to the firm touch, stiffening against the fabric of her push-up bra. A pulse started beating low in her belly. As goose bumps broke out over her skin, she tried sucking in a calming breath, but that only expanded her chest, pushing her flesh more insistently against his fingers.

They tightened again on her arm, then . . . pressed back?

No. It had to be an accident. But another round of prickly heat washed over her flesh. Her thin shawl was caught on her elbows and she wished she'd worn something heavier, a sweater, a coat— thick wool to smother all her suddenly leaping nerve endings.

As they continued walking, one of the fingers circling her arm straightened, then stroked against the side of her breast.

Bailey's breath caught in her lungs.

That wasn't a mistake. He did it again.

She flicked him a sideways glance. His expression was closed, and she was on his left side so couldn't read anything in the patch that covered his eye. He caressed her once more.

Her knees melted.

"Okay?"

His tense, low-voiced question shivered down her spine. Okay? She was simmering like soup in a pan and he wanted it that way. He couldn't pretend not to know what he was wreaking with those secret strokes.

"Bailey? Okay?"

What was she supposed to say? *I sat through a dinner that made me want to cry and now I'm walking down the street and needing you and that makes me want to cry too.*

Honesty didn't seem the right way to go, but she had to come up with *something*. She looked down at her bare hands for inspiration and said the first dumb thing that popped into her dizzy brain. "I'm thinking I don't have so much as a promise ring, let alone one that proclaims we're engaged."

Finn's step hitched. His jaw hardened.

Bailey felt like an idiot. "I'm kidding, I'm kidding." Then she sighed, knowing there was no joke, no laugh, nothing that would make walking down the street with this elephant between them possible Sighing, she stopped short to turn and grip the lapels of his coat.

"I'm confused, Finn."

"About?"

The dinner we just had? And now your hand teasing my breast? "You and Ayesha," she said. "The two of you . . ." Stupid how hard those words were to say. But of course he'd moved on with his life. She cleared her throat. "The two of you were in love, right?"

He was staring down at her fingers on his coat. "What makes you say that?"

"Mr. and Mrs. Spencer couldn't have made it any clearer without taking out an ad."

There was a long silence, then he dropped her arm.

"You're wrong. They're wrong. Sort of." His gaze focused over her head, down the dark street. "She had feelings for me. Maybe . . ." He shrugged. "But we worked together and I didn't think it was a good idea to take things in that direction."

"So you *didn't* have feelings for her?"

"Damn it!" The barked words caused a passing couple to give them a startled glance, then hurry off. His fingers curled into fists. "Do we have to do this? Do we have to talk *now*?"

But Bailey wouldn't back down, ironic as it was that at the start of the evening she'd been dreading a personal conversation. "No. We can go back to Coronado, leaving forever the mystery of why you brought *me* tonight and why—"

He grabbed her shoulders and pulled her up on her tiptoes so they were face-to-face. "Why I want you so bad I'm walking with a flagpole in my pants? Why your nipples are so hard it looks like you stuffed cherries in your bra?"

She jerked back in his grasp. "Finn—"

Her bad boy kissed her quiet. Fierce, demanding, all hot lips and needy tongue, and the only things swept clean were the sensible objections from her head.

December 13
Bell ringing at Christmas is a holdover from pagan times when noisemakers were sounded to frighten away evil spirits during winter solstice festivals.

Chapter 13

Towing Bailey in the direction of his loft, Finn knew he'd had too much to drink—though he wasn't anywhere near binge drunk. Christ, that would be easier. Then he'd be on his way to passing out and feeling nothing, not the grinding loss of Ayesha or the greedy hunger for the woman beside him. There was disaster in the offing, he could feel it, smell it like cordite in the air, but he didn't give a flying fuck about his sixth sense this time.

"What are we doing? Where are we going?"

He shut her up again by hauling her close for another kiss, thrusting his tongue in her mouth to ensure she kept quiet. There'd been enough of talking tonight and now every cell and fiber of him craved action.

For days, months, hell, it felt like *years*, he'd been living in the past. Tonight he needed something more than memories and regrets. Something that was *now*.

The rest of the world might wait until December 31. For Finn, this was the moment to usher out the old and bring in the new.

He set Bailey back on her heels. Her eyes were wide. Her mouth was wet. She licked at his taste on her bottom lip, and at the sight of her pink, velvety tongue, his cock jerked against the hot skin of his belly.

"I'm going home," he told her, his voice hoarse. Dark, like his mood. "To my loft. Are you with me?"

Without waiting for an answer, he grabbed her hand and pulled her into the lobby of the next building.

"Why do I hear an 'or against me' in the air?" she asked, even as he gave a nod at the security guard and pushed her into the waiting elevator.

When the doors shushed shut, he backed her into a corner and circled her waist with his hands. Desire was pumping like a steady back rhythm in his blood, a beat on two, a beat on four, driving up his temperature. Driving up his desperation.

"I'm not playing word games, GND. I want to

touch you. Feel you." She started to say something, but his right fingers pressed briefly against her lips. "In silence."

She blinked. "Silence?"

He slid his hands up the bumps of her ribs to stop just below her breasts. Her short, fast breaths pushed the edge of his fingers closer to their soft rise. "Near silence, then. You're allowed 'like that,' 'there,' 'please,' 'more.' Nothing else."

Bailey had never asked for his touch in her life, but he needed to be sure tonight was without words. Without emotions.

With only that insistent thump of blood in his veins.

She swallowed, a flush rising on her throat. "Finn—"

His hands cupped her breasts, squeezed. "Decide."

The elevator doors opened before she had a chance to reply. He tugged her through them and then to his front door. It opened, then shut with a firm click, leaving them alone in the locked privacy of his loft.

He pushed her against the gunmetal gray paint, staring her down in the dim glow of the one lamp he'd left on in the living area. "Sex, or no?"

She wanted him, he didn't doubt that, but she could still roll her heaven-blue eyes. "Oh gee, stop with the hearts and flowers, will ya?"

He wouldn't tell her he'd broken the bank in the

hearts and flowers department ten years ago and she'd run away before he could prove it to her. That was then; this was now. "Why are you complaining? From what I can tell your bed's been empty lately."

She stiffened. "You really investigated me?"

"Didn't have to. I know you, remember?" Action. Bending his head, he tongued the curve where her jaw met her throat. "You're picky."

She shivered under his hands. "I . . . I picked you, didn't I?" The words sounded shaky. "Wh-what does that say?"

He feathered kisses from her ear to her mouth. "That you're talking too much. *We're* talking too much."

Without words, remember? Without emotion. His teeth nipped her bottom lip.

She arched against him, and he heard that tell-tale swallowed moan that was the muted sound of Bailey turned on.

Just like that, the two and four rhythmic pound of his blood expanded to a heavy metal–band blast beat. In music production it could create a wall of sound. In Finn it created an explosion of want.

He pressed his erection against her soft mons. "Decide."

"Finn . . . Is this smart?"

"Talking too much. Thinking too much." His

mouth moved to her ear and he licked the lobe. "It's simple. Sex, or no?"

"Neither . . . one . . ." Her head tilted to give him better access to her neck.

"Neither one what?" He licked along the pale column.

"A word . . . you said I could use."

He smiled against her lips as he kissed her. "Add 'sex' to the short list."

A heartbeat passed. A second one. Then her arms slid up his chest as she offered her mouth to him again. "Oh, fine. It's Christmas, isn't it? Please, Finn. More."

So many words when only a single would do. Wasn't that just like a woman? But as he went lip-to-lip, need exploded inside him again like sound inside an echo chamber, reverberating like another pulse. Reminding him this wasn't just any woman in his arms. This was Bailey.

Her mouth opened under the pressure of his and he swept his tongue along the slick surface of her teeth. He tickled the underside of her upper lip and she crowded closer to him. His hands fell to her ass and he tilted her hips against his, grinding against her with no more finesse than a teenager dry-humping his way through a slow dance. His cock pulsed. Ready to go. Ready to go off.

He groaned, pushing her away. "I need air."

Her palms flat against the door, she leaned back,

her mouth red, her breasts heaving in that pretty dress.

And just like that, touching her was imperative again.

There was a wide belt at her waist. He pretended not to notice his shaking fingers and her shuddering breaths as he unfastened it. When he peeled it back, it took the sides of the Bailey-blue dress with it, unwrapping the garment like the petals of a flower.

Underneath the fabric she was wearing a strapless, black lace bra, matching panties, thigh-high stockings that clung to the sweet inner flesh of her legs.

Heat flashed over him. He'd never seen the Girl Next Door in black lace. Then it had been tiny undershirt bras. Cotton panties with rainbows or clouds.

Now it was pushed-up here, pulled-high there, all designed to knock-him-over, suck-him-under, do-him-in.

As he backed away, his hand grabbed the center of his chest. "You're killing me."

She smiled. Brazen. Grown-up. And took a step forward.

Leaving the dress behind. In slow motion, Finn watched it slide off her rounded shoulders, catch on the bend of her elbows, tickle along her forearms to drop to his hardwood floor. The second step of her black high heels cracked like a gunshot.

Time sped again, and he found her in his arms. Fragrant. Hot. He buried his face in the valley between her breasts and pressed his lips together to keep words from rushing out.

You. Me. Past. Present. Anything. Everything.

"Bailey." He mouthed it against her hot skin, feeling the fast tattoo of her heart against his lips. "Bailey."

Her hands stroked his hair and he lifted his face, needing her mouth, needing her taste to distract from all the emotions that threatened to overtake him. Sometimes he drank, sometimes he drove too fast, but this time he had Bailey to make him forget.

He bent his knees and curved one arm around the back of her thighs, the other around her shoulders, and lifted her against his chest. Bed. Yeah.

But the shortest route took him past the couch in the living area. A vision flashed in his brain. Bailey in her black lingerie. Bailey in her black lingerie and on that slick black leather of his couch.

There was a distraction sure to make him forget an entire lifetime of unrequited emotion and what-might-have-beens.

She sucked in a breath when he set her on the cool, slick surface. But he was there to warm her up, his knees on the floor and pushing her thighs apart to move between them. All the better to take her mouth again.

It turned him on even higher, heat shooting up

his spine, his cock going harder, that she was near-naked and he was fully clothed, her body sandwiched between his and that firm, motorcycle-black leather. Bracing his palms on either side of her head, he shifted his mouth to make the fit of the kiss *their* fit, falling naturally into the familiar angle that fused their lips. Like old times.

No. His hand drifted down to trace the edge of her stocking.

New times.

He sat back on his heels and lifted one of her ankles to tip off her shoe. Then the other. His hand slid high so his fingers could curl under the elastic lace at the top of her leg. He glanced up at her face. Then froze.

Her big blue eyes were watching him.

She never watched. She always closed him out when it came to undressing, just as she always swallowed the sounds of her passion.

New times.

His heart shuddered, and without looking away from her intent gaze, he rolled down each of her stockings. Then his hands traveled back up bare skin.

"Finn," she whispered, as his thumbs met over the triangle of her black panties.

"Hmm?" He broke their gaze as he stroked over the lace, compelled to watch his fingers move. He heard her gasp as he tucked his thumbs under the stretchy fabric and found other petals, already opening, already wet. He rode their slickness, down, then up, opening her more and finding their hard little center. He leaned in to kiss the place, still covered by the panties. His tongue stroked the damp lace. Such a sweet flower.

"Finn."

He glanced up. His breath caught.

She was *still* watching him. An odd spike of embarrassment jolted through him. Had she ever known how much he worshipped her body? How much power that gave her over him? Could she tell now?

"Like that," Bailey whispered. "Please. There. More."

His heart jerked. Bailey. Watching. Asking. Without breaking their gazes, he continued playing beneath her panties, playing with *her*, sliding, circling, drenching his fingers in her arousal, until they were slick with the feel of her and he was intoxicated with need.

Her fingers flexed into black leather, her eyes long since having turned from blue to dark. "Finn," she said again. Then she leaned forward and twined her fingers in his hair. "*Sex.*"

Desire spiked. He caught her panties in one hand and yanked them down her legs, scooting back to pull them free. His jacket, tie, and shirt flew across the room. Then he fumbled with his belt, his zipper, freed himself so that his cock was heading straight for heaven. Kneeling between her legs again, he flipped open the front clasp of her bra and filled his palms with her creamy breasts. He fingered the stiff crests, then couldn't resist tasting them, which meant tasting her too, as he licked and sucked the lingering dampness he'd transferred there from his hands.

She stroked his hair and it was so good. So good.

He leaned closer, his cock kissing her wet heat. They both groaned. He gripped her waist and pulled her nearer to the edge of the seat cushion, then he lifted his head to look into her eyes as his hips flexed, starting to push—

"Condom," they said together.

Finn's muscles locked up. He commanded himself to move back. He didn't want to move back.

"I'm—" They spoke together again.

"—on the pill."

"—clean, hospital says so."

Bailey inhaled a shuddering breath. Her palms caressed his hair. "Come to me."

He sank into her slick heat. Tingles shot up his spine as his nerve endings registered the sensation. Tight like a fist. Wet. So soft. No condom. Tight, wet, soft. Heat.

Finn and Bailey.

Bare and bare.

Her muscles fluttered around him but he resisted the urge to move. Instead he trailed his knuckles over her cheek. "Okay?"

Her top teeth biting into the pillow of her bottom lip, she nodded.

But, damn it, now silence wasn't going to work. "Talk to me, baby."

She smiled, a gentle finger tracing the strap of his eyepatch. "More, Finn. More sex."

Permission granted, his body sank deeper. His chest touched hers, her nipples scraping against his sensitive skin. Tingles shot up his spine again, but he didn't let them take over as he pulled out, then dropped back into her body, finding a rhythm that was matching the insistent beat of his heart.

Bailey widened her thighs to make more room for his hips and he crowded closer to her. He licked his thumb and forefinger and once again found the center of that pretty, hot little flower she was sharing with him. Her hips jerked up, arching toward him as he rolled and rubbed.

His body pumped harder as he watched a flush move up her belly and fan outward over her naked breasts.

He'd never felt anything this good.

He'd never seen anything so beautiful.

Heat wrapped around his balls, yanked them upward, as more heat invaded his belly, his chest, his throat.

It felt so tight, he could hardly breathe.

Bailey's back arched and her breasts kissed his chest. She was almost there. He was about to take off.

Another wave of that strange heat rose inside him again, from belly, to chest, to throat.

The heat jumped higher, stinging his one eye.

He came forward in a deep plunge, his thumb strumming over her clitoris. She cried out, her inner muscles squeezing squeezing squeezing, and his body spasmed in a matching fierce release, over and over and over.

As tremors twitched through both their bodies, he leaned against her, fighting to reclaim his breath. Trying not to think too much about it, he quickly wiped away the moisture on his cheek. Then he half lifted to ensure she was all right. Their bodies still joined, he brushed her hair off her face with his hand.

He'd wanted to usher out the old, and he'd done it, by God. He'd surely brought in the new.

New times.

Bailey on black leather.

Her eyes open, her body open to him, naked to him in every way, and he felt that strange heat rise inside him again, from belly, to chest, to throat, to—

Say something, he told himself hastily. Thank her, compliment her, something. Then something—God, the wrong thing—spilled out.

Grasping her hips in his palms, he heard himself demand an answer to a decade-old question: "Why the fuck did you leave me?"

* * *

Bailey lurched back against the couch, but there was nowhere for her to go, not with Finn still inside her, around her, staring at her with such dark intent. Her fingers bit into the cool leather on either side of her. "I . . . Now? No . . ."

He pulled out of her, standing up to stalk away, but he was back before she regained her wits. He threw a bathrobe at her, then stepped into a pair of worn jeans, the fabric split over both knees. "Now, yes," he said, staring down at her, his arms crossed over his bare chest.

Behind him was a wide picture window, and through it, a spectacular view of the cityscape. Pretending a fascination with the glittering lights, she shifted her gaze away from him and scrambled into the huge terry-cloth robe, trying to buy herself some time. The soft fabric smelled like Finn, but that wasn't any comfort as she belted it around her waist and then sat down again to draw her knees up under the fabric.

How could she explain in terms he'd understand and accept? She was going to have to make it clear—

Suddenly he let out a harsh laugh. "What a stupid question." he said. "I'd been a screw-off for years. No wonder you dumped me."

Her head jerked toward him. "It wasn't about you. Not exactly, anyway."

"So it was about you. Your feelings changed. I get it." He turned his back, and went about the room retrieving his tossed clothes.

"It wasn't exactly like that either!" Frustration caused her voice to rise. This wasn't fair. Finn was fifteen steps ahead of her. She was still reeling from her rash decision to give herself an early Christmas gift and get naked with him, still bowled over by how good it had been between them . . . again, and he was already over it and ready to delve into their past. No—take that back. Now it seemed as if he was finished with that too.

She pressed her palms to her eyes. "Listen, I know we had made plans—"

"You were starting college in New Hampshire in September, but we were supposed to have the whole summer together." He bent to grab his slacks. "The beach, trips into Mexico. You made a list."

On the last day of his Christmas vacation at his grandmother's. She'd sat in the circle of his arms, swallowing back the tears she always hid from him when he was leaving, as she itemized their upcoming summer adventures.

"But then right after high school graduation I was given the chance to attend an inter-session for incoming business majors," she said. And she'd leaped at it.

"You didn't write. You didn't call. There was no good-bye."

She jumped to her feet. Could he ever understand? "But don't you see—"

"I see that we didn't mean the same thing to you as we did to me," he said, snagging his tie off a lampshade.

Bailey wrapped her arms around herself. "It could only have ended badly, Finn."

He turned to stare at her. "What do you call how it *did* end?"

"Smart. Sensible. Okay, maybe immature in some respects, but I'd make the same choice today." His look of disgust caused her stomach to churn. "You don't get it."

"Try me."

With a sigh, she dropped back onto the couch. "It was going to blow up in our faces. If not in June or July or August, then in September. Or the next September. Sometime. I wanted to make a quick, clean break. Get out . . . get out before it got ugly."

He made a quick gesture with his hand. "You couldn't share this with me?"

"Wouldn't you have tried to talk me out of the feeling . . . the knowledge? We thought it was magic, Finn. But there's no such thing."

He studied her for a moment, then, shaking his head, he started to laugh. "God, it's rich."

"What? What's rich?"

"You always were smarter than me."

Her scalp prickled. "What do you mean?"

"Ten years ago, I *would* have argued that very point with you. What else could it be but magic that brought together the bad ass and the golden girl next door?"

"Finn—"

"But I'm a believer now. A believer in *your* theory, thanks to the very fact that you walked out on me without a word." Laughing again, he dropped his clothes to the floor and sprawled on the couch beside her, resting his dark hair against the leather.

He rolled his head to look at her, then groped for her hand, found it. Squeezed. "GND, I should be thanking you. And as a matter of fact, I do."

His reaction curdled in her belly. "Finn . . ."

From somewhere in the bundle of clothes at his feet, a phone rang. The smile on his face died. His big body froze. "Fuck," he whispered. "Something's happened to Gram."

"What? Your grandmother?"

He pawed for his cell. Flipped it open, brought it to his ear. "Jacobson." As he listened, his tight expression eased. His chest rose, then fell as he blew out a breath. "No kidding. Terrific. Sure, I'll go wake her up. You're right. She'll want to know."

He was smiling again when he hung up. Grinning, actually, in such a carefree fashion that it seemed as if he'd forgotten they'd had sex. That they'd delved into ancient history. Or maybe it was that her answer to the Big Question had put their past to rest, just as Bailey had wanted it to.

"Well, what do you know?" he murmured, sliding his phone into his pocket. "Let's get moving, GND. It's a happy day."

So why did she feel so lousy?

Bailey Sullivan's Vintage Christmas Facts & Fun Calendar

December 14

At Christmas, Greek children walk the street singing songs and playing instruments for treats or money. There are no Christmas trees, but gift giving occurs on St. Basil's Day (January 1).

Chapter 14

Tracy clutched an armful of glossy papers to her chest as she hurried toward the recycle bin beside the hibiscus hedge. She wanted them out of her house and off her mind. She wished the same thing for the man who had put them on the porch. Dan had left her, so now he should leave her alone!

She reached out to lift the plastic top, then froze as she caught sight of her neighbor, Alice Jacobson, on the other side of the hedge. Her heart gave a painful squeeze. Finn's grandmother looked two sizes smaller than she had a month ago and she was walking with short, cautious steps. The elderly woman had a stack of newspapers under her arm and was heading for her own matching blue can.

"Alice! How nice to see you," Tracy said, hoping her smile hid her dismay. "How are you?"

The older woman's answering smile was still bright. "I'm feeling all right. How are you this beautiful morning?"

Tracy glanced around, for the first time aware that the morning *was* lovely. There'd been fog during her first cup of coffee, but the sun had burned it away, leaving blue skies and twittering birds.

She inhaled a breath of the clean air. "I hear congratulations are in order. A great-grandson?"

"Ten pounds, three ounces."

Tracy winced. "Mom's okay?"

"Hale and hearty. So is Miguel Finn Jacobson-Vasquez."

"Oh, named after his uncle Finn. Cute. A big baby like that needs a big name." Tracy shook her head. "Harry was not quite nine pounds and I thought *he* was a monster."

Alice lifted the top of her bin. "How is our Harry?"

"Taking to college like a duck to water. I'm so happy for him." As with all her friends' living-away children, the cell phone kept them in amusing and constant contact. He'd called twice the day before. Once to ask if he could bake chocolate chip cookies in a microwave oven. The second time had been to relate in detail the storyline of a *Family Guy* episode he was certain she'd like. She hadn't understood a thing about the TV show, but she'd laughed anyway. And later awarded herself a virtual medal for not nagging him about studying instead of watching TV.

"How about happy for you?" Alice asked, dropping her papers and shutting the bin. She rested her hands on top of the heavy plastic.

"Happy?" Tracy echoed. "Me?" She'd been working so hard on not feeling *anything*.

"I remember my daughter-in-law had a tough time when her youngest, Janet, went away to school. She said the house was too quiet."

Tracy's gaze shifted to the older woman's hands. How frail they looked, the skin papery and the nails bluish. There were bruises on her forearms too. Tracy remembered how fragile her mother's skin had become as she aged, the slightest bump causing a wound or discoloration.

She dropped the papers she carried on top of her bin to make a quick once-over of her own flesh. It was a little dry, maybe, but still unblemished. All the bruises were on the inside.

"It looks like you're planning a trip." Alice nodded at the colorful pamphlets spread out on the top of the bin. They covered the gamut from Las Vegas to Lichtenstein.

Tracy flushed and gathered them up again. "Dan picked them up at an agency."

"Travel would be a lovely treat for you." Alice beamed.

"I don't think I'm much in the mood for a treat," Tracy admitted. Then she thought of Bailey, whom she'd dragged back home as her second marriage deteriorated. And worse, whom she'd likely traumatized during the demise of her first. "And probably not deserving of one either."

"Nonsense," Alice said. "It's time for you to celebrate Harry's launch."

Tracy shrugged. "Winter isn't a good time to travel." She didn't want to admit that any trip she'd take, she'd be taking solo. Though it was probably all over town that Dan had dumped her, Alice was ill and maybe unaware of what was really going on next door.

"There are other seasons, Tracy."

"Sure." She tried to smile. "Spring, summer, fall."

"Other seasons of your *life*. Maybe you're grieving for the end of one, but soon you'll walk out of that grief and into the next phase."

"I'm not sad." She wasn't anything. She was carefully collecting all her hurt and sending it to that locked-away place she'd told Dan about. Safely hiding it behind secret doors. In her head she pictured herself writing in the center of a piece of paper "divorce," "Dan," "empty nest," and then folding it into an origami figure—a protective lion, or maybe a bird that could fly it away.

Better yet, an ant, the painful thoughts minimized to bug size.

"Then what are you, dear?" Alice asked.

Tracy whispered the first thing that popped into her head. "I'm not anything." Her gaze jerked up to the older woman's, expecting to have shocked her. Tracy was shocked herself that she'd spoken the words aloud. But it was the truth. And more shocking, perhaps, was that she was beginning to like the buffer of immunity that nothingness provided.

Alice only smiled. "I've known you since you were born, Tracy. I have great faith in your capacity to bounce."

Her eyebrows drew together. Bounce? "Huh?"

Alice was already turning back toward her house. "Go in and make yourself a cup of tea." She waved. "You'll see I'm right."

Shaking her head, Tracy turned too. A cup of tea didn't sound bad. As she approached the back door, she could hear the phone ringing.

Harry, probably ready to wheedle her into putting more money on his Starbucks card, *again,* or maybe he needed to know what else he shouldn't try in a microwave. As she reached for the receiver, she realized she was still holding the travel brochures close to her heart.

Rolling her eyes with disgust, she dumped them on the kitchen table, then picked up the ringing phone.

Harry didn't know how to manage a coin-operated laundry. As she started walking him through the details, a disturbing thought came to mind. He'd been gone how many weeks?

To calm herself, she started paging through the glossy pictures, and found herself thanking Dan instead of cursing him. A week on Corfu provided a worthy distraction to mental visuals of three-month-dirty sweat socks.

December 15

The custom of the Christmas bonus was brought about in 1899 by department store owner F. W. Woolworth, who wanted to ensure his employees worked hard during the busy season. Five dollars was given for every year of service, not to exceed twenty-five dollars. It was considered a nice sum at the time.

Chapter 15

Movie night. In The Perfect Christmas's back room, Bailey cursed idea person, ex-principal Peggy Mohn as she cocked an ear to the dialogue of the 1947 version of *Miracle on 34th Street* and stuffed tissue paper in the man-sized Santa boots. She had her head down and her hair was covering her face when she heard the door open, shut.

"Trin. Thank God. Give me an update on where we are in the movie. The courtroom scene? Have they dragged in the big bags of letters? Oh, never mind," she said, before the other woman could reply. "If the audience has to wait a few minutes for me—I mean, Santa, to show up and pass the cookies, so be it. But if one more person calls this albatross of a store an institution—"

"Landmark."

Bailey jerked up, steadying herself on the small worktable beside her. "What?"

Dressed in jeans and a red pullover, sleeves pushed to his elbows, Finn stood with his shoulders against the door, one foot crossed over the other. "Landmark. On my way in, I overheard a grandmother telling her granddaughter this place is a landmark."

She could only stare at him in reply. The night—early morning, rather—that he'd dropped her off after their . . . interlude in his loft had been the last time she'd seen him. A flush blossomed over her skin and crawled up her neck. It was one thing to look on the man who'd been her first lover and suffer a nostalgic little shiver. It was quite another to recall in immediate, *intimate* detail what he'd felt like pushing inside her, his hot length invading, the cool leather at her back. How she'd felt when he'd caressed her between her legs, what the sound of their harsh breathing and the scent of Finn's shampoo and sex had been like in the emotion-charged air of his loft.

Which were exactly the wrong kind of memories to be reliving in the workplace. There was a passel of customers in the next room and everyone knew she was all-business Bailey. She had to get him out of here.

The tissue shoved in the toes of the Santa boots crinkled as she took a cautious half step back. "I don't have time to talk. There's forty-something Whos from Whoville out there, Whos who'll be clamoring for the promised refreshments as soon as the movie's over."

"You're missing the Grinch-green face paint, but you've got the outfit. Nice." He nodded at her.

She glanced down by instinct, then wished she hadn't. Without a better Santa substitute, she'd had to settle for herself. So far she had on the boots and the big red pants, held up at her shoulders by suspenders. But of course it was all too big, so red fleece bunched at her boot tops and gaped at her hips. On top she wore a skinny-ribbed tank top, because she'd yet to don the pillow she'd brought from home and the red jacket that would go over all of it.

"What do you want, Finn?"

"I thought we could talk."

"I told you. I don't have the time." Stacked on the worktable was the tissue she'd been using, along with a jumble of other items. As she reached for another sheet, her gaze snagged on the pieces of the vintage heart ornament she'd dropped the week before. With a big ocean swell coming in from the south, no one had gotten around to trying to repair it. By the twenty-sixth, though, it wouldn't be the only battered and broken thing in The Perfect Christmas. *Nothing flocked can stay.*

She looked back up at Finn. "Go away. I'm busy."

"I've come to the conclusion we can't unring the bell."

Her fingers slid off the sleek white paper. "What do you mean by that?"

"We had sex. I can't just forget about it."

Who was forgetting? Finn's body had changed in a decade. What had been bony and boyish had become muscular and manly. There'd been dark hair on his chest that had once been smooth and she'd wanted to touch it, run her fingers through it. His thighs were different now too, heavy with muscle. The thick length of his erection had been longer, felt smoother, hotter without a condom. More flames rose along her neck and she looked down at the stack of tissue, ruffling it with her fingers as she tried to play it cool.

"I was thinking . . ." Finn drew the word out until she looked at him again. "How about a replay or two?"

She stared. Was he insane? This was a man she'd known for only about, what, oh, seventeen years? Okay, he wasn't anywhere near a stranger, but still . . . It wasn't going to happen.

"Just because we rang the bell once, Finn,

doesn't mean we have to go all merry and jingle it again."

"Don't you think it would be . . . fun?"

Bailey wiped her damp palms against the dumb red pants. "I'm only here until the twenty-fifth."

"Brief fun, then. Even better."

Oh, but she didn't want brief! She wanted hours with him. Long hours to explore him in all the ways she'd never dared when she was seventeen and so afraid of how he made her respond. What would the curve of his biceps feel like under her tongue? Would his nipples harden beneath her fingers as hers did at his touch? Even thinking about his touch.

She crossed her arms over her chest. "Can't we chalk it up to a one-night stand?" There was the practical solution.

"A one-night stand?"

"Come on. That's all it was. You needed someone that night, and I happened to be there. That's why we ended up together."

He frowned. "Are you telling me it was a pity fuck? Thanks a lot."

Through the door, she could hear swelling music. Santa needed to get of here. Bailey too. "Look, I didn't mean to hurt your feelings."

He pushed off from the door and stalked closer, appeared anything but wounded. Instead, he looked . . . predatory.

Bailey took another step back and then another, until her shoulders hit the far wall.

"I know how you can make it up to me," he said softly.

Her palms pressed against the cold surface behind her. "Finn . . . I thought we agreed there was no such thing as magic."

He smiled and reached out to slide his forefinger under one suspender. "I'm not talking about magic, sweet thing." His finger rode the elastic until his knuckle bumped into the hard nub of her nipple. "I'm talking about all the ways I didn't get to touch you. Taste you."

"No fair." Those were *her* daydreams.

His finger slid back up to toy at her breast. "Aren't you just the tiniest bit . . . tempted?"

There wasn't enough air in the room. And the air that there was smelled like Finn, the spicy scent she'd inhaled the first day she'd seen him again and realized he'd grown up—but maybe she hadn't grown out of her overwhelming attraction to him.

However, surrendering to attraction and temptation was what she should be fighting against. Yes, it was self-protective, but it was also smart. When she was eighteen she'd decided it was safer not to bother committing to anyone too much. Then she would never have to feel the soul-destroying hurt that she'd witnessed at the end of her mother and father's marriage. That she was witnessing now with the demise of her mother's relationship with Dan.

She cleared her throat. "Don't you think this is a little weird? Admit it, two days ago you still resented me for the way I left you."

His wandering finger halted. "I'm a man. I compartmentalize. And the compartment that's getting all my attention right now is the one that has me in it, with you, naked."

While unfortunately that was quite an intriguing one to her as well, something suddenly wasn't jiving in Bailey's mind. There was a hard look on Finn's face that you *could* take for pure lust, but the hair on the back of her neck was now rising in a completely unsexual way.

Her hands pressed harder against the paint, her eyes narrowing. "So, um, what have you been up to since last we met?"

"Downloading photos of my new nephew. Downloading more photos of my new nephew. Driving Gram to a couple of doctor's appointments." His finger traveled from her breast to her chin, so he could tilt her mouth toward his. His voice lowered to a raspy whisper. "Thinking about you."

Bailey swallowed, still not buying it completely. "How is your grandmother?"

His hand dropped. "On the road to recovery." He pivoted away from her and stalked toward the door. "So do you want to get it on or not?"

"Gee, there you go with the hearts and flowers again."

He stomped back. His face was furious now, but she held her ground. He grabbed her right hand and pressed it against his breastbone. "I've got your heart." His slammed against her palm with an angry beat. Her left hand he forced to cup the hard rise of flesh between his legs. "And I've got your flowers right here."

And with those two rough gestures he had Bailey all over again. Not because she appreciated rough—but because that wasn't the kind of man he was. He'd always, always been so careful with her, and this attitude told her that something besides sex was driving Finn, something dark and tangled and that maybe he wasn't even aware of.

He might as well have been whispering, "I can't do it, Bailey. I don't think I can do it alone."

Just like that, finding his way once more into her damaged heart.

"Maybe we can cut a deal," she said, sliding her left hand from under his and away from his erection. More sex shouldn't be on the table—*that* wouldn't be a high-IQ move on her part—but maybe there was a win-win option available.

"Yeah?" He caught her escaping fingers in his, held them.

Her heart stuttered a little. "Yeah. I have a business to run, customers waiting, and you fill out the Santa suit better than I do."

His eye narrowed. "So I ho-ho-ho for you and then you'll h—"

"Tell me you're not about to mention me and 'ho' in the same breath."

He grinned, and she felt some of the tension leach out of him.

Some tension left her too. *Congratulations, Bailey.* He'd taken the bait. By the time he was done with Kris Kringle duty, perhaps he'd be too tired or at least too diverted to think that sex was the answer to whatever was driving his mood.

Almost three hours later, she still hoped she was right. At the end of the film, once the sentimental moviegoers had sighed over the sight of ol' Kris's cane left beside the fireplace of the new Santa believers, Bailey had trotted out her Kringle-for-the-night and called upon Trin to help pass around refreshments. Then the customers had proceeded to do what all good customers should . . . they'd lined up at the cash registers, many of them purchasing their own copy of the *Miracle on 34th Street* DVD as well as the ornaments, cards, and other memorabilia commemorating the movie that she'd hastily stocked.

Then she'd sent Trin home to her baby and husband and let Finn help her stack the chairs she'd rented and put the displays back to their original position. It was almost midnight when they stood by the door and she flipped off the lights.

"Thanks for everything," she said to Finn. He

had to be as ready to call it a day as she was. Sex, please God, was the last thing on his mind.

He put one hand on the doorknob. The other he curled around the back of her neck, underneath her hair. "I have an idea. Let's stay here."

Earlobes could goose bump, she realized. And maybe sex *wasn't* the last thing on Finn's mind.

"Let's stay here and eat . . ." He let the sentence trail off, then added the one word guaranteed to seduce her. "Donuts."

No fair! Her stomach growled and she could already taste them on her tongue. Finn knew she was a goner for greasy, sugary stuff. Bailey slid a glance toward him, his expression telling her nothing more than it had when he'd marched into her back room demanding to once more ring her chimes.

It was such a bad idea. But he wasn't suggesting sex again, exactly, was he?

Leaning closer, he whispered in her ear. "Bailey." A hypnotist, and she was halfway to being mesmerized. "*Donuts.*"

Oh hell. Some things were just worth the risk.

December 16

The Christmas flower known in the English-speaking world as the poinsettia is named after Dr. Joel R. Poinsett, a U.S. diplomat who served as minister to Mexico in the 1820s. The shrub, native to Mexico, blooms in midwinter with star-shaped crimson blossoms. Mr. Poinsett returned home to Charleston, South Carolina, with enough cuttings to begin growing the plants in more northern climates.

Chapter 16

When Finn returned to The Perfect Christmas bearing a pink box and the best four bucks could buy from Dee Dee's 24/7 Donuts around the corner, he found the front door unlocked but no sign of Bailey in the dimly lit store. "GND?" he called softly, locking the door behind him.

At his first step, a reindeer standing on an eye-level shelf swiveled its head his way. Finn started, nearly dropping the box. The movement triggered more action on a display table to his right. Jack-in-the-box-style, a Santa popped out of a chimney. Shaking his head, he took another step and saw the lights strung along the banister to the second floor spring into action. Red and green alternated, racing upward at a dizzying speed.

Getting the hint, he made for the staircase, then almost swallowed his tongue when something touched his leg. He looked down and left—a knee-high angel was waving her arms about, gesturing him onward with a lighted plastic candle. As he reached the landing, a stuffed moose hanging on the wall broke into song, its mouth moving, its ears twitching, the wreath around its neck blazing with light. "I wish you a Merry Christmas too," he muttered, then kept moving, senses alert for Bailey's next surprise.

A train steamed down its track laid along the hallway as he reached the top of the stairs. Taking the indicated left turn, he continued forward. Three snow globes sitting on a narrow table lit up and started spinning in their bases, snow whirling in tiny blizzards as he passed by. Finally, a moving Santa and Mrs. Claus gestured him into the smallest second-floor room, half dark like the rest of the store.

In one shadowy corner stood a real Christmas tree, decorated more simply than those downstairs.

White lights twinkled through its bows and it was wrapped in strings of cranberries and slices of dried orange.

"Another popular myth busted." The amused voice of the woman he wanted sounded in the room. "Apparently men *can* follow directions."

His head shifted left. He looked up. Perched on a short stepladder, Bailey gazed down at him with a half smile curving the usual pout of her full mouth. She had a glitter-covered ornament in her hand and he saw a streak of glitter across her cheek.

It was like that night in Gram's driveway when he'd thought she'd been dipped in stars. He'd ached for her then. He ached for her now.

For some reason she wanted to fight going into his arms again, but he would overcome her resistance. Rushing her wasn't going to work, he'd tried that in the back room at the store. So he'd settled on seduction. By sweet treats, by sweet words, by whatever damn thing necessary, he was going to get her naked and him inside her again.

Bare to bare.

Battling his Bailey-lust the past couple of days had only been making things worse for him and everyone who came in contact with him. The tension he'd vowed to uncoil this Christmas had instead only been wrapping tighter. He'd nearly clocked the receptionist at Gram's oncologist's that morning.

Don't tell him the holiday season was a bad time to be terminally ill.

Bailey stretched high, taking his mind off everything but her, as she reached to place the ornament in her hand near the top of the tree. Finn remembered the balance beam her stepfather had built for her in her backyard. He'd watch from his side of the hedge as she practiced, fascinated by the grace in her flips and turns. Fascinated by the slender line of her strong legs and the way the sun caught in her blond hair. Bailey then.

Bailey now. A woman.

As if sensing his thoughts, she looked down at him. Their gazes met, and deep inside him, at his center, there was a shift, like something fallen over finally rerighting itself.

"What?" Bailey asked, and when he didn't answer, a puzzled smile took over her face. "*What?*"

It was the attraction, Finn told himself, pulling the bakery box closer to his chest. That's all. His need for sex moving from his groin outward.

"Finn?"

"Get down from there," he ordered softly.

Her body twitched, swaying a little on the ladder.

He reached her in one stride, steadying her with his hand on her thigh. The top of his head reached her hips. "Be careful."

She stared at his hand on her leg. "Don't you get it? I'm trying, I'm trying."

"Then come on down, sweetheart." He squeezed her denim-covered flesh.

Her gaze didn't leave his hand. "I, uh, think we should talk."

"Talk?" Yeah, he'd sworn to do whatever necessary to get into her pants again, but, hell, she was hot against his palm and he just wanted to get her naked. "Talk about what?"

She cleared her throat, looked up, down, back at his hand. "I don't know. Tell me about . . . about Tanner."

"Tanner?" *Tanner?* "Why the hell would you want to talk about him?"

She shrugged. "He's an old friend. And I—"

"How well did you know him?" Finn had never considered it before, but Tanner Hart and Bailey Sullivan were two golden peas in the beachside pod of Coronado. Heat shot up his spine to pool at the base of his skull. "Damn it, did you date him when I wasn't here?"

"Why are we talking about dating?"

He ground his back teeth. Tried convincing himself he shouldn't yank her off that ladder, yank down her pants, thrust himself inside to make clear whom she belonged to. But he wasn't that kind of bad ass anymore. And she wasn't "his" in any long-term kind of way either. He'd never trust in that stupid idea again.

"You wanted to talk," Finn muttered. "You brought up Tanner."

"I'm wondering how the two of you connected, that's all. I wouldn't have said you had a lot in common."

He laughed, and it released some of the tension in his neck. "Ah, but you didn't see me that summer, did you? I'd cut my hair. Passed the GED and even had one semester of community college under my belt—all A's."

"You're kidding."

He dropped his hand from her leg and took a moment to send some sympathy to the poor lovesick sap he'd been. "I wanted to surprise someone." He'd wanted to impress Bailey.

"Finn . . ."

The note in her voice had the coils tightening again, and he couldn't have that. "Now don't go feeling sorry for me, GND. Wanting to be more your style and speed got me out of the gutter, and just that was worth the price of admission, okay?"

"Still, I'm sorry."

He leaned over to drop the bakery box on a nearby table. He hated the fucking pity in her voice. He had to find a way to get rid of it.

"You want to make it up to me, GND?" His voice was dark and his fingers cupped the inside of her ankle to travel slowly up her inner thigh. "Because I have some suggestions."

She froze as the blade of his hand found the intersection of seams on her jeans. It was hot there. He pressed closer. Damp. She moaned.

He rubbed his cheek against her hip as one hand unfastened her jeans.

"Finn . . ."

"Shhh."

Her body trembled as he slid down the zipper. A triangle of red panties showed in the now-open vee and he bent his head to press his mouth right *there*.

Her fingers slid through his hair. "Oh, Finn," she said in a throaty voice.

His skin rippled over his muscles as his pulse started to drum in his ears, at his groin, in the tips of the fingers that curled in denim to yank her pants past her knees. The beat sounded so loud in his head that he couldn't hear if she protested when he sent her panties in the same direction. He stepped closer, then kissed the sweet, soft hair at the juncture of her thighs.

Her nails bit into his scalp.

He groaned against her, greed, need, want flaring.

The constricting clothes at her ankles didn't afford complete movement, but it was enough. He lifted one leg, separating it from the other, so he could prop her knee on his shoulder. Then he opened her with his thumbs, pushing against the soft, swollen folds to see her secret flesh glistening. For him.

His sixth sense kicked in, trying to sneak a

warning through his haze of lust, but Finn knew one sure way to shut up that irritating voice. Leaning forward, he buried his mouth in Bailey's wet flesh.

She shuddered. Her nails bit again. That voice inside him tried speaking louder.

None of it deterred him. Instead he flattened his tongue and took in all the sweet tastes and slick surfaces that he could reach. His fingers held her open still, not letting her hide behind even her own flesh.

Mine. All mine.

He strung kisses along the crease of her thigh and pelvis. Made matching bites on the high inside of her thighs and then licked the sting away. He latched on to the hard center of her sweet, delicious flower and sucked until she bucked against his mouth.

And he still wanted more.

He pulled her off the stepladder and laid her under the sparkling tree. Then he threw off his clothes, his heart slamming as he watched her struggle out of her own. Bailey, going naked for him.

It turned him on so much he had to taste her again. This time he pushed her thighs wide, his palms just above the new marks he'd made on her flesh, and watched her sex unfurl for him. Then he dove down to accept her erotic invitation. Her body arched upward as he descended and he filled her with his tongue, trying to get to the very center of her. She cried out, the passionate sound piercing him to the gut.

He glanced up and saw that she was wide open to him, her legs splayed, her arms spread wide, her eyes not squeezed tight, but open too, trained on Finn. On Finn pleasing her.

Bailey, vulnerable, open, giving him everything. Trusting.

His heart hammering against his chest, he reached up to squeeze her breasts and thrust his tongue once more toward her heart.

She screamed, climaxing against his mouth.

Gratified, satisfied, feeling pretty damn puffed-up even with his cock cryin' the my-turn blues, Finn slid up Bailey's still-trembling body. Soft, wet, her body took him in like a key sliding into a lock. He groaned into her ear.

She let out another small scream.

He lifted his head. "Christ, I must be better than I thought. Again already?"

"S-Santa. Santa's watching."

"Huh?"

"Finn, do something."

He followed her pointing finger. In the doorway stood her two red-robed gatekeepers. While Santa appeared benignly interested in the sight before him, Finn had to admit that Mrs. Claus wore a pinched look of disapproval behind her wire-rimmed granny glasses. Glancing back at Bailey, he surrendered to the inevitable and clambered to his feet.

When he got close, Mrs. C tried to wave him off.

"Prude," he muttered, then relocated the figurines out of sight. In a flash he was back to the naked woman who was his ticket to paradise.

Naked, donut-stealing woman.

"It's not refreshment time," he scolded, staring her down. Sitting up, she had a powdered sugar treat in one hand and was rummaging through the box with the other. "We're not done yet, lady."

She smiled and held out the half-eaten donut. "I'll share."

"Damn straight you will." Lying back beside her, he shoved the pink box out the way, then pushed her down to make his place between her legs again. He bent his head to lick up the powder that had fallen onto her breasts.

"Mmm," she said. "Maybe I don't need a donut after all. Maybe I'm hungry for something else."

Finn's head shot up. His gaze jumped to her flushed face.

Her knees clamped his hips. He let them sink lower to find her and slide into her again, once more trying to plumb her depths. The donut fell from her hand and her damp nipples rubbed against his chest.

Mine. All mine.

December 17
Ancient people thought that mistletoe was magic, and a connection between earth and the heavens because it grew without roots. It was thought to keep evil away and was also a symbol of peace. Warring soldiers under mistletoe would call a temporary truce.

Chapter 17

After that night in The Perfect Christmas, Bailey gave up resisting and decided to embrace her inner sex fiend. So when Finn showed up on her front porch that afternoon to help her with the surprise light stringing at her mother's, she merely laughed when he held up a ribbon-wrapped bundle of mistletoe. Without hesitation, she went on tiptoe for his kiss.

Their mouths met and he tasted like cinnamon again. She savored his flavor, savored his kiss, her hands spearing through his dark hair. When they came up for air she fell back to her heels and rubbed her cheek against his hard shoulder, giddy with his nearness. She was like a cat with a catnip toy, she thought, drunk on his scent and ready to take a bite. As she smiled to herself, her teeth nipped at him through his soft flannel shirt.

He yelped, then pushed her away, his expression bemused. "Good God. Has someone kidnapped my real GND?" He hooked a finger in her T-shirt and pulled it away from her body, copping a look at her chest in the process. "Nope. Those are indeed your lovely breasts."

She batted away his arm, someplace between embarrassed and pleased with herself. Who knew she could be such a physical creature? Her fingertips trailed along his hard abdomen, and he responded by holding up his mistletoe again. He glanced at it, glanced down at her face. Expectant. Confident.

Bad boy.

Fine. She kissed him again, giving him tongue, making it sloppy and wet until his free arm came around her hips and tilted her against his growing hard-on. Her knees sagged. Then "Good King Wenceslas" sounded in the near distance, and she came to her senses and stepped back, clearing her throat.

"The neighbors are out," she said, nodding across the street where Mr. Lantz was up on his roof, adjusting the plastic Santa that was trying to stuff a pretend big-screen TV down the chimney. "We don't want them calling the police."

Waving the leafy bundle over her head, Finn grinned. "We'll blame it on the mistletoe."

She took a second step back from temptation. Six feet, two inches of hard-muscled male, of *Finn*, had become her personal, sexual switch. When he smiled at her like that, heat shot up her calves, flooded her belly, even made its sneaky way toward her chest. She rubbed there and took a breath of air, clearing away the giddy effervescence that was fizzing her blood and fogging her mind.

"You know that plant's a parasite, don't you?" she said, pointing upward. "It has those leaves to produce its own food but it would rather root into its host and take *its* water and nutrients. There's no way to get rid of the stuff either, nothing short of amputation, anyway."

He grimaced, his hand dropping to his side. "Gee, thanks for ruining a perfectly harmless custom. Has anyone ever told you you're a wet blanket?"

Shooting him a cheeky grin, Bailey walked away. Sex fiend was fine, but better a wet-blanket sex fiend than a shattered romantic with a thing for one man's body. Despite their attraction and her physical capitulation, she was still committed to keeping her emotions unengaged and unscathed. "It's what comes from working with dozens of ferocious divorce attorneys."

He caught her elbow, hauled her back. "What? I thought your firm was family law."

"Oh sure, we've got your ugly one-night-drunk paternity suits, your siblings at each other's throats over who gets the soup tureen, your fed-up folks wanting to emancipate their bratty teenagers, but we're best known for our take-you-to-the-cleaners divorce department."

His hand loosened, but she felt his gaze still studying her as she walked over to retrieve the boxes of lights she'd stacked nearby. "Sometimes I'm sorry I can see inside your head," he said.

"Orderly, practical." Unswayed by the fact that multiorgasmic was no longer just the subject of an article in *Cosmo*. "What's not to like?"

He didn't answer the question. "But I don't get this Christmas lights thing. You, Ms. Grumpy Grinch, volunteering to do more decorating?"

"It's for my mom." There was the mailbox bow, the front-door wreath, the garland on the stairs, the tiny tree in the kitchen. Bailey had hung Christmas guest towels in the powder room downstairs and stacked holiday mugs in the kitchen cabinets. So far, though, no sign of her mother at The Perfect Christmas. Not even a whiff of interest in what was going on at the business. Not a good sign.

"I've got to snare her into the season." Bailey gathered the boxes of lights and turned to Finn. "You said you'd help. You're not changing your mind?"

"I'm not changing my mind about anything." Taking the boxes from her, he set them aside. Then he put his arms around her and dragged her into a shadowy corner of the porch. "Let's go have more sex."

"Finn!" His mouth was already on her, though, hot on her neck, then trailing toward her collar-bone. His hand slithered under her tight T-shirt, and her belly quivered as he found his way to her breast.

Making her giddy again. She pressed into his hand and moaned when he rubbed the edge of his thumb across her nipple.

"I want to do it in your room," he whispered in her ear, his breath hot. "On your bed, in your shower, every place you've ever been naked that I haven't been with you."

Lust tightened her throat, her thigh muscles, her womb, even as another—possibly perverted—part of her thought the line was kind of sweet. "Finn . . ."

"On your desk. I want to sit you on the very edge with your legs open and your heels on my shoulders. Then I'll write an essay about all the things I like about your pretty pu—"

Definitely perverted, she thought, her mouth fastening on his, heat shooting everywhere now, toes to fingernails, breasts to thighs, ankles to neck, because that line wasn't sweet at all and still she liked it. His tongue thrust inside her lips, and giddiness evaporated as her temperature soared. All she wanted was Finn.

Finn forever.

The last two words froze in her mind. Chilled all her heat. Once again she broke away, chest heaving. To hide her new uneasiness, she worked at plastering on a casual smile.

Finn said nothing, his one-eyed pirate gaze watchful. Suspicious.

She swallowed. "I only have a couple of hours before I have to be back at the store. Can we, uh, pick this up where we left off tonight?"

He turned to retrieve the lights. "Tonight might be a problem. I have a dinner thing."

A dinner thing? Her stomach tightened. What kind of dinner thing did a sexy, piratical man have? Her uneasiness washed away and something else took its place. She saw red, then green, and a little spike of temper burned through her blood. A dinner *date* kind of dinner thing?

"I see," she said, keeping her voice calm, though. Noncommittal.

His head whipped around, his eye narrowed. "Oh no. No. You've got it wrong."

"What do I have wrong?" She thought she got incredulity just right. "I don't know what you're talking about."

"You have that braided-bracelet face on."

Oh hell. In an instant she knew what he meant. She'd been jealous once, fine. She'd kicked up a fuss, probably flounced off in a huff, and then refused to speak with him until he'd cut that butt-ugly bracelet off his wrist. He'd handed it to her.

Later she'd flushed it down the toilet.

Now she felt her face turning red. "I still don't know what you're talking about."

"GND." He snagged her with an arm around her waist and drew her close to his body again. "I'm meeting some people about a job."

She meant to pull away, but his words surprised her. "A job? You have a job."

"Yeah, well." It was he who let go this time, he who moved off to make his way down the porch steps with a box of lights, his destination the ladder she'd propped against the side of the house.

She had to trot to catch up with him. Her fingers curled around the sides of the ladder as he started to climb. "What are you talking about? What's this job?"

"There's a local company. They have contracts with the Department of Homeland Security. Over the past couple of months they've been giving me the big recruiting rush. I've decided I should hear what they have to say."

Her jaw dropped. "Oh. I, uh, thought you were pretty into working for the Secret Service."

"We get pretty tight because of the long hours and all the travel." His long arm stretched to loop the string of lights on the hooks screwed into the eaves. "You follow a diplomat around for a month. Then you're working the Super Bowl for a couple of weeks, next you're called on to chase down some loon who's been sending the White House threatening letters. The saying goes that if the Secret Service wanted you to have a family, then they would have issued you one."

"You . . ." Bailey's chest ached, just a little. "You want a family?"

"That's not the point." Finn descended the ladder and she moved aside for him to adjust its position.

He was tense again; she could tell from his jerky movements and the closed expression on his face as he climbed back up. Which meant she shouldn't press for more, she told herself. A sex fiend didn't need to know the interior landscape of the object of her lust.

"Well, what *is* the point?" she heard herself ask anyway, proving that even fiends couldn't keep their minds on just sex and just sex only.

"I don't know if I can work for the Service anymore." He continued stringing lights, as if the admission meant nothing to him.

Bailey stared. "Why?"

"The job requires skills I've . . . lost."

Whoa, that was news. "Like what?"

"My observational skill, for one," he replied, his voice matter-of-fact. "You've seen it a hundred times, the president or some important dignitary doing the grip-and-grin along a rope line, Secret Service at his or her shoulder. Agents have to be observant enough to detect the first sign of trouble. Missing an eye, I'm not so good at that."

The cool way he said it abraded her nerve endings. "But . . . but . . ." She craned her neck to get a read of his face. "There's got to be other duties—"

"Sure. Desk job. Counterfeit work."

That wasn't so much to his taste, obviously. "But you said 'skills.' Your vision, that's one skill. What else have you lost?"

He didn't bother looking at her. His voice went cold and hard. "Nothing you can give me, GND."

The simple words hit her square in the chest. *Back off,* he might as well have told her. *I don't want you to know any more about me.* She stumbled away, surprised by how much the rebuff hurt. Her palm rubbed the ache between her breasts. She wasn't supposed to feel pain when it came to Finn.

When it came to any man!

Rattled, but determined to hide the fact from him, Bailey retreated from the ladder and moved toward the front of the house. Maybe a glass of water or one of the Christmas cookies she'd brought home from the bakery would settle her back down.

A luxurious motor home rolled to a stop across the street. That wouldn't have caught her attention without the pumping strains of "Start Me Up" blasting from the half-open driver's window. Her stomach clenched, tight enough to make her belly ache along with her chest.

A man with a lion's mane of gray hair leaped out, exuding enough energy and charisma to replace his beloved Mick on any concert stage. "Bailey!" he crowed as he jogged across the street.

She hadn't seen or spoken to him in two and a half years.

"How the hell are you, little girl?" He enfolded her in a sinewy embrace.

Her mouth moved into a smile. It always did. Even when she'd been dragging his suitcase to the car for him as he prepared to leave her forever, she remembered smiling at her daddy.

She'd smiled at him maybe a dozen times since: often at Christmas when he'd drop by without warning. Once on her mother's birthday—he'd mixed it up with Bailey's. At her high school graduation.

Her father moved back, clapping his palms together in his hearty way. "Surprised, huh?"

Her smile flitted again. "Surprised."

"But tell me this is a good time to visit." He propped his fists on his hips.

"A great time. It's always great to see you."

It was always great to be reminded of the hard lessons of a lifetime, she told herself, especially when the two men who had meant the most in hers were suddenly so close again.

Taking a step away from her father, she checked over her shoulder. Finn was still high on the ladder. The distance from the both of them made it easier to breathe.

December 18
England's King Henry III was known to put a merchant out of business if he didn't like the size of his end-of-year cash gift.

_____

Chapter 18

Finn watched Bailey close the door to The Perfect Christmas, the bells on the handle chiming cheerfully, in direct contrast to the scowl on her face. "Thank God that's over," she said, peering through the glass at the thirty four-year-olds marching down the short front walk. "I'll need at least the next hour until we open to wipe their finger smudges off everything."

She made her way toward his place by the cash register, then stopped short by one of the round display tables, her scowl deepening. "Will you look at this? Somebody mixed up the reindeer ornaments. Now the antlered ones and the ones without antlers are all mixed up."

Finn rubbed his chin. "I think I noticed a few of your, uh, guests playing with them. They wanted to start some reindeer families."

Bailey looked up. "What?"

"How else are you going to make reindeer babies?"

Shaking her head, she started resorting the ornaments into their side-by-side baskets. "Who invited the little Santaholics anyway?" she muttered. "It's not as if any of them had a dime in their itty-bitty pockets to spend. We need cash flow, not a crowd of penniless browsers."

Preschoolers, penniless browsers. Okay. Finn swallowed his grin and threaded his way through the displays. God, he couldn't resist her, not her smiles, not her scowls, not even her bad temper over being stuck with the store this Christmas. Yeah, he was still having his own bad moments, times when he felt like he was an eyelash away from putting his fist through a wall, but just a stroke of Bailey's skin, the touch of her lips eased his edginess.

She was the channel for all his frustrated energy.

Standing behind her, he brushed the hair away from her nape so he could kiss the soft, warm skin, and tried to keep the laughter out of his voice. "Wouldn't that be you?"

Her fingers went lax at the touch of his lips. She leaned her head back against his chest and he kissed her temple and then licked the lobe of her ear. She shivered. "Wouldn't that be me, what?"

"Who invited the Santaholics in?" She was melting like butter against him and he cupped her shoulders, then ran his hands down her arms so they could link fingers. "Wasn't that you who came in early today to host this special visit?"

"I came in early today, but I didn't *invite* them to make this 'special visit.' That would be the bedpan-wielding battle-ax Mrs. Mohn. It was a reflex from the days when she was my school principal. I had to say yes when she phoned. She has a mean voice."

And you don't have a mean bone in this pretty little body of yours, no matter how hard you try to make people believe it. Finn snuggled his cheek against hers. "Admit you liked them here, GND. Admit you love The Perfect Christmas."

She stiffened in his arms. "Give me a break. You know how I feel about this place. About the whole stupid season."

He thought he really *did* know and suddenly it seemed imperative for her to admit it. "Bailey—"

"Let's talk about you instead." She pulled free of him and spun around, crossing her arms at her chest. "How did your dinner go last night?"

"Fine." Damn it, she was dodging. And damn it, he was dodging too, but this was his line of questioning and he needed to follow it through. "But let's get back to—"

"You." She dropped her defensive arms and moved forward to wrap them around him instead. Her smile was as much crafty as it was seductive. "You left my inner sex fiend panting yesterday. You had her all hepped up with no place to go." She rubbed her hips against his, the witch. "Or come, as the case may be."

He groaned, knowing any protest was futile. He was a goner against this grown-up GND. "Bailey . . ." She cut off further words by drawing his head down and sliding her tongue into his mouth. Heat rocketed up his spine and his hands splayed along her back.

"I'll make it up to you now," he said against her mouth. His lips trailed to the sweet spot behind her ear. "Don't make me wait until tonight."

She stiffened against him again. "I'm . . . I'm afraid I have something I have to do tonight."

"What?"

"My, uh, father stopped by the house yesterday." She pushed his chest away. "When you were dealing with the lights."

"I didn't see Dan."

She shook her head. "Not Dan. My real father. He shows up from time to time. The law firm told him where he could find me and he stopped by on his way to go beach camping in Mexico. He wants to take me out to dinner tonight."

There was a weird, forced little smile on her face, which caused Finn's sixth sense to start whispering in his ear. "Maybe—"

The jingle of the front door bells broke in. They turned their heads, then separated from each other as two people—a woman and a little boy—entered the store.

"I'm sorry for the interruption," the woman said. She had on red sweat pants and a white sweatshirt. An official-looking badge from Beachside Preschool was pinned on her collar and stated her name was "Miss Michele." Her mouth pursed and she sighed as she glanced down at the scruffy charge by her side. "Angel has something to say to you."

Naming her son Angel must have been wishful thinking on his mother's part. If his dark, wavy hair had been clean and combed at some point, he'd long ago found some sand to rub through it. There was a rip in the pocket of his shorts, and the neck of his stained T-shirt was stretched out as if he'd been hanging from it.

His black-lashed eyes were trained on the toes of his grubby sneakers that had parted company with the soles. If Finn had to guess, he'd say the kid was pretending he was somewhere else.

Miss Michele gripped the little boy's upper arm, giving it an impatient shake. "Angel?" She cast an apologetic look at Bailey. "This one causes us trouble."

Finn felt himself twitch. *This one causes us trouble. The class would be quiet if it wasn't for this one. This one got us all kicked out of the museum. We'd have peace in the family, Rita, if it wasn't for this one.*

Frowning, Bailey flicked him a glance as if she'd noticed his reaction, then she crossed her arms over her chest and shifted her gaze between Angel's face and Miss Michele's. "What's the problem?"

Miss Michele shook the little boy again. "An—"

"You can let go of him." Bailey had enough ice in her voice to build igloos at the North Pole. Finn didn't know if she was pissed at the woman, the kid, the interruption of her morning's work, or all three. "Just tell me why you came back."

"One of the other children let us know he broke something," Miss Michele answered, dropping the little boy's arm.

Bailey gazed around the room. "Broke what?"

Still staring at his toes, the kid dug his fingers in the pocket that wasn't ripped. Out came a palm-sized, ceramic figurine of Santa Claus, now decapitated. He held the two pieces out in both grubby hands.

"The children were told not to touch anything," Miss Michele intoned.

Bailey face appeared etched in stone. "I remember. I believe I was the one who made that request." She stepped forward and the little kid jolted back, as if expecting a slap.

Finn froze. Then he shot a look at Bailey, wondering if she'd read it as he had.

"Accident," the kid mumbled. "Didn't mean to."

Miss Michele sighed, looking less of an ogre now, and more just worn out. "Yes, well, Angel, you sure have a lot of didn't-mean-to moments. The preschool's sorry, Ms. Sullivan, and I'm sure Angel is too."

It was Bailey's turn to say something. "I—"

"Santa won't bring me nuthin' will he?" Angel's words rushed out and he looked up, his gaze latching on to Bailey like a laser beam.

She stilled—the pose of a deer hoping she'd be lost in the forest camouflage.

"My brother says there's no such thing as Santa. And that my mom won't bring us nuthin' either." Angel didn't blink. "What do you say?"

Slowly, oh-so-damn-slowly, Bailey turned her head and looked at Finn.

He didn't know what the hell she was thinking, but he could imagine any number of things she might say in response to the boy.

You might as well find out now, kid . . .

Nothing in life comes for free . . .

Or perhaps what she'd told Finn in his loft that fateful night: *We thought it was magic. But there's no such thing.*

His gut clenched, his breath backing up in his lungs.

With a little shrug, she turned her gaze back on

the boy. "Angel. Buddy." She took the ceramic pieces out of the boy's hands and fitted them back together. Then she held up the almost-as-new figurine. "All I can tell you . . ." She cleared her throat, started again. "All I can tell you is that you just gotta believe."

Finn and Angel exhaled in identical relieved puffs of air. Even Miss Michele had her holiday face back on. Finn walked the boy and the woman to the front door. The two left for the Beachside Preschool with a happy jingle of the front bell. He thought he saw the little guy skip a couple of times down the sidewalk.

He turned around to find Bailey at the front counter, organizing the already organized space. "GND—"

"Do me a favor. Call that preschool. Get that boy's last name. Get his brother's name. And see if you can charm them into an address."

He stared at her, silenced.

Her head jerked up. She pinned him with glittering eyes. "What? What are you thinking? Did you suppose I was going to spread my cynicism instead of holiday cheer? Thanks a lot."

"Bailey—"

"He was just a little boy!"

A little boy with a label Finn knew only too well. He'd noticed the child during the class's visit to the store, because he'd recognized the kid's buzz of energy, his too-big movements, the way the teachers rode herd on him before he even had a chance to breathe.

And still he'd broken something.

Finn had broken dozens of things in just that very same way, until he'd stopped caring about the "bad" label they'd given him and started embracing it instead. Then had come Bailey.

Never impressed with his bad-ass attitude. Never put off by it either. He supposed he'd fallen in love with her that very first day when she'd sprayed his sullen, sorry face with a blast of cold hose water.

And, he realized now, his heart slamming to a stop, he was still in love with her today.

Finn hung around The Perfect Christmas the rest of the day but steered clear of Bailey, which was easy enough to do because there were customers all over the store, not to mention the welcome—though surprising—presence of both of the surfing sales kids. He could have gone back to Gram's, but she was spending the day doing a salon thing with her friend Jeanette. He could have gone back to Gram's anyway and used the alone time to dissect his reaction to dinner the night before.

The job offer. The very nice money that went along with it. The notion of never being a Secret Service agent again.

Trying to forget about that, he could have gone to Hart's and hit the booze. A few drinks to take the sting away and smooth out all his rough edges.

But neither peace and quiet nor company and whiskey would help erase the latest screw-up in his life. When he was supposed to be plastering over ten months of uninvited emotions, he'd just added another lethal feeling to the mix.

Love. For Bailey.

Fuck.

His throat felt dry at the thought, and he reconsidered a quick trip to the bar. That first shot would go down quick and the beer chaser would go down easy. But no, there was something that scared him more than the idea that she still had his heart, and it kept him nearby.

He was afraid she was going to run from him again.

Late afternoon, he was outside the back of the store, looking for fresh air and some hope that he wasn't really once more at the mercy of the woman who'd already eviscerated him. A car stopped in the narrow alley with its "No Parking" signs, and Bailey's mother, Tracy, slipped out.

Her face registered the same surprise he felt. "Oh," she said. "Uh, Finn."

He sketched a wave. "Mrs. Willis." His gut cramped. Her mother's return to working at The Perfect Christmas would send Bailey speeding to her other life for sure. She'd be gone—*poof*—before he figured out how to hack out of himself the part that still belonged to her. "Back at the store?"

"No." The word was quick. "I'm only dropping off some things."

Relieved, of course he volunteered to help her with them. So he let her load him up with an armful of boxes.

"For the Grandma's Attic room she told me about," Tracy explained, as she held open the door that led to the rear storeroom for him. "I had some things tucked away that came from who-knows-where. She might be able to use them."

"You like the idea of selling vintage?" he asked.

A smile flitted across Bailey's mother's face. "It's a very Bailey idea. Timely. Smart . . ."

"Profitable," they said together. Shared a smile.

He set the boxes on the room's worktable as Tracy sidled up to the half-open door that led to the downstairs display rooms. He followed her there, watching her watch her daughter at the front register. For all her anti-Christmas rhetoric, Bailey didn't appear unhappy to ring up yet another sale.

"She fits here," Tracy murmured. "More than at that cutthroat law firm she runs."

Finn cocked a brow. "She can be pretty cutthroat herself." He had the old scars to prove it, and worried like hell he was on his way to only more wounds.

"Sometimes . . . sometimes people hold the knife, keeping others away to avoid being hurt themselves."

"But Bailey—" He swallowed his words as Tracy jerked, sucking in a gasp. "What?"

Her gaze trained on the older man striding through the front door, she edged back, her heels just missing Finn's toes. But he wasn't giving an inch, not when it was obvious something was up. Not only was Tracy's body quivering, but so was his sixth sense's antennae.

Bailey was wearing that weird forced smile again. "Dad!" he heard her say to the newcomer.

The lean man had a headful of wind-tousled gray hair and a careless smile. He beamed it about the room as he turned in a circle. "I haven't been in here in twenty years."

"Twenty-three," Tracy murmured.

"I thought you weren't picking me up for dinner until six," Bailey said, her voice sounding thin and anxious. "I can't leave right now."

The other man—her dad—turned back to her, his smile no less dim. "Ah, here's the deal, honey."

Bailey's face betrayed no emotion as he gave her a litany of excuses. People he promised to meet for margaritas. A possible business deal in the making. No raincheck because he was on his way first thing in the morning after overnighting at a local state beach campground.

His daughter didn't seem to notice how flimsy it all sounded, and even gave him that soulless smile again. "I'm sorry it didn't work out." Her hands lifted. "I guess this is Merry Christmas then."

"I'm sorry too, honey. I get so busy . . . But I make the important stuff, right? Like your college graduation."

In front of him, Tracy's muscles started humming like a tuning fork. "He didn't make her college graduation," she whispered furiously.

It was as if Bailey could hear her. "You, uh, didn't come to college graduation, Dad. But you were there for high school, though. Remember? I did a reading of Eleanor Roosevelt."

"That's right." Her father slid his hands in his pants pockets. "All those words of wisdom. And I gave you mine too, remember?"

Bailey's face blanked. Even if that wasn't enough to make Finn's antennae go wild, the conversation was triggering memories right and left. He'd spoken with her on the phone the day before her high school graduation. She'd seemed tense, nervous about her role at the ceremony, but had let nothing slip about plans to leave town. To leave him.

A few days later she was gone.

After that visit from her father. His scalp prickled a warning.

"I remember your wisdom real well, Dad," she said now, her voice low.

"It works, right? In relationships, jobs, hell, marriage. 'Get out before things get ugly.' I live by it."

Bailey nodded. Then she made a big play of looking at her watch. "Hey, Dad. If you're going to make those margaritas . . ."

He slapped his hands on his thighs, clapped them together, then turned toward the door. "Smartest daughter I have."

"Only daughter he has," Tracy said through her teeth.

Finn swallowed a painful laugh as he watched Bailey usher her father through the front door. Getting him out before things got ugly.

But it was probably too late, Finn thought. For all of them.

December 19
Victorian-era gift giving might include a cobweb party.
Each family member was assigned a color and then all
were taken to a room criss-crossed with cobwebs of
multicolored yarn. Persons had to follow their color to
find their presents.

Chapter 19

Tracy tried everything she could to control her anger. She wrapped herself up
in a feather comforter, visualizing it as
her buffer of nothingness, and watched
five hours of television. When she found herself
aiming the remote at the TV like a sword and
viciously stabbing the buttons, she took herself
to her bedroom and a book.

The letters in the sentences kept rearranging
themselves, creating new words. *Adultery. Disloy-
alty. Revenge.* Like the feelings boiling up inside of
her, they were all too big to write on a piece of

paper and fold into something small enough to fit into her mental compartmented cabinet.

At dawn, she backed out of her driveway. The quiet street with its competing Christmas decorations didn't lighten or appease her spirits. On her way, she passed The Perfect Christmas and saw old Charlie Baer in his Retired Citizen Service Patrol car parked out front, sipping from a cup of coffee. She was going so fast she didn't think he had time to jot down her license number.

The three red lights she sped through, she took to be good omens.

Red matched her mood.

At her destination, it was beyond easy to find him. There was the car he'd used to drive away from 631 Walnut. It was a 1972 Corvette coupe, a car he'd coveted, and that she'd given to him after saving out of her paycheck for years. He'd probably cheated on her in that car.

She parked behind it and got out, breathing deeply through her nose. The cool air seemed to be swirling around her in a wild wind, and her heart pumped in time to match it. Despite the cold, her body felt too hot, though she was only in a pair of jeans and a thin T-shirt.

She couldn't keep her gaze off that car.

The wind still twisting around her, she fumbled with the lock on the trunk of her old sedan, her hands shaking. It opened, and her gaze shifted from the Corvette to what was inside the deep well.

A couple of greasy rags. Some plastic oil containers. The windbreaker Dan had been looking for in August before a sailing trip. Half hidden beneath that, a crowbar.

She didn't know why it was there.

Without thinking, she reached in and lifted its cold weight in her hand. Her palm folded comfortably around it. It was painted red. Like the stoplights. Like her mood. Like the color of her blood pumping with fierce anger through her body. It looked like permission.

Heading into the whirlwind, she strode around her back bumper and approached the Corvette, where it was hitched to the motor home, probably in preparation for the all-important Mexico trip that superseded a visit with the daughter he'd betrayed as much as he'd betrayed Tracy.

Get out before things get ugly.

She lifted her arms over her head and brought them down on the Corvette's back windshield.

Glass shattered, cracks spiderwebbing from the point of impact. Like her heart had once been damaged.

The impact shuddered up her arm to her shoulder, but she ignored the little pain and strode through the tempest to the side window. This time she swung the crowbar like a bat. Another satisfying smash.

"Hey!"

She ignored the voice, but saw someone emerge from the RV parked nearby. It was a woman, in flannel pajama bottoms and a long sweatshirt. She had two inches of gray roots and a pillow crease across her face. It was like looking in a mirror. Tracy, post–Dan's defection.

Walking around to the other side of the vehicle, she shot the woman a look. "I paid for this stupid car. He used it to leave me." *Bam!* She took out the other side window.

"Oh," the woman said, already retreating. "I never trust a single one of them."

Neither had Tracy, she all at once understood. Not after what Kevin had done.

He emerged just as she was contemplating the front window. "Tracy. My God. What the hell are you doing?"

It was calm where she stood now, she realized. She'd made it into the eye of the storm. Yet *she* wasn't calm. Her heart was pumping, the anger jumping, all the emotions that she'd been hiding, secreting, controlling for all these years were pouring into her blood. If someone took a picture of her right now, all they would capture was a flame.

"Tracy . . ."

She turned her head. Kevin had aged well, she thought idly. He was older than she. Thirty-four when he left her and Bailey, but he had no soft spots now. Lots of hair.

Get out before things get ugly.

But still no soul to speak of.

The wind picked up again. Maybe it picked up on her mood, too, because it seemed to come from the east now, a California Santa Ana gust that tasted like heat and sand on her tongue.

"Tracy . . ." He started to approach, halted when she lifted her crowbar again. There were others from the campground exiting their RVs, but when they saw that Kevin wasn't coming nearer, they kept their distance too. He pushed a hand through his hair. "What's this all about?"

She bared her teeth at him. "You shouldn't have disrespected me. If you didn't like what we had, if you were unhappy, you should have said something." Her fingers tightened on the crowbar, then her arms dropped. The front window cracked.

"You should have followed through with the raising of your child"—her arms rose again—"because she never, ever got ugly." *Swak!* Another crack ran through the glass.

"When you decided you didn't want me anymore, instead of sneaking around behind my back and lying to me, the woman who'd married you and borne your child, you should have had the goddamn decency to treat me with honesty and kindness. You should have treated me like a *person*." And as if the weight of the world aided her last swing, the crowbar crashed down, demolishing the windshield with a final shatter.

Someone in the small crowd of onlookers clapped.

Tracy just stared at the damaged car, its glass fragmented into thousands of pieces. No more than her heart was broken into, she realized, as all the painful misery she'd stored inside it leaked out.

Shaking his head, Kevin had just let Tracy drive away. Maybe he had just enough soul left to realize he deserved what she'd done. Now her wrist hurt, her shoulder, her chest. She focused on her physical pain instead of her emotional state, holding her right arm tight against her body and steering with her left as she took another route away from the campground. Some ice would help, and she'd get that later, but she had a stop to make first.

Everyone knew where the Crown Palms condominium complex was located. Not only was Coronado just that small, but it had a reputation as *the* singles haven in town.

She cruised the parking lot until she located Dan's car. Pulling up behind the vehicle, she braked and climbed out of her sedan.

They'd bought his Volvo three years ago because it was loaded with safety features and they had a new driver. Though the air bags had never once deployed, Harry had managed to dent the front fender, scrape the back one, and snap off the radio antenna four times. Compared to the experience of their friends, they'd considered themselves lucky.

Tracy ran her fingers over the cold white metal . . . and then she moved on, forcing her leaden feet along the meandering, pebbled paths that led through the lush garden setting of the complex's three-story buildings. It was still quite early, still quiet, but as she passed the orgy-sized hot tub and the Olympic pool, she noticed a man and a woman already swimming laps. Another woman, wrapped in a sunny yellow beach robe, was adjusting a lounge chair to catch the first rays of the sun. Under her arm was a glossy fashion magazine.

A spurt of resentment nudged aside the throbbing pain from Tracy's arm. Oh, wouldn't that be nice? A morning swimming or sunning, with nothing more pressing than daydreaming about a runway wardrobe. A morning without trying to accomplish some of the chores a five-bedroom, four-bathroom house piled up before heading off to open the downtown store. A morning without having to cajole a zombie-eyed teenager out of bed, out of his room, out the front door with his backpack, his homework, his sports bag.

Did he have enough gas to get to school?

Lunch money?

Anything close to qualifying as "breakfast" in his stomach?

With a sneer, Tracy watched the other woman stretch out on the lounger. Yeah, wouldn't that be the life? she thought.

And then realized it *could* be her life.

The store was running along fine without her. The zombie teenager was a college student living on his own. Most of the five bedrooms and four bathrooms at 631 Walnut went unused. Unneeded.

Like herself?

Brushing away the paralyzing thought, she turned from the pool and scanned the nearby doors. Dan had given her his condominium number when he'd first moved out. She'd never thought of needing to know it.

She'd never forgotten it either.

Determining it to be in the next building, she set forward on heavy legs, nodding as she encountered other people along the path. Ignoring their curious glances.

What, didn't she make the height requirement for all the fun rides here in DivorceLand?

Up ahead, a door on the ground floor opened. A man slipped out, the back of his hair in a pillow-mussed disarray. She watched as he spoke to the lush-bodied, dark-haired woman who stood on the other side of the threshold, holding a short apricot-colored robe closed at the throat.

It looked as if these two had just taken their turn on the Sex-o-Coaster.

The man, wearing long, silky basketball shorts, T-shirt, and flip-flops, turned to leave.

Tracy gasped.

Dan's head whipped her way. Their gazes met.

What had the woman at the campground said?

I never trust a single one of them.

He shoved a hand through his already messy hair. Bedhead hair. "Trace." He hurried toward her and she found herself frozen, staring at his tan, muscular legs, seeing him swimming laps in that pool. Visualizing him pulling himself up and over the side to lie wet and gorgeous on the lounger beside that woman and her magazine.

Or *that* woman in her apricot robe.

"What are you doing here?" Dan said. "Has something happened? Is someone hurt?"

She shifted her gaze to his face. Concerned eyes. "What?"

He glanced over his shoulder. "I was fixing Brenda's shower. It wasn't draining. Were you looking for me at my place? Tracy?"

When she didn't answer, he touched her right arm.

She gasped again, in pain this time, and rocketed back.

"What's happened?" His gaze traveled down to her hand. "And why the hell are you carting around a crowbar?"

Her fingers tightened on the heavy metal. Why was she carrying it? Why had she brought it with her? She'd walked past the Volvo without that burning compulsion she'd felt to damage her Kevin's Corvette. But surely she didn't have it to hurt Dan, though thinking of him riding the rails with that . . . that bitch by the door made her want to do something violent.

"Trace?" Dan stepped closer. His fingertips brushed her cheek in a gesture so tender that tears stung her eyes. "What's going on? What's with the crowbar? You can tell me."

She *could* tell him, she realized, as the emotion that had broken free of her locked heart at the campground rose from her leaden feet and heavy legs to fill her chest. He *had* been fixing that woman's shower drain. It was the kind of thing Dan would do. Cheating on her was not.

"Trace?" His voice sounded bewildered and just the tiniest bit scared.

As she'd been when he'd left her. Or the shell that had been she. When Harry had gone to college she'd felt as empty as his bedroom, with only that stony nut of her heart rattling around inside her bones for company. That's how small and hard it had become, over all the years of protecting herself from getting hurt again.

But instead of opening up to Dan she'd closed further in, and lost him in her blindness to his hopes, dreams, and dissatisfactions.

She held the crowbar out to him. "It's evidence," she said. Did he understand it was all who she was? The best, the worst, the pain, the joy, the criminal, the saint? "It's evidence that I have a heart after all. That there's life still in me. That I want to spend the rest of it with you."

That she could bounce.

December 20
The first outdoor electrically lighted Christmas tree on the West Coast was at the Hotel del Coronado in December 1904.

Chapter 20

Finn's cell phone rang at four in the morning. He fumbled to find it on his bedside table, then flipped it open. The GND.

"Is something the matter?" His voice was surly, but damn, *he* was surly. Not only had he been sleeping when thirty minutes ago he'd thought it was impossible, waking up only reminded him of the hell of a mess the Girl Next Door had gotten him into. At that absolute worst time of his life, he realized he was still in love with her. "What do you want?"

"I'm being very naughty. Want to come join me?"

"What?" He held the phone away from his ear

to stare at it. There was a slap-happy—not sultry—note to her voice that told him the kind of naughty she meant wasn't the kind of naughty he wouldn't be able to resist. "No."

"Don't be such a stick in the mud."

"I'm not." But the accusation jabbed a sore spot. Among his other worries, he'd been wondering about his stubborn reluctance to consider altering his career path since losing his eye. Was refusing to resign from the Secret Service a stick-in-the-mud move? The job could never be what it once was for him.

"Come on, Finn." Her voice beguiled. "Look out your window."

Gritting his teeth at his own weakness, he swung his legs off the bed. Striding to the glass overlooking the street, he slipped on his eye patch. Outside, the block was dark, all the residents and the long lines of visitors to the many Christmas displays snugly tucked in their beds with their sugarplum dreams. Where he should be.

"I don't see anything," he said.

"I'll wave. See me now?"

There she was, dressed in pants and a parka, on the lawn across the street. He squinted. "What the hell are you doing?" It looked as if she was replacing the reindeer in a sleigh display with plastic elves from a different decorative setup a few doors away. With the elves at the end of the reins it was a weird, somewhat kinky, effect, until he saw she'd replaced Santa with Rudolph as well.

Or maybe that made it even kinkier.

"GND—"

"You once called me little Miss Perfect and I have to prove to you I'm not."

He sighed, even as he pulled on a pair of jeans and slipped his feet into running shoes. "You're proving you're nuts."

"Christmas does that to me."

When he peered out the window again, he couldn't see her. "Where are you now?"

"Do you know that the Smiths at the end of the block have a life-sized Elvis dressed like Santa on their front porch? Now that's wrong. Just plain wrong."

He let himself out of Gram's house without making any noise. Yesterday he'd thought the best way to deal with his renewed addiction to Bailey was to go cold turkey, yet already he was succumbing to temptation. Another man might have let her gallivant around in the dark, breaking laws of man and nature and holiday, but not Finn, even though he figured he'd regret it.

At the Smiths', he found her on the sidewalk, dragging a buxom Mrs. Claus toward the trashy Elvis.

"He looks lonely," she whispered, and he could feel hyped-up energy radiating off her. "And it turns out she's a fan. She thinks he's much hotter than Mr. C."

Without a word, he wrestled the life-sized Mrs. C away from Bailey, the dummy's sensible red shoes and orthopedic hose bumping his shins. "Christmas really *has* made you nuts."

She gave up Madam Claus with a pout, and trailed him as he returned the figure to her rocking chair beside a faux fire. "I never denied it."

"Yeah, but why? I get that your family runs a Christmas business, but it seems that might make some people more sentimental about the holiday."

"I'm sentimental about *nothing*." She said it with an almost-feral smile, her whole body still humming with that inexplicable force.

Finn picked up the meowing cat twining his ankles and placed it on the soft lap of Santa's wife. "All right. But to what do we owe this manic mood?"

"Celebrating some good news." Her hand waved a dismissal of further explanation as she gazed about the neighborhood, obviously trying to determine what havoc to wreak next. When she headed off again, he followed closely behind, then in stoic silence put to rights the results of each of her little pranks: restoring wooden soldiers moved into I-surrender positions back at parade rest, removing penguins that were piled into a red toy bag and replacing them with the original wrapped gifts, rescuing an innocent ice skater figurine from the clutches of a fake woolly polar bear.

"You're worrying me, GND," he said, yanking an oversized Styrofoam candy cane out of her hand. He didn't like the way she was eyeing it. "What's going on with you?"

"I just have to get this out of my system."

But get *what* out of her system? Shaking his head, he told himself he should leave her to it. Why not go back to bed and recharge his batteries? He was going to need all the energy *he* could get to get over her.

With his warm sheets and his good sense beckoning, he started to cross the street on his way to Gram's. Glancing over his shoulder, he saw Bailey approach a family of peacefully grazing animals that would glow with white lights when the power was on. As he watched, she grabbed one of the unsuspecting beasts and started to—

"Bailey, for God's sake!" he whispered, as loud as he dared.

Frowning at him, she whispered back. "Sheesh. Loosen your tie a little. I think that Secret Service gig has been a bad influence on you."

The insult turned his feet back around. "What the hell's that supposed to mean?"

"Just that you used to be more fun."

This from the woman who was doing something obscene with two of the lighted reindeer. She had repositioned one so that it appeared to be scr— uh, climbing the back of the other.

Dismayed, Finn froze. God, *had* he become a stick in the mud? He was censoring his own thoughts.

Still, he crossed his arms over his chest. "Someone's going to catch you doing this, GND. It's time to stop." And furthermore, it wasn't in character, and neither was the odd, frantic mood she was in.

"What's wrong with you?" Her eyes narrowed. "Don't you take chances anymore?"

"Well, if we're going to indulge in character criticism," he said, shouldering her away to reset the reindeers back to their previous G-rated positions, "can I say that you've turned as brittle as a stick?"

He didn't have time to regret the words. Just then, at the corner, headlights turned into the street. Acting on instinct, he spun around to yank Bailey by the arm and then behind an igloo located to the right of the reindeer. She bumped into it and the damn thing belched with a hollow sound.

"Shhh!"

"That's not me, it's the milk jugs."

His eye on the approaching car, he reached out to inspect their hiding place. She was right. Someone had constructed a bigger-than-life-sized Eskimo domicile out of empty plastic milk containers. All right, maybe she *wasn't* the only one whom Christmas made a little crazy.

The car cruised toward them at a slow speed. "Cop," he said, noting the profile of the vehicle, including the strobe on top and the cowcatcher on the front grille. He pulled Bailey closer to his body and tucked her head against his neck. The scent of her rose around him, and he couldn't stop himself from sucking it in.

"Hey, Finn, if the nasty ol' police person pulls over maybe you can scare him off with your big flashlight." She wiggled her butt against it.

He thought about strangling her. "That's just plain mean to mention," he ground out. "I can't control that."

"Mean is better than a brittle stick."

"Oh hell. So I'm sorry. I'm sorry I hurt your feelings." The car was passing them by. "Now be quiet."

Of course she wouldn't shut up. "I'm sorry too," she whispered. "I don't want to fight with you, Finn. Not now. Not . . . tonight."

He was about to ask about that little hesitation, when the police cruiser braked in the middle of the road.

"Oh, it's only Mr. Baer," she said, relaxing against him. "The Retired Service Patrol guy. You know." The car was pulling into a driveway across the street as they watched.

"That's some late patrolling he does."

"And early too, my mother says. I think he's out at all hours. After his wife died—"

She gasped as the car suddenly leaped toward the closed garage door. Finn tensed, spinning Bailey away to give him a clear sprint toward it. His muscles bunched—

Brakes shrieked. The car halted inches from the metal door, its body rocking on the chassis.

"God! Is he all right?" Now Bailey moved, but Finn held her back.

"Look, look, he's moving. He's okay. Just mistook the gas for the brake, I'd bet."

"Maybe we should check on him." She craned her head around the igloo.

"No. Leave him with his dignity. Plus we don't want him to know we're out here, remember?"

"You already put everything back the way it was," she grumbled. "And you called me a wet blanket."

He tousled her hair. "Let's not call each other anything."

She stepped close enough to rub her chin against his chest. "Does that mean we're kissing and making up?"

Now her voice had that sultry note he didn't want to resist. But he should, damn it.

His hands circled her waist. "Only if you'll tell me why you felt the sudden need to—"

"Be naughty?" she whispered.

He couldn't look away from her mouth. "Bailey . . ."

"I'm in a good mood."

"Yeah? Why is that?"

She rose on tiptoe to breathe into his ear. "Remember what you said? About wanting to get naked with me in my shower? Let's do it. Let's do it right now."

His spine jerked straight at the thought. He cleared his throat. "Your mother—"

"Isn't at the house. It's empty. Unless you and I—"

"Fill it up." He slid his hands under her butt and boosted her high. She put her legs around his waist. What man could keep cold turkey on his mind when he had the chance at warm water and slippery soap?

And Bailey. "I'm going to fill *you* up," he promised.

He'd never been allowed in her bedroom, though he'd probably frittered away more than half his teenage years imagining it, imagining *her*, pulling down the shades, pulling down her pants, pulling him to her with just one wanton look as she toyed with the clasp of her bra.

Of course Bailey had never been wanton.

Before.

Now, now the skin along his spine prickled as she shut the bedroom door behind them both. Then she turned, her soft, tender mouth curving as she toed out of her shoes and shimmied out of her jeans. She'd dumped her short parka at the bottom of the stairs, so now she stood before him in nothing more than a thin T-shirt and a teeny pair of panties.

"The bathroom's this way," she said, pointing to another doorway at the end of the room. Then she padded off in that direction.

He stayed where he was, frozen. The ruffles, the rumpled sheets, the confident sway of her hips shooting the needle high on his personal Lust-o-Meter. She paused in the bathroom doorway and looked at him over her shoulder.

Smiled like a witch.

Crossing her hands in front of her, she drew the T-shirt off, then let it fall to the floor. Naked shoulders. The tiny back vee of satin panties. The peach curves of her ass. No bra.

Then another graceful move.

Now no underwear at all. Just Bailey, tousled blond hair to bare bottom to bare heels. Pink and white and that ripe peach, right in the center.

Her eyes gleamed like blue jewels as she gave him another look over her shoulder and decamped.

The disappearance got him moving. He couldn't lose her so soon.

The tiled bathroom was already turning steamy once he made it inside. For a few minutes he stood, transfixed by the sight of Bailey under the spray, her body blurred by the bubble glass of the shower door.

That odd pitching movement started up in his

chest again—like that night in The Perfect Christmas—and he held his palm there to calm the movement. To calm him.

The shower door clicked open. A flushed face peered out. He saw one rosy breast. A wet knee.

"What's a girl gotta do to get a man?"

This man was already hers. Still, he went slow. Slow removing his clothes, slow to cross to the shower, slow to open the door and climb in.

Slow to touch her with his hands, even as all her wet flesh pressed against his like a full-body French kiss. He bent his head to meet her mouth, but she stopped him with a hand to his cheek.

"Can your eye patch get wet?"

He caught her fingers and kissed her palm, tasting the water on her skin. "It doesn't matter."

Her fingers went back to toy with the elastic strap. "It doesn't matter to me either."

"There's nothing to see," he said. "It's not ugly, it's not anything. It just looks as if my eye is closed."

"Then let me touch you everywhere," she said. "With nothing to hide behind."

When still he hesitated, she whispered the most sultry thing of all. "Trust me."

So he let her draw the patch away even though he had so few secrets left from her. Her face betrayed nothing of her thoughts as she gently traced the few scars that showed on the outside. At the touch, he felt the old sharp ache in his bones, a phantom pain that would show up at times of stress. He tried breathing through it, but then lost his breath altogether as she went on tiptoe to press kisses to his usually protected flesh.

"Oh, Finn," she whispered against the missing part of him. "How much you scare me sometimes."

He groaned, his palms cupping her warm shoulders. "Bailey . . ."

"Shhh." She ran her lips down the side of his face to his jaw. Her mouth sipped at the moisture on his neck, his collarbone. She found his nipple and tickled it with her hot little tongue.

Leaning against the tiled wall, he groaned again and refused to let his eye drift closed as it wanted to. He had to feel her *and* see her, searing the image of her going down on her knees in his mind for all time.

Her hands were slick with water. She stroked him, cupped him, ran her fingertip around the pulsing head of his cock. Then she circled him with one slow lap of her flattened tongue.

He pressed his hips against the tile, then forced his left palm against it too, only allowing his right hand to tangle in the wet disarray of her hair.

Her gaze lifted as she licked him like a lollipop. "I always wanted to do this."

Christ! What was he supposed to say to that?

I always wanted you to do this. I stayed awake during years of math, English, and social studies classes, dreaming of you doing this.

Her tongue slid back down his steely flesh. "Do you mind?"

Her little cat smile told him she already knew the answer. Still, he tried to sound casual about it instead of ready to beg. "I've always tried to be neighborly."

It must have been the permission she was waiting for, because she bent over him and drew his cock into the wet heat of her mouth. His breath sucked in, his eye flared wide, he thought he could die happy.

Even happier, as she teased him with her mouth, setting his blood on fire and his pulse beating against his skin. His head clunked back against the tile and he stroked her hair as he watched the water sluice down her naked back and his flesh disappear between her pretty lips.

Then it was all too much. As his balls yanked tight to his body, he yanked her to her feet. "No more," he said harshly.

"But—"

He half dragged, half carried her from the shower. Laughing, she snagged a towel and managed to throw it down on the bed before he tumbled her there. She tried scrambling to a different position, but it only inflamed him more.

He had to have her now.

With his hands on her hips, he flipped her over. She stilled.

No longer laughing.

No longer a saucy flirt with the upper hand.

"Get on your knees," he whispered, his voice rough. They'd never made love like this. Teenage Finn would never have dared. He came behind her as she slowly moved higher and then he slid his knees between hers to widen them. His palm slipped from her hip to spread across her belly, his pinkie finding the slick wetness that wasn't from the shower.

"Finn?" She glanced over her shoulder, her wet bangs in a tangle over her eyes, her mouth swollen. Her voice . . . unsure?

"All grown up now," he said. He fit himself to her body, key to lock. Pushed inside as she jerked back against him, her pretty ass snug to his groin. "All grown up."

Then he rocked, and the hand that held her tight against his body took in the rippling movement of his invasion and her surrender. Of them becoming one. She arched her back and he kissed the place where her wings would meet if she was truly not of this world.

And didn't just feel like heaven.

His mouth went dry as she moaned and pushed back against him, harder. He surged deep, holding there, as his pinkie played over her clitoris. She jerked back again, arched again, and he pressed his mouth to her damp spine as they both came. Adult to adult. Lover to lover. Angel to man.

Afterward, Finn thanked God he hadn't held on to his idea to go cold turkey. But he couldn't say anything to Bailey. Not yet. His throat was too tight, his chest too heavy, his head overflowing with memories of how it had been with them this time. So he cupped his body around hers and pulled the covers over them both, burying his nose in the drying hair at the nape of her neck.

He had no idea what she thought about. If she dozed.

If she dreamed.

But as dawn filled the room, casting pink light across her bare arm, he knew she was awake. Her skin goose bumped as he drew his forefinger from her shoulder to her elbow. He sensed the tension in her body.

"Bailey?"

She stiffened. "What?" As if afraid of what he might ask next.

Leaving him with only one question he could speak aloud.

"French toast?"

Gram's kitchen was quiet, and so was Bailey as she watched him make coffee and then turn to the refrigerator for eggs and milk. He'd taken her there knowing it was stocked with all the necessary ingredients.

"You don't really cook," she said.

"All grown up." He shot her a look, noticing the new color flushing her cheeks. So she hadn't forgotten that moment, or the new connection they'd forged. It satisfied him for now, just knowing she couldn't pretend—he'd given up on it, of course—that they were merely two people waxing nostalgic.

This wasn't scratching an old itch.

This was stroking new skin, caressing a brandnew version of a first love.

It was more than they'd ever had before.

All grown up.

She cleared her throat. "Finn, I think we should . . ."

Her voice trailed off as Gram walked into the kitchen. She stopped short in the doorway, a smile breaking over her pale mouth. None of her bright lipstick today. "Bailey."

The GND popped up from the table. "Mrs. Jacobson!" She rushed around the chairs to embrace the older woman in a gentle hug, as if afraid Gram might break.

Finn frowned. Bailey had a funny expression on her face as his grandmother lifted a thin hand and stroked her blond hair. "I enjoy hearing your voice in this kitchen," Gram said. "What a treat."

Bailey cleared her throat again as the two women moved apart. Then she held out a chair for Gram. "Let me bring you some coffee."

Gram smiled again. "Spoiling me like Finn."

The GND turned away and he saw her knuckle away a tear from under her eye. His frown deepened and he glanced over at his grandmother. She didn't look so bad . . . did she?

But his gut clenched as he saw her through different eyes. When had she become so shrunken? When had the shadows beneath her eyes become so dark?

He hurried forward with her plastic container of pills and a glass of water. Then he stepped back, almost plowing into Bailey. She put a hand on his back, gave him an absent pat.

He felt it to his heart.

She slid a mug in front of Gram and sat down beside her. "He says he can do breakfast," she said. "What are the odds?"

Gram's gaze flicked from his face, then back to Bailey's. Her smile went secretive as she picked up the hot coffee. "Take me to Vegas right now. I'm feeling lucky."

The women chatted. Finn moved about the kitchen, then suddenly stopped, an egg in one hand and his coffee in the other. *I'm smiling at nothing*, he thought. *I haven't felt so relaxed in months.*

Still smiling, he tuned back in to what the women were discussing.

"Actually," Bailey said, "my mom and Dan are doing well. Better than well." Her laugh tinkled like glass breaking.

The sound sliced down Finn's spine. His sixth sense stirred. He turned.

She was looking into her cup of coffee. "They're back together. It's official. As a matter of fact, they'll be opening the store this morning."

Her eyes lifted to Finn's face. "That was my good news. What I felt like celebrating about." Her gaze jolted back to her mug. "I'm going back to L.A."

Finn's hand tightened, cracking the egg he held, mirroring what his suddenly coiling emotions were doing to that poor battered organ in the middle of his chest.

Trust me, she'd said in the shower, and he had. Dumb sap. Because there was nothing new in the fact that she was going to be leaving him. Again.

Here came the get-ugly part.

The night before, when her mother had finally called to tell Bailey where she was and why she wasn't coming home, Tracy had urged her to take the next day off. Yet at midmorning, Bailey still found herself at The Perfect Christmas anyway. Because she wanted to make sure her mother and stepfather were *really* together, she told herself.

Not because she missed the store already.

Not because she had to get away from Finn, so close by next door.

God, and Mrs. Jacobson! Finn had said she'd been sick, but her frailty turned Bailey's stomach inside out. Just another thing to run from . . . and now she could.

The bells jingled their familiar tune as she pushed open the door. It wasn't quite opening time, but on the hospitality table, the cookies and chocolates she'd ordered last week sat on the holiday platter in perfect circles. The coffee urn beside them gleamed. A rich java smell mingled with the store's distinctive scent.

She saw her mother unpacking a box and hanging an ornament on the tree by the register. "Mom!" She hurried over. "I think that one looks better with all natural ornaments. Just the shells and coral and such."

Tracy looked down at the glass figurine in her hand. "No Little Mermaid?"

"Oh! Well." Embarrassed, Bailey stepped back. "Of course you can do it however you want."

"There she is!" From the back room, Dan strode out, a happy grin on his face. His gaze met Tracy's, and Bailey swallowed, watching them exchange a secret communication. She remembered it from the past.

Then Dan swept her up in a strong embrace. She clung, even aware that she was doing it. But couldn't she be happy for them? Her cheek pressed against his shoulder, hard. *Shouldn't* she be happy for them?

Dan's arms didn't let go. "There, there," he said, as if she were eight years old and had fallen off her bicycle. His palm stroked the back of her head, as Mrs. Jacobson's had done in her kitchen. Bailey blinked away a tear.

Silly me. Nothing hurt here.

She broke away, and smiled as wide as the empty place in her chest. "It's great to see you guys back at the helm."

Her mother and Dan telegraphed another quick thought. Indecipherable to Bailey. "We're glad to be here together," Tracy said. Her hand reached out and Dan clasped it, that goofy grin back on his face.

"We'll always be together," he said.

Good luck with that, Bailey thought, another stupid tear welling.

She cleared her throat. "Can I do something? I know you said to take the day off . . ."

Tracy's gaze cut to Dan's, then back to her face. "Well . . ."

"Or if you don't need me, I was thinking about heading home."

Tracy stilled. "Home to . . . to Walnut Street?"

"No." She shook her head. "*Home* home. L.A."

An awkward silence welled.

Dan rubbed his hand over his gray-less head. "Here's the thing, Bay—"

"Harry will be home day after tomorrow," Tracy interjected. "Can't you stay through the holiday? We're only open until noon on Christmas Eve."

Bailey frowned. "You're going to be closing at

noon? The Christmas Eve afternoon hours are primo time, Mom. All those people on the way to holiday dinners making a quick stop for the perfect hostess gift—which means the quick hostess gift. I was planning to put the most expensive stuff at the front of the store and also right beside the register. Christmas Eve shoppers are desperate."

"Noon on Christmas Eve," Dan said, his voice firm. "We're going to start doing things differently."

She shrugged. "Okay. It's your store."

"That's what we wanted to talk about on Christmas Eve afternoon," Tracy said, the words rushing out. "The store. I mean, that it's ours."

Bailey frowned. "Well, it is."

"We might as well tell you we're thinking of making some changes in our life," Dan said, his gaze gentle on Tracy's face.

Her mother swallowed, hard, her eyes unwavering as they met Bailey's. "And we want to give The Perfect Christmas to you."

December 21

In Mexico, the Christmas season includes the tradition of the *posadas*. People travel to one another's homes, reenacting Mary and Joseph's search for lodging, with some taking on the roles of mean innkeepers and others the Holy Family. What follows is food, fun, piñatas, and fireworks.

Chapter 21

"Of course I told them no." Bailey rocked from one foot to the other while Adam Truehouse, ragdoll-asleep, drooled on her neck.

Trin continued fanning cocktail napkins across the surface of her dining room table. "So what are they going to do with the store?"

Bailey shrugged. "Sell it, they say. They want to do some traveling, explore other options."

Trin swung around, her eyes widening. "What

if the new owner doesn't want to keep it The Perfect Christmas?"

Adam's little red velvet shoes had come from the store. Bailey ran her finger over the soft fabric. "Then it becomes The Horrid Halloween or The Excellent Easter or even The Freakin' Fourth of July," she said, her voice matter-of-fact.

"But it's—"

"An institution, I know."

Trin frowned. "I was going to say landmark."

Albatross. "Whatever." She wasn't going to feel bad about the loss of the family store. After all, she'd done her very best, hadn't she? She'd kept it going these past weeks so there *would* be something to sell to someone else.

"I bought Adam's first Christmas ornament there," Trin said. "This year's ornament too. He picked out that cute little jointed panda bear, remember?"

"No." It wore a green-and-white striped cap and carried an even tinier teddy bear. She looked up, straight into her best friend's annoyed glare.

"Bailey—"

"Give me a break, Trin. I don't like Christmas. I don't like the store." Though she'd given in to pressure once again and agreed to stay until the morning of the twenty-fifth. Her mother wanted her to have Christmas Eve dinner with the family and there was her half brother Harry to consider too. He'd be back home and eager to tell all of them about his college experience.

Trin stalked toward the kitchen. "The whole town will be upset about the store changing hands . . . if it even stays a store at all. Word gets around fast, you know. I bet some people at the party tonight will already have heard about it."

Wincing, Bailey followed. She'd hoped to be hours away before that news hit Coronado. Mrs. Mohn might come after her with a bedpan. "Surely not. I don't think my mom and Dan will say anything right away."

"What about Finn?"

"What about him?" Bailey inspected the trays of cookies lined up on the counter. She wasn't going to feel bad about that either. Both of them had gone into their fling eyes-open. That it was ending now . . . it was nothing more than they'd both expected.

Of course yesterday morning in her bed . . . She'd wanted a memorable last time with him, but it had been like nothing she'd expected or ever before experienced. His heart had beat like a drum against her back; it had been like her heartbeat. Their heartbeat.

"Is Finn going to let you run away again?"

"You mean is Finn going to wave good-bye as I head home like I intended from the day I drove back into town?" She recalled the cool expression on his face when she'd dropped that little bit of info in his grandmother's kitchen. "I think he will."

"Well I'll just ask him," Trin said, as she peeled plastic wrap off a plate of fancy-cut sandwiches.

Bailey clutched Adam tighter to her chest, so that he made a sleepy bleat of protest. "Did you . . . did you invite Finn here tonight?" She'd managed to avoid him since the French toast the day before. Maybe he was ducking her too, but because she'd spent all her time at the store today, even coming straight to Trin's without a stop on Walnut Street first, she didn't know.

"Yup."

Bailey pasted on a calm, upbeat smile. Why not? She *was* calm. Upbeat. Her trip to her childhood home couldn't have ended any better.

She should be feeling on top of the world.

It was closing in on midnight and Trin and Drew's party was winding down. Telling herself her lowering spirits were just postparty letdown, Bailey volunteered for leftovers duty and busied herself in the kitchen. In a lower cabinet, she found two shelves full of jumbled plastic containers.

She looked up as Trin's footsteps clacked on the tile floor. "I know we're all grown up when I see you have a full complement of Tupperware. But something tells me this isn't one of the areas you've baby-proofed."

Trin didn't laugh. Bailey didn't either, as three words echoed in her head. She stared back down at the disorganized plasticware, so different than the by-size and by-color stacks in her own cupboard in L.A. *All grown up.* Finn had whispered that in her ear. Finn, who had never showed up at the party.

"Bay . . ."

Her gaze shifted back to Trin. The Christmas cheer was gone from her best friend too.

Bailey stood so quickly, her head spun. She shot out a hand to catch the lip of the counter and steady herself. "What's the matter? What's wrong?"

"You know how news travels fast around here."

"Sure." Seventy-five hundred households. Seven point four square miles. Nosy. Cozy.

"Somebody just heard from their babysitter who heard from her mother who heard from another friend . . ." Trin glanced over her shoulder, then grimaced. "I know why Finn didn't come tonight."

Foreboding trickled like a tear down Bailey's spine. "Why?"

"His grandmother's been terminally ill for months and this morning . . . this morning she passed on."

Bailey's face must have been so blank that Trin felt the need to be even clearer. "Bay, Mrs. Jacobson died."

┌୨୨୨୨୨୨୨୨୨୨୨୨୨୨୨୨୨୨୨୨୨୨
Bailey Sullivan's Vintage Christmas
Facts & Fun Calendar

December 22
The Yule log goes back to pagan times. A special log
was cut and burned during the winter festival to ward
off evil and to bring safety to the home and its inhabi-
tants for the coming year.

Chapter 22

Bailey drove directly to Hart's. It was the
same as the first time, sticky floor, loud
music, muscled, clean-cut young men
and the much-smaller number of decorative females. As the door closed behind her, from
somewhere by the pool tables a male voice yelled
out "Hooyah!" and three other guys beat their
chests in response.

Neither the hooyah-er nor any of the chest beat-
ers was Finn.

"He's not here," Tanner said, suddenly appear-
ing by her side, causing an approaching young

man with a prominent Adam's apple and a full bottle of lite beer to veer off.

"You heard . . . ?"

He nodded. "He called this morning. After breakfast, Mrs. Jacobson decided to take her usual rest. When he went to check up on her an hour or so later, she'd died in her sleep. All things considered . . ."

Bailey swallowed the lump in her throat as she thought of the lady who had been her next-door neighbor all her life. They'd shared French toast the morning before. And a hug. She was glad for that last moment even though she hadn't know it was good-bye.

She'd always been lousy with those anyway.

Her throat felt thick and she swallowed again. "You said Finn called you?" He hadn't contacted Bailey. Even if he didn't know her cell phone number, he could have reached her through the store.

"Yeah."

"But he hasn't been by tonight? I tried calling the house and no one answered. I figured he was here."

"Oh, he wouldn't come here." Tanner shook his movie-star hair.

Bailey frowned. "Why not?"

"He knows that I wouldn't serve him any liquor unless he'd talk first."

"Well surely that's good, the talking, I mean," Bailey said. "He's got to be feeling—"

"That's the whole problem, Bailey," Tanner put in. "That's *Finn's* whole problem. He doesn't want to be feeling anything at all."

She didn't waste any more time in the bar. On the sidewalk outside, she hesitated a moment, thinking through her options. Finding Finn wasn't the issue—that had to be done. But where to look first?

"You're Finn's friend," a voice from the shadows said.

Bailey jumped, then swung toward the stranger stepping into the light over the bar's door. The young woman had long, straight dark hair, exotic eyes, and coltish legs in tight, bleached jeans.

She held out her hand and gave a winsome smile. "I'm Desirée."

Ah. Desirée, sometimes referred to as Desirée al-Maddah, sometimes Desirée Bryant, depending upon whether the press was describing the celebutante as the daughter of her Middle Eastern prince of a father or as the daughter of her famous model mom. Bailey shook her cool hand. "I'm Bailey Sullivan. I recognize you from the, uh, kiss."

The younger woman grimaced. "Don't mention it to Tanner, will you? And don't tell Troy you've seen me here, okay?"

Which reminded Bailey she had yet to see Finn

and he shouldn't be alone. "It's nice meeting you, but I have to go now."

"You heard about Mrs. Jacobson?"

"Yes." Bailey hesitated. "By any chance, you wouldn't happen to know where Finn is, would you?"

"Well, I—"

The bar door swung open. A male voice growled through the night air. "What the hell are you doing here again? Haven't I already told you to get lost?"

Desirée flinched, then lifted her chin to face the behemoth who stomped outside to confront her. "It's a free country, Troy."

"I thought I ordered you to stop hanging around the bar when you showed up here the other day." He crossed his arms over his chest, looking half genie and mostly scary with his bulging biceps and shaved head.

Bailey frowned. Troy appeared angry and Desirée defiant, but there was something else buzzing beneath the surface of their conversation. Something hot and—

"We don't want you here," Troy stated.

Apparently unwelcome.

"*I* don't want you here," he clarified.

Very unwelcome.

Desirée blinked, swallowed, and despite her mulish expression, Bailey had the distinct feeling she just might cry.

To preserve the younger woman's dignity, Bailey slid her hand through her elbow. "We're on our way," she said, guiding them both toward the parking lot.

Desirée looked back, just as the bar's door slammed shut. Bailey felt her flinch again. Then she slipped free of Bailey's arm to wrap her arms around herself in a sad self-hug.

"Thanks," she said, her winsome smile now turned wry. "I thought it was bad when Tanner was mad at me, but then I met Troy and . . . I don't know why I let him get to me. Especially when he doesn't bother trying to soft-pedal the way he feels."

Bailey lifted a shoulder. "Sometimes you don't have any choice."

"Yeah." Then she reached out and touched the top of Bailey's hand. "And speaking of men with chips on their shoulders, I saw Finn's SUV parked at the north end of the beach."

Bailey stopped her Passat behind Finn's big, black car. It was a no-moon night, and with her headlights off the darkness wrapped around her like a blanket. A safe blanket.

She could go home.

No. She couldn't leave him out here alone.

At Trin's, she'd changed out of her work clothes, and she realized she should have changed back, because her high-heeled sandals were impractical sand gear. She slipped them off as she reached the beach and let them dangle in one hand, shoving her other inside her jacket pocket to grip her cell phone.

The sand was slippery cold against the soles of her feet. Her toes curled into it as she gazed up and down the beach. The only clear thing she could see was the white froth of the incessant waves.

There! she thought, squinting. There was movement.

A spark pierced the darkness and then kindled into a small fire a quarter mile down the beach. Still gripping her cell phone in case it wasn't the man she was looking for, she headed for it. As she drew closer, she noticed the pallets and other shadowy pieces of wood piled nearby, enough to keep the darkness at bay all night long.

When she neared, Finn didn't look away from the fire he'd started in the cement circle. He was sitting beside it, a flask in his hand. As he lifted it to take a drink, the light of the flames flickered yellow and red against its silver surface, a bright contrast to his black eye patch, the dark night, the murky ocean with its ever-changing frothy skirt of white sweeping back and forth, back and forth, across the wet sand.

Bailey's shoes dropped from her suddenly sweaty hands. She followed them down to the sand, leaving that ring of fire between her and Finn. She filled her chest with a long breath of the cool air, tasting the salt on her tongue and wishing it was words instead.

When she'd thought about finding him, she'd never thought about what she would say once she did.

Comfort, she told herself. She was here to offer sympathy, provide support, be his friend.

Somehow make the loss easier for him.

Flames glinted against the flask again as he brought it to his mouth for another swallow. "Go away."

She jerked at the sudden sound of his hard voice, and flashed back to poor Desirée and her reaction to Troy's rejection. But it wasn't the same at all, she thought. The sexual, romantic part of her relationship with Finn wasn't unrequited, it was O-V-E-R.

So she dug her butt into the shifting sand and refused to be scared away.

Finn said nothing more. Through the flames she saw him reach out to the pile of fuel and grab another piece. He tossed the length of wood into the blaze. It had twigs and leaves attached, and as they caught, they crackled with the sound of candy wrappers, then smoked like a wizard's spell.

But not the kind of alchemy that worked magic. Finn remained silent. She didn't know what to say herself.

Maybe companionship was enough.

"Go home, Bailey."

He thought he didn't even want companionship, then. But she was stubborn too. "I'm fine. The fire is keeping me warm."

More minutes of brooding silence followed. He drank. She waited. Then he picked up another length of wood and fed it to the leaping flames. Took another swallow. Added more wood to the fire.

Finally Bailey couldn't take the tension. "She was a wonderful woman," she offered. "I'm sorry I didn't know she was so ill."

He hesitated, flask in his right hand, wood in the other. Then his left arm dropped, the piece of fuel slamming into the fire.

Sparks exploded, and Bailey flinched, but kept on talking anyway. "You didn't say a word about that, Finn." It was the first thing that had struck her when Trin told her the news. "You insisted she was going to get well. Didn't you know—"

"I know what the doctors said." He hurled a second piece of wood into the blaze. Embers sprang high, as if trying to escape.

"Then why—"

"Because I didn't want to think about it, all right?" He swigged from the flask, wiped his mouth with the back of his hand. "I didn't want to talk about it."

"Or believe it?"

Another piece of wood crashed into the fire.

Silver turned red as he brought the drink to his lips again.

She dug her fingers into the sand, though the unstable stuff offered nothing solid to hang on to. "It's no crime to grieve, Finn. Grief is normal, natural—"

"Oh, I'm done with grief." His voice was more caustic than the acrid smell of smoke in the air. "I've been living with it grinding my guts into sausage meat since I woke up in the hospital and found out that Ayesha was dead eleven months ago."

He tilted his head back and sipped again from the flask. "There's nothing left inside of me for it to chew on."

The wind off the ocean fluttered the ends of Bailey's hair. "Then you don't need to be out here all alone. Let's go back to my house . . . or to the bar. Tanner's there."

"I can't deal with Tanner's guilt tonight too."

Oh, Finn. "Your grandmother wouldn't want you to feel guilty. You know that. You know you didn't have the power to stop what happened to her."

"But then there's Ayesha." He tossed another piece of wood into the crackling blaze even as he took another drink. "You can't say I didn't fail her."

Confused, Bailey shook her head. "What could you have done about that either?"

"I was her supervisor." He stared at his reflection in the surface of the flask. "I should have seen something. Sensed something."

She lifted her hand, sand sifting between her fingers. "You couldn't have known about that assassin. You can't read some murderer's mind who shows up out of nowhere."

"Oh, baby, you've got it all wrong." He shifted his gaze from the booze to spear a long, thin stick into the middle of the blaze and watch it light up.

It looked like an accusing finger, she thought, and Finn had pointed it toward himself.

"You're right that I couldn't know the assassin was going to pick that target, that day, that time," he continued. "But I knew Ayesha. And I should have suspected what she might do."

"Her job." Bailey heard the sharp edge in her voice. "You said she did her job."

"Yeah." The stick was burning now like a tongue of flame. "But the problem is, see, I don't know that her actions were dictated by the mission. There were other ways for it to play out that day which didn't involve her standing up for that bullet. I wonder . . . was she thinking of me? Was she trying to impress me? Save me? I don't know. But I should have seen, I should have sensed in those days and weeks before, that she wasn't operating in pure agent mode. I should have worried about how far she would go for love."

The smoke was stinging Bailey's eyes. Blinking

them away, she had to clear her throat too. "How could you look into someone else's heart?"

"Easy." His laugh sounded short and rough, and then he took a long draw from the flask. "I only had to look as far as my own. I was the same for you, Bailey, once upon a time. I would have done anything for you—hell, I did. I cleaned up my act, went to college, joined the Secret Service as my way of impressing you. A bullet? I would have taken that too."

"I . . . I don't know what to say." She didn't want to think about all she'd lost by running away.

"Good-bye will work." He was staring down at the booze again. "Oh, that's right, you tend to duck those."

It stung, but this time she wasn't leaving, even though the smoke was making her chest feel tight now too. "That's not fair. I came here tonight, didn't I? I came to talk to you about how you feel. I came here to . . . to be your friend."

There was a charged moment of silence. Then he shot to his feet. Bailey twitched at his sudden movement, staring at him and how the light of the flames on his jeans and black sweatshirt made it appear as if he'd caught fire himself.

"My friend?" he repeated, his tone incredulous as he stared at her through the leaping blaze. "You call yourself my friend? You want to know how I *feel*?"

"Well, I . . . yeah."

He threw back his head and laughed, a dark sound that made her think of pirates again. Or devils. "Be careful what you wish for, baby."

Though it was clear that the alcohol, or his emotions, probably both, had caught up with him, Bailey needed to see this through. "I can take it."

"Then how about this." He snagged another piece of thick wood and threw it into the blaze. More sparks exploded, flying upward. "I feel torn to pieces over Ayesha. I feel pissed off that I lost my eye and my ability to do the job I love."

More fuel was dumped on the fire, and pieces of ash swirled around him. "I hate that I couldn't stop a disease that was leaching the life from Gram."

Turning, he dropped his flask to the sand, then bent at the waist to pull something from the hodge-podge of wood beside him. When he straightened again, she could see it was a full-sized Christmas tree—but an old one, its needles dried to a rusty brown. "I'm damn depressed that it's the holidays and I can't think of a single thing worth celebrating." With one strong movement, he lifted the tree over the concrete ring and jammed its trunk into the sand and into the center of the leaping fire.

As the needles burst into flame, crackling and popping, their corner of the beach turned bright as day. The heat forced Bailey to scoot back.

But not far enough to miss Finn's next words, harsher and more biting than all the others. "And at the top of my list, I feel like letting you know you're not my friend. Friends are people I trust. And you just don't qualify."

She was on her feet, backing away from the burn, but he still seared her.

"You, Bailey, you are nothing to me."

December 23
Guidelines from a department store Santa Claus training school include admonishing Santa not to leave his
chair even if a child has an "accident" and to always
keep gloves and beard scrupulously clean. They further
advise that it never looks quite right for Santa to flirt
with the elves.

Chapter 23

Finn saw in another dawn. Three days
ago it had been in Bailey's bed, yesterday
on the beach, today he sat on the wicker
chair in the corner of Gram's small porch.
With his boots propped on the railing, he sipped
another of the endless cups of coffee he'd been
mainlining since dumping the last of his flask
into the sand after running Bailey off.

Bingeing on booze no longer appealed—and he
hoped was no longer necessary.

He took another swallow from his mug and

paged through Desirée's—aka the Mad Gift Giver's—latest present. The poor little rich girl continued to come up with outrageous ways to assuage her guilt in the whole assassination debacle and to thank him for saving her father's life— even though that father had little use and even less time for her.

Sort of like someone else he knew.

But he pushed that thought from his mind and turned another page, his gaze widening at the latest position detailed in the Kama Sutra pop-up book that had been left on the doorstep. A note in Desirée's own handwriting guaranteed it was a one-of-a-kind faithful rendering of the ancient text on sexual behavior. "May it inspire you to great lengths for love," she'd written in that perfect, boarding school handwriting of hers. He wasn't sure she even realized the double-entendre.

And love wasn't something he wanted to be thinking about either.

Despite himself, he glanced over at the house next door. Bailey's Passat was still on the street. He couldn't wait until she left town.

Then he could hunker down to make it through Christmas. Gram had specifically prohibited a funeral or memorial service, so his parents had encouraged him to head out to the Midwest to be with the rest of the family, including his new nephew, but he'd taken a pass. He didn't plan on wallowing his way through the holiday so much as it didn't feel right to leave Gram's home empty right now.

Gram. Somehow, her memory didn't hurt. That last morning, his sixth sense had failed him again. He'd had no clue that she'd pass on peacefully in her sleep, but he could accept that now. They'd had plenty of time to talk about her wishes and her attitude toward the end of life. More important, he could hear her telling him as clearly as if she were sitting beside him right now, over seventeen years she'd shared with him how to live it.

A car clattered its way around the turn at the end of the block. Finn placed his feet on the ground and craned his neck to see what was happening as the junker came to a stop behind Bailey's car.

The passenger door popped open, and a young man unfolded from the seat. Then he ducked back in to pull out a backpack, two roly-poly duffels, and a shopping bag of wrapped gifts that he propped against the pole of the ribbon-bedecked mailbox. One more reach inside, and he drew out an extra-long sleeping bag that appeared to be stuffed from mummy toes to cinched neck with— Finn squinted as items spilled from a rip in the side—clothes. Having once been a college student himself, Finn hazarded a guess they were *dirty* clothes.

The boy grinned at the driver and waved a

good-bye. Harry, Finn thought, home at last.

It was like that Christmas coffee commercial, when Peter arrives in the early A.M. to surprise sister and sleeping parents. But this prodigal son didn't make it so far as the kitchen. Instead, suddenly the Christmas lights blazed on next door, and Tracy, Dan, and Bailey poured out of the front door and onto their porch.

Finn drew deeper into his corner so they wouldn't see him, but he watched the reunion. Dan grabbed his son first, clapping him on the back, the sound loud enough to wake the neighborhood. Tracy got him next. Harry swung his mother up, and she hugged him close with one arm around his shoulders. Her other arm curled out to her husband, inviting him into the embrace. What followed was a Willis family huddle.

With Bailey smiling from several steps away.

Finn couldn't force his gaze off her. She looked rumpled and like the teenager he'd first fallen for in her flannel PJ bottoms and little T-shirt. The Christmas lights lent her blond hair some punky red, green, and blue highlights as she absently reached over to the wreath on the front door and straightened it to an even greater degree of perfection.

The woman who had saved the day at her family's store, the woman who had decorated the family's house despite her avowed aversion to Christmas, stood alone, outside the circle.

Get out before things get ugly.

Bailey, always withdrawing before she got too close.

Before anything could hurt too much.

That fissure in his soul began to bubble again.

Shit. Rubbing his chest, he squeezed shut his eye and felt that familiar ache in his facial bones. And here he'd thought the beach bonfire had purged all the pain out of him. He was sure after spilling all to Bailey that night that his emotions had finally been scraped clean.

Anger, guilt, frustration, sadness consumed in the flames. It had been a hell of a way to release the coil of emotions that had put him in knots for months, but he'd thought that with Gram's death and the subsequent confession time on the beach, it was all, finally, gone.

That he was free. And back in cool, utter control.

But now he realized he was still under the influence of one final emotion he didn't want to feel—love.

That night by the fire, he'd thought he'd told her the truth. *You, Bailey, you are nothing to me*, he'd said. And in his anger and hurt, he'd been desperate for that to be right.

He opened his eye, his gaze zeroing in on Bailey. Still standing alone. As Dan and Tracy chattered to Harry, she moved into the deeper shadows of the porch.

Just as Finn had hoped to hide how he felt about her.

But it wasn't going to work, was it?

Gram's voice sounded in his head. She'd already done it a few times in the past couple of days and he imagined she'd be doing it for a while yet. "There's a reason we celebrate Christmas at the darkest time of the year, Finn," he heard her saying, just as she had a few weeks before. "To remind us that hope and light will always arrive."

He didn't know about hope and light. But he had held on to something for ten years—and this was just the right season to give it away.

Bailey Sullivan's Vintage Christmas
Facts & Fun Calendar

December 24
Headline over an editorial in the September 21, 1897,
edition of the *New York Sun*: "Is There a Santa Claus?"

Chapter 24

The cyclone fence gate clanged shut, a depressing sound to go with the day's weather. After weeks of clear afternoons, the sun had been no match for today's thick fog. The dreary stuff weighted down roofs, wrapped itself around stoplights, wiggled between the leaves of the trees. It made it even easier for Bailey to turn her back on the mint-green stucco apartment complex she'd just visited. No, she wasn't sad to leave the depressing place, just as she wasn't going to be sad to leave anything else in Coronado.

Telling herself she should be happy to check off one of the final impediments to her departure, she turned toward her car, then stumbled as she stopped short.

"Watch out, GND," Finn said, materializing out of the gray gloom. "If you trip and fall on Christmas Eve, it'll mean a long afternoon in the emergency room waiting your turn among the results of all those family brawls and ugly scotch tape incidents."

"Who's the cynic now?" she murmured, ducking her head to observe him through the shield of her lashes. Since that beach bonfire, his car had come and gone from his grandmother's house and she'd seen people knock on the door with casseroles in hand and then go away without them, but she hadn't seen Finn. Today he was all cool pirate again, his expression unreadable, even with bright presents stacked high in his arms.

"It looks as if we both can be soft-hearted on occasion," he said. "Unless you only dropped by our friend Angel's place to debunk the Santa myth this time."

All I can tell you is that you just gotta believe.

She'd told the little boy that, which meant she'd had to follow through with providing a small measure of Christmas magic, didn't she? Gifts from a couple of near-perfect strangers should do that.

"The family isn't home," she told Finn, which she thought made the whole thing even better. Anonymous gifts were pretty darn close to Santa

Claus, weren't they? "But I left mine with the landlady and she promised to pass them along once they return later today."

"I'll do the same," he said. "Thanks for the tip." With a businesslike nod, he started to move past her. As if *they* were near-strangers.

"Finn."

He paused. "Yeah?"

"Well . . . Um . . ." Bailey wiped her palms on her jeans and tried not to remember that this was the man who'd made love to her with such fierce tenderness that she could still feel the imprint of his mouth on the skin between her shoulder blades. She tried not to remember the heated scorn in his voice when he'd told her on the beach she was nothing to him. That he didn't trust her.

She'd known from the beginning he was a man without patience for pretending.

"My mother wanted to invite you over for Christmas Eve dinner." Bailey didn't add that she'd immediately nixed the idea, but Tracy would be happy to add another plate to the table even now. "We're having turkey and all the trimmings around five."

"You tell her thanks for me . . . but no." He made to move off again.

Move out of her life. Okay, she was the one leaving, but just like . . . like this?

"Finn."

He turned again.

And he was so beautiful to her, she didn't think she could choke out a good-bye. Maybe she didn't deserve one.

"GND?"

Bailey jerked the thoughts out of her head. Tried a smile. "Nothing. Just . . . nothing."

And the last she saw of him was the shrug as he walked away.

The fog deepened as she traveled the half block to her car. Champagne bubble–sized drops of moisture clung to the ends of her hair. As if there was anything worth celebrating, she grumbled to herself, unlocking her door.

Except, of course, the fact that she would be back in L.A. tomorrow.

She slipped inside, then reached over to dump her purse on the passenger seat. It was already occupied.

On it sat a small package, wrapped in Christmas paper printed with mistletoe. As if it might bite, Bailey put out a finger and touched the cool top. There wasn't any gift tag.

But it had to be for her. And she knew of only one person whose early career included breaking into cars.

There weren't any instructions included either. Nothing that said, "Wait until Christmas" or "Open me now."

There didn't have to be. Even without any

words, it was already shouting at Bailey. *Get out before things get ugly.*

When is that? Bailey thought, staring at the package. Maybe she should have asked her father the question ten years before. When is it too soon . . . and when is it too late to save what's left of your heart?

Bailey Sullivan's Vintage Christmas
Facts & Fun Calendar

December 25
Charlie Brown asks in *A Charlie Brown Christmas*: "Isn't there anyone who knows what Christmas is all about?"

Chapter 25

"You're sure you won't stay for Christmas dinner?" her mother asked, as Bailey stowed her suitcases in the trunk of the Passat.

She shook her head. "If I leave now, I'll get to L.A. before the holiday afternoon traffic heats up. Anyway, we had the good stuff last night and for breakfast this morning. I think I'll pass on the tuna noodle casserole."

Tracy smiled, her gaze turning to the basketball game going on between her son and husband in the driveway. "I suppose I shouldn't have promised dinner tonight would be Harry's choice."

Looking over, Bailey had to smile too. Her little brother had been inhaling food since the first moment he'd walked in the door. Apparently Cheerios, Hot Pockets, Flamin' Hot Cheetos, and rocky road ice cream were not available at UC Berkeley, or didn't deliver quite the same punch of flavor.

"I'm sorry I couldn't get him to commit to the store." She'd cornered him during his third piece of pumpkin pie and floated the notion that he might want to take over The Perfect Christmas after college.

"Oh, honey," her mother said, reaching out to tuck a lock of Bailey's hair behind her ear. "Don't feel bad. Not only wasn't that your job, but Harry's too young to commit to *anything*."

Bailey nodded. "You're right. I remember myself at that age." Running away from home and from Finn. See? Too young to get in too deep. Smart enough to realize that.

Tracy laughed. "Oh well, *you* on the other hand . . ."

Me on the other hand? Better not go there. Bailey shut the lid of the trunk with a decisive click. "I should get on the road."

"You always knew what you wanted the minute you saw it."

Finn.

"Yes, well, I'm pretty good at knowing what I don't want too."

Finn.

Tracy's expression turned sad, and she brushed at that errant piece of Bailey's hair again. "I was miserable for a long time, and I'm afraid I made you miserable right along with me. I should have been your rock, and instead you were mine."

Bailey's calf itched and she used the toe of one sneaker to attack the phantom bite, hoping that easing the scratch would ease the memory of broken sobs echoing in an empty bathtub. "Mom—"

"I can't help but think I taught you that trusting people could get you hurt." There were tears in Tracy's eyes.

Bailey turned away from them. "It's okay, Mom."

"It's not. What I have with Dan . . . I wouldn't want you to miss out on that." She let out a watery laugh. "Okay, okay, I see by the expression on your face that you're not entirely convinced that Dan and I are on strong footing again."

"Maybe I'm convinced of the strong *feelings* . . . but just not about how long they will last. Dan's a good man, I know that. But Mom, are you sure you want to take the chance again?"

"I can only answer that the way I answered when you asked me why I let you date Finn. I don't feel like I have any choice." Her mouth curved as her gaze drifted toward her husband, crowing because he'd just beat Harry for the rebound.

Inside the house, the phone started ringing.

Tracy grimaced. "I doubt the men will stop their game to answer that."

"I'm on my way, Mom. Go ahead and get it. I'll call you when I get home."

Tracy flapped her hand. "Who would I want to talk to over you right now? The phone can wait."

But Bailey couldn't. Everyone knew good-byes weren't her thing, and she was ready to get this one over with. She reached out to hug her mother. Ran over to give Dan and Harry quick embraces. Then she was back at her car and she jumped in before things could get any stickier.

The last thing she saw in her rearview mirror was her own gaze, which she resolutely ordered away. It fell on the mystery gift that she'd placed on the dashboard, still unopened. So then she had to order it from that too.

Look ahead.

Starting for the bridge that would take her to the freeway and then on up to L.A., she heard sirens. They sped closer and she pulled to the side of the road as emergency vehicles rushed past her and then took the next corner.

She grimaced. It looked as if somebody's Christmas wasn't going to be a happy one.

It made her think of little Angel, and that made her think of Finn, and *that* got her back onto the street, her foot on the accelerator. Those sirens were still wailing, though, and the sound seemed to collect inside her empty chest. She slowed as she crossed the intersection where the vehicles had gone right, and she peered in their direction, but could see nothing amiss.

Curiosity killed the cat, she reminded herself, but even as she felt guilty for her sudden nosiness, she flipped her right clicker and made her own turn.

Ambulance chasing wasn't such a difficult art in a small town with wide streets on a quiet Christmas morning. Today was clear of fog too. She cruised slowly through each intersection, looking for signs of trouble, and didn't find any even as she approached downtown.

The hairs on the back of her neck prickled as she realized she was definitely getting closer to the siren sound. She unrolled her window an inch to get some fresh air in the suddenly close car.

It's probably just a tourist gone apoplectic after getting a load of his hotel bill from the Del, she told herself. Or maybe the security alarm at the boutique next door to The Perfect Christmas had tripped accidentally again.

Then she smelled something burning.

Then she turned a corner and saw the emergency vehicles, lights flashing, gathered at a familiar block.

Then she got closer and realized they were parked outside The Perfect Christmas and that over the tall profiles of the bright red vehicles, there was smoke rising.

* * *

It took several hours for the emergency workers to put out the fire to their satisfaction. They figured that after old Mr. Baer finished his morning coffee in his patrol car outside the store, he'd mixed up the brake and the accelerator—Bailey had only mentally added *again* when they told her about it—and though they'd managed to extract him from the car that was lodged in the first floor before the fire started . . . well, then the fire had started.

The whole town had shown up at one time or another to watch the action until the fire trucks had pulled away. A little something to do between Christmas breakfast and the hour the ham had to go in. Tracy, Dan, and Harry, who had arrived on scene short minutes after Bailey, had expressed appreciation for the community support, but now they were gone too, off to the hospital to visit Mr. Baer. He was checked in for observation but expected to make a full recovery.

The same could not be said for The Perfect Christmas.

The police had strung yellow tape around the destruction—what Mr. Baer's patrol car hadn't gutted, the ensuing fire had finished off. All that was left were remnants of the outside frame. Most of the roof had collapsed.

Bailey sat alone on the curb across the street and watched ashes flutter up, then drift back down in the afternoon breeze, a little like snowflakes.

A stiffer wind drove a flurry of them all the way across the pavement, where they floated in the air around her.

She'd done it, a semihysterical voice said inside her head. Though she might not have saved the store, she'd brought snow to Vermont.

A couple of blocks away, the Methodist church was playing carols from its bell tower. It seemed almost too plain—one simple melody at a time—after night after night of the unlikely and sometimes boggling carol collaborations at Christmas Central.

Bailey didn't look away from the blackened shell that had once been the family business when a body sat down beside her. Her peripheral vision took in battered jeans and motorcycle boots.

Finn.

"I talked to your mother," he said. "I promised I'd stop by and see how you're doing since she said you're not answering your cell."

How nice of him. Neighborly. Being her mother's friend.

"You look cold," he continued. "Do you want my jacket?"

She didn't feel the temperature. Her hand waved absently. "I have something in my car."

"I'll get it."

He was back in moments, and he draped her short parka over her shoulders, then dropped back down beside her. "Maybe you should head over to Walnut Street. Take a shower to get that smoky smell off you."

"I really need to get on to L.A.," Bailey said. She sounded numb. She felt numb. "They'll be expecting me back at the office in the morning."

"The day after Christmas?"

Bailey shrugged. "In retail, it's December. It's like March is for tax accountants. For divorce attorneys, the busy time is right after the New Year. Folks who've vowed not to spend one more Christmas with their spouse du jour."

He didn't have a response to that. Maybe because the idea depressed him as much as it suddenly did her.

The breeze picked up, another gust fluttering the yellow police tape. More ash swirled. Through the store's blackened exoskeleton, Bailey saw a charred beam finally lose its battle with gravity, crumbling as it dropped.

Her spine crumbled with it.

She curled into her knees, pushing the heels of her hands into her eyes. Though she couldn't move away, she couldn't watch any more of this.

"Bailey?" She felt Finn's hand hovering over the back of her head, but then it was gone.

She wished he'd touched her.

"What's wrong?" he asked quietly.

She didn't know. "Nothing should be, right? This is all I've ever wished for, isn't it? I called the store an albatross and now it's gone. No one would blame me for not wanting to take over the nothing that's left, would they?"

"I guess not."

"Yes. So . . . so, it's happy holidays to me."

But instead of being relieved, she was all at once angry. "I hate it," burst out of her mouth and she jerked straight, her hands curling into fists.

Suddenly she wanted to have every tantrum she'd swallowed, she wanted to cry every tear she'd held back, she wanted to scream with all the frustration of a five-year-old who had lost her trust that a family would last forever. "*I hate it.*"

Her nose started to run and she swiped her hand underneath it, smelling the smoke on her own skin. Another puff of air tried cooling the heat of her face, but it only burned hotter as a piece of charred paper fluttered by. The remains of a Perfect Christmas shopping bag.

She snatched it out of the air and squeezed it in her fist. "Here's my secret," she said, learning it herself as each word exited her mouth. "It was never Christmas I hated, but December 26. We'd go back into the store and it wasn't pretty anymore. You'd see all that was left was damaged or broken, just like what happened to my family."

"Bailey—"

"I *hate* when things get ugly. When they aren't perfect anymore. It's why I wanted to leave by the twenty-fifth. But this time the ugliness came too early."

As quick as it had appeared, the anger inside her extinguished. Her voice sounded as weary as her soul. "This time it came too early."

"I'm sorry, GND."

She opened her fist to stare at the scrunched paper and ash in her hand. "I held some of the vintage things back so there'd be new stock the day after Christmas. But I guess they're all gone too."

Glancing over at Finn, she saw that he was staring at what was left of the store. "I don't know why I'm so upset about this." She managed a hoarse little laugh. "It's almost funny, now that I think about it. I joked to myself I wanted to burn the place down. I even told Mr. Baer that first night I came back that nothing flocked can stay."

She sighed, looking around the quiet block. "Nothing stays. Nothing lasts. Nothing."

The street had been deserted after the fire engines left, the lookie-loos having gone home and the stores around them closed for the holiday. But in the distance she could see a small, ragtag parade heading their way. Shepherded by a couple of young teen girls in new pastel-colored hoodies, a half-dozen littler kids were tooling along the sidewalk on skateboards, scooters, and bicycles, each one buckled into a gleaming helmet.

Trying out their new gifts, Bailey decided. When she and Trin were girls, they used to speed up and down the streets, hair flying free, never thinking of what accident might lie around the next corner. Kids were so much safer today.

Finn didn't appear aware of their approach. Without looking at her, he dug his hand in his jacket pocket. "I don't know if this will help," he said, holding out the gift he'd left in her car. "But I noticed you haven't opened it yet."

Bailey stared down at the present. "I . . . I was afraid to," she said, surprised by her own honesty.

Finn smiled. "It's a gift, not a weapon."

"I have nothing for you." She still didn't touch it.

"Maybe not, but that's okay too. It's for you, GND, no strings attached."

Her hand was slow to take it from him. Even slower to tear through the paper. Her nervous pulse pounded in her ears as she lifted the lid. Inside the box was another, smaller box, and—

"It's my vintage ornament. The one I dropped," she said, holding it up. The old, ruby-colored glass swirled and dipped. Somehow the fractures barely showed. She glanced up. "You unbroke the heart."

"You made something more of me, a long time ago, so I'm happy I could return the favor—even in a small way."

Holding the glass in the palm of her hand settled her nerves somehow, and made it easier to open the second box. Shocked, her pulse jolted back into high gear.

Finn cleared his throat. "I brought it with me that last summer when you were gone. I designed it myself, had it made. It's a promise ring."

Gold and silver, a B entwined around an F. Tears stung the corners of her eyes.

"Bailey, it's still my promise to you." He held out his left hand. The heavy ring he'd worn on his little finger was gone and on that bared knuckle was the same insignia. A B entwining an F. The only tattoo he'd never removed.

She couldn't look away from it. "No." *No!*

"Yes. I was in love with you then. I'm in love with you now. It didn't go away. It's not going away. If nothing else, well, I can promise that lasts."

"On the beach—"

"I wasn't ready to admit the truth."

"Finn . . ." Her voice trailed off as she realized they were surrounded by the parade of kids she'd seen tooling toward them before. They took no notice of the adults, just pushed back their brand-new helmets to survey the ruins across the street.

One of the little kids, she saw now, was preschooler Angel, balancing on a spangled banana seat while a pair of training wheels kept him steady. The miniframe was red with black handlebars, and a flashy water bottle was clipped to the side.

She caught Finn's eye, nodded to the boy. "Bicycle?" she whispered.

He smiled, shrugged, then rose to his feet. "Anyway, GND, happy life."

"You're . . . you're leaving?" She looked down at the ring, and then back at his impassive face. Had she dreamed him saying he was in love with her?

"I told you," he said, gesturing to the items she cradled in her lap. "Those are gifts. Not weapons, not strings. Maybe they'll bring you some warm memories as you're expediting those divorces up in L.A."

At her glass and steel building where she spent so many overtime hours that she was too tired to realize the matching soullessness of her condominium. Sure there were communities in L.A., but where she lived and the way she worked didn't encourage them.

She had never encouraged them in her life. It had always been easier to avoid disappointment by keeping her distance.

Finn turned and started off down the sidewalk. She stared after him. He was walking away from her as he'd done outside Angel's apartment building. Walking away and taking all his gifts with him.

Except for . . .

She looked down at the repaired heart. The promise ring. B and F entwined forever.

He was in love with her?

"Wait!" she heard herself call out.

He paused, slowly turned. The kids' helmets

swiveled too, all of them looking at her, expectant.

The church bells were ringing louder with peal after bright peal, or maybe it was really the shattered shards of her heart, tinkling, clattering, finally coming together after having been broken that day she heard her father say, "Get out before things get ugly."

Finn was in love with her. How could that ever get ugly?

And how could she let him walk away when she was in love with him too? But it would mean she would have to take off her metaphorical helmet, and . . . and . . .

If nothing else, I can promise that lasts.

She'd have to believe.

Jumping to her feet, she snatched up the water bottle clipped to Angel's bike frame. "Hey!" he protested.

Glad to find it full, she squeezed it hard, shooting the water into Finn's wary, then surprised, then annoyed face.

"Hey!" he said, in the exact same tone as the little bad boy on the banana seat beside her. "What the hell?"

Bailey laughed. Now that she was whole, she felt as if she could fly. "You looked like you were sulking again."

He flicked water off his face with one hand, his gaze wary. "That's how I get when I can't have everything I want."

"Oh, Finn." Her feet took off and she did fly, like a reindeer, like an angel, like a woman who wanted to be pressed against the man she loved. "I think it's about time you were rewarded for all your good behavior.

"I love you," Bailey said against his mouth. His arms held her tight. She believed in him, them, magic. How else, to paraphrase Finn, would the girl next door get the bad boy of her dreams?

She'd been called home to save the season, but in the end, she realized, it had saved her. "Merry Christmas."

Author's Note

Coronado is a lovely place to visit any time of year. While I tried to give the flavor of the "island" in the story, with very few exceptions I made up street names and other details. (Don't go looking for Christmas Central on Walnut Street!)

Please visit www.christieridgway.com for more Christmas trivia, recipes, and fun. Wherever you are this season, I wish for you hope and light.

*S*till stuck on what to get your mother or best friend this holiday season? Perhaps you're thinking of buying them a gift certificate—again? Well, worry no longer—you can't go wrong with gifts of love and romance!

*A*von *presents* these four spectacular Romance Superleaders—two by the prolific Suzanne Enoch (one historical and one contemporary romance), and the latest and greatest offerings from Judith Ivory and Christie Ridgway.

*T*reat yourself, and a friend or two, to some of the most delightful and sweeping romances this season, where the hero and heroine always get the perfect gift.

Avon presents . . .

Something Sinful

**by Suzanne Enoch
(September 2006)**

Lord Charlemagne "Shay" Griffin excels at everything he puts his mind to, especially when it comes
to business—which is why he never expected the al-
luring Lady Sarala Carlisle to best him at a business
transaction! Sarala sees herself as an equal to any
man, and she just couldn't resist the chance to put
the arrogant lord in his place. But Shay is not one to
admit defeat and launches a plan of seduction against
Sarala.

***

$\mathcal{B}$y the time Shay reached Carlisle House his brain had
begun to sort things out rationally, and he was able to resist
the urge to pound on the door and smash the pots of ferns on
the front portico. The chit obviously ran wild, so he wouldn't
deal with her. Business was business, and business was for
men.

A large, gray-clothed man opened the door. "Yes?"

"Charlemagne Griffin, here to see Lord Hanover."

The butler blinked. Someone in the household knew
him by name, at least. He stepped back, gesturing Charlemagne to follow him inside. "If you'll wait in the morning room, I shall fetch him."

The morning room was small, tasteful, and, unless he was

mistaken, smelled of cinnamon. The scent forcibly reminded him of the chit who'd bested him. And considering what she'd been doing with him in his dreams, it almost felt like a double loss on his part. And he didn't like to lose.

Before the butler could finish closing him into the room, he heard a rush of footsteps and a hurried, muttered conversation. A second later the door swung open again, and the lady herself practically skidded into the room. She wore a frilled dressing gown, one sleeve hanging to reveal a tantalizing view of smooth collarbone and shoulder. That black hair was everywhere, half up and tumbled down, caressing her cheek and sagging into an unfinished knot at the back.

The angry comment Charlemagne had been about to make vanished back into his throat, making him cough a little. Glory.

Belatedly she tugged up her sleeve. "Lord Charlemagne."

Mentally he shook himself. *Business, man. Business.* "You stole my silks."

"I did no such thing. You informed me of a potentially lucrative business opportunity, and I acted on that information."

He narrowed his eyes. "I discussed my business with you because I was under the impression that you were an admirer—not a rival."

She snorted. "Then you made two mistakes."

Charlemagne took a step closer. "Where's your father? I came to speak with him, to discuss the return of my property in a rational manner."

Lady Sarala gave what might have been a brief frown, then lifted her chin. "This is *my* affair, and you will discuss it with me, or not at all."

Good God, she had some nerve. And her sleeve had sagged again, so that he could see the pulse at her throat and the quick lift of her breast. "Then return my property," he said, returning his gaze to her soft mouth.

"It's not your property. But for a price, I will let you have every stitch."

He knew he shouldn't ask, but he couldn't stop himself. "What price, then?"

"Five thousand pounds."

His jaw fell open, then clamped shut. "*Five thousand pounds?* So you would steal from me and then overcharge me to recover my own goods?"

She looked him right in the eye. "Once again, I did not steal anything from you, or from anyone else. Make me a counter offer, or bid me good day and leave."

Incredulous, he shook his head. "This is ridiculous. Where's the liquor?"

"Over there." Lady Sarala pointed toward the cabinet beneath the window.

Her fingers shook, and he grabbed her hand, pulling her up against him. "You're not frightened of me, are you?" he murmured.

"Is that your intent? I'd heard you were a fearsome opponent, but you seem to be harping on one point of contention, which does neither of us any good. Make me a counter offer, my lord."

He lowered his head and kissed her upturned mouth. Sensation flooded through him, all the way to his cock. He didn't know how to describe what she tasted like—sunshine, warm summer breezes, heat, desire.

When she began to kiss him back, he forced himself to lift his face away again. "How was that?" he drawled.

Sarala cleared her throat, belatedly recovering her hand and backing away. "Fair. But hardly worth five thousand pounds."

Avon presents . . .

Angel In a Red Dress

by Judith Ivory
(October 2006)

As a special treat, we're re-issuing the wonderful classic, originally titled *Starlit Surrender*, with a beautiful new package and title . . . Golden-haired innocent Christina Bower is totally captivated by the Earl of Kewischesteran, a lethally charming rake whose touch alone can melt her heart.

$\mathscr{A}$drien led the way deeper into the garden, perfectly polite.

Christina felt a fool. He wasn't disapproving or making harsh judgments of her. A gentleman, she realized as she followed him. Whatever else he was, he was that. Not a sham, no deceit, genuinely upper class. Like the sound of his voice. She envied his speech. It had taken her so long, and several girls' schools, to achieve something similar.

They went around the last bend in the path, and there stood a little house made of nothing but glass. "What—" She halted.

He held the door open. "The roses are toward the back."

He motioned, then guided, putting her in front of him. His hand touched lightly at her back. She had to quell a little shiver.

The greenhouse was not particularly small, but it was

crowded with plants. Orange trees bloomed. Lemons. Pine-
apples. And at the rear, a wall of roses. Beautiful, peach-
colored blooms. He pointed to them.

"Oh," she said. "They're lovely!"

He moved around her, brushing her shoulder as he passed.
She was more aware of him—of his body, its solidness and
peculiar grace—in the crowded quarters. As he bent toward
her, his chest came up against her arm and breast, and he
murmured an apology. As if this were perfectly excusable.
He picked up some shears from the workbench.

One, two, three . . . a dozen. Methodically, he cut the flowers. When he offered them to her, she didn't know what to say.
His smile, his pleasant friendliness, his sharp features were
so magnetic. She damned all handsome men as she stood in a
cloud of confusion. After a moment, she reached out. Then
stupidly, promptly, dropped the roses onto the floor.

"Ow—" Blood oozed from the tip of her middle finger.

His hand wrapped around hers. He took her finger into
his mouth.

She was stunned.

His mouth was warm. She could feel the gentle pressure,
a drawing of his teeth and tongue. It took her much too long
to retrieve her hand.

"Sir," she reprimanded softly. She looked away.

He bent to pick up the flowers at her feet. And the little
glass house began to feel close. Where he squatted, he
aligned the flowers—six, seven, eight . . . Christina flattened her hands into her skirt to hold it back, to avoid stepping on his fingers. She tried to take a step back, but a low
shelf caught her, pressing into her bottom. It was strange,
but this was somehow alarming. She felt agitated, fidgety.
She looked at her finger. It had begun to throb lightly. There
was a pinprick of blood.

He stood, the bundle of roses in his hand, and reached
above her—his chest against her face. The smell of him
again. Soap, tobacco, leather. Was he doing this on purpose?

Christina felt suffocated by him. She held her breath rather than breathe in his warmth, his humidity. She raised her hands. Lightly against his chest. Not knowing how to push him back without touching him. Then, on his own, he moved back. As if it were nothing. As if she weren't there. She was nonplussed, a woman left in midair. She couldn't look at him. Yet, in nervous glances, couldn't stop keeping track . . .

He wrapped a piece of paper about the stems of the roses, then set the tidied parcel on the workbench and took another step back. He rested an elbow on the upper shelf and looked at her. There was a faint, ironic smile on his lips.

"I've frightened you," he said.

She was quick to shake her head. "Oh, no—"

He laughed. "Oh, yes. I'm sorry. I didn't mean to." He reached and caught her hand again.

She was half flustered, half piqued at the apology followed by the same trick. She flinched as he turned her hand over and studied it. Her hand was clammy. It shook slightly. His was steady, smooth.

He let go. She huffed a wounded breath and pressed her palm to her chest.

"It will be all right," he said. He cocked his head to the side. "The cut, I mean." As if he could have meant something else. "And I am sorry for the moment ago. Only your finger just suddenly looked—" He shrugged, smiled. "It's what I do with mine. Honestly." His smile broadened, a flash of white teeth as brilliant as a bolt of electricity through a dark sky.

Christina blushed, turned her head away. She caught sight of the door at the far end, down that corridor of plants. She really must leave, she thought.

Then she heard him laughing. "If you make a break for it, I'll drop you to the ground flat out. Wrestling team, you know, all the way through university. I'm a smash as a takedown."

Her eyes went wide to him.

His soft laughter again. "Sorry." He made a self-conscious apology with his shoulders. "Only pulling your leg. You look so bloody green." More soberly, "But I'm just a little insulted. What you must be thinking."

"I wasn't thinking anything."

"Only that I'd as soon ravish you as look at you. Which is not true. I find looking at you exceptionally pleasant." He paused. "Why did you come out here with me if I frighten you so?"

No answer. Though it remained a very good question.

Avon presents . . .

Billionaires Prefer Blondes

by Suzanne Enoch
(November 2006)

Former thief Samantha Jellicoe is enjoying her new legitimate career and her romance with billionaire Richard Addison. Then she spies someone she'd thought dead—her father, Martin Jellicoe—and she knows he's up to no good. Her worst fears come true when a new painting that Rick purchased goes missing and her father is under suspicion. Rick and Samantha's relationship will be tested like never before.

"*S*amantha?"

Damn. She looked back up to the head of the stairs to see him gazing toward the far window with its missing pane. He had good vision, but hell, not that good. "Yes, Rick?" she said, echoing his tone again. *Never give anything away.* That was one of the thieves' rules as quoted to her by her dad on a regular basis, until Martin had ended up in prison and then dead just over three years ago.

"There are a dozen coats and two briefcases in the entryway," Rick was saying. "How did you pass them by without realizing I was here with company?"

"I was distracted. Have fun with your minions."

"And why would you walk through the front door and up the stairs with a dress wadded up under your blouse?"

"My hands were full."

"With that missing window pane up here, by any chance?" He descended the stairs again. "You broke into the house."

"Maybe," she hedged, backing down to the first floor. "What if I just forgot my key?"

Rick joined her at the foot of the stairs. "You might have knocked at the front door. Wilder is here, and so is Vilseau," he said, tilting his head at her, his eyes growing cool.

He hated having her try to pull one on him, whatever the circumstances. Samantha blew out her breath. At least she knew when to give up. "Okay, okay. Boyden Locke talked to my boobs for forty minutes while I sold him on some security upgrades for his town house. And then I went shopping for the dress, and I just kept noticing . . . things."

"What things?"

"Cameras, alarm systems. Everything. It was making me crazy. Plus we're going to an art auction tonight, at Sotheby's, no less, I was just feeling a little . . . tense. So I decided to subvert my bad self by busting in somewhere. I picked a safe place."

"And I caught you again." He reached out, curling a strand of her auburn hair around his fingers. "The last time I did that, we broke a chair afterwards, as I recall."

Technically, this time he'd caught her well after the fact and only because of a huge mistake on her part, but as the raw, hungry shiver traveled down her backbone she wasn't about to contradict him. She drew her free hand around the back of his neck and leaned in to give him a deep, soft kiss. "So you want another reward, I suppose?"

He nuzzled against her ear. "Definitely," he whispered.

She was going to explode. "Why don't you get rid of your minions, then, and I'll reward you right now?"

Rick's muscles shuddered against her. "Stop tempting me."

"But I broke into your big old house. Don't you—"

He pushed her back against the mahogany bannister, nearly sending them both over it as he took her mouth in a hard, hot kiss.

Ah, this was more like it.

Avon presents . . .

Must Love Mistletoe

by Christie Ridgway
(December 2006)

When her feuding parents cause the family business, The Perfect Christmas, to flounder, self-admitted "Scrooge" Bailey Sullivan returns to resort town Coronado, California, to try and salvage something. She plans to stay from December 1 to 25—but even that seems too long when she discovers that Finn, the bad boy next door she loved a decade ago, is also home for the holidays. Still, no matter how magical her love for Finn had once felt or now feels again, Bailey's certain that no love lasts. Or can it?

*T*he summer Bailey was fourteen she cajoled Finn to the beach with her every afternoon. His kiss came one July day—her first. She hadn't known to open her mouth for his tongue, and her skin had heated like sunburn when he whispered the instruction. Then his tongue had touched the tip of hers and he'd tasted like pretzels and Pepsi and saltwater. Going dizzy, she'd clutched his bare shoulder, her fingertips grazing across gritty, golden sand sprinkled on his damp, tanned flesh.

Two years after that, the darkness of her backyard and the ghostly glow of the soccerball-sized hydrangeas. The fresh scent of night-blooming jasmine. The flinch of her stomach as his bony boy fingers touched her belly skin on their first, bold approach to her breast. The instant pebbling of her nipple beneath her neon bikini top and her naive, desperate hope he wouldn't notice.

He had.

"Something wrong?" he asked now.

He'd always paid such close attention.

She tossed her hair back and crossed her arms. "Nothing access to my car won't fix right up."

"Give me a sec."

She let herself watch him stride off, his long legs so familiar, the wide plane of his back and his heavy-muscled shoulders so not. What had he done to earn that beefcake physique? What had he done with his life? What had happened to his eye?

He'd been such a bad boy.

Her bad boy.

But the bad boy had grown into a one-eyed stranger who was already back with a hammer and who didn't appear interested in talk.

Or interested in her.

So she clamped her mouth shut, too, and watched him move away the big crate.

She then ducked into her car, turned the key, and slipped it into reverse.

Not putting voice to her questions, though, didn't make them disappear. Just as wishing her memories of him to a cobwebbed shelf in the back corner of her brain didn't immediately send them there, either.

But the fact that he didn't appear the least bit affected by her presence—or their past—should make the banishments not far off. Just, say, five minutes away.

Before that could happen, though, a knock on her driver's door window made her jump. The one-eyed pirate who was moments from being out of her mind forever was giving her another expressionless look from his one dark eye.

Bailey unrolled the window, trying to appear as if she'd already forgotten who he was and what they'd once meant to each other.

It certainly appeared as if *he* had.

"Yes?" she asked. "Did you want something?"

"Just checking."

She frowned at him. "Checking for what?"

"That you're still into skipping good-byes." And then he turned, leaving without another word.